RETURN TO MARS

by
Gary Gentile

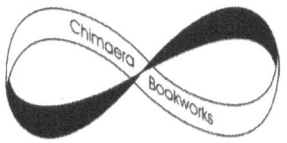

Chimaera Bookworks
P.O. Box 57137
Philadelphia, PA 19111

Additional copies of this book may be purchased from the same address by sending a check or money order in the amount of $15 U.S. for each copy (plus $3 postage per order, not per book, in the U.S. Inquire for shipping cost to foreign countries). Alternatively, copies may be purchased from the author's website, and paid by credit card:

http://www.ggentile.com

Front cover photographs courtesy of NASA.

International Standard Book Numbers (ISBN)
1-883056-20-9
978-1-883056-20-9

Original copyright - 1982

Printed in the U.S.A.

Many a hearth upon our dark globe
    sighs after many a vanish'd face.
Many a planet by many a sun
    may roll with the dust of a vanish'd race.

               Vastness
               Alfred Tennyson (1809-1892)

Chapter 1

From the ten-thousand-foot-high promontory, the vast ocher plain of Syrtis Major fanned out like a calm lake, stretching interminably to the pale pink horizon. The barren sand was striated with monotonous shades of brown — from the slightly reddish mineral colors to the duller, grayer sediment — blended together like the drab dress of a pauper forming a hodgepodge, irregular pattern. Small craters dimpled the ancient seabed like miniature oases, giving relief to the otherwise flat and featureless desert. Here and there small dust spouts churned inexorable paths across the sweeping panorama. Sand was continually being picked up and deposited: dunes moved dynamically over the inanimate surface.

The dull yellow orb of the sun hung limply in the soft orange sky, its weakened rays easily penetrating the thin envelope of carbon dioxide. Bold shadows spearheaded distant crater peaks. Despite the dim light, the planet was illuminated in sharp contrast, the dust-laden atmosphere having an almost effervescent quality that sparkled brightly. An overall deep pervading silence reigned.

Altogether it was a bleak and desolate landscape. It was a harsh world of airlessness and desiccation and subzero temperatures. It was a world of lifeless continuance. It was a world of nakedness.

It was Mars.

I shuddered, inwardly retreating from the cold and passionless vista. My gut reaction was one of not quite revulsion, but more than imminent dislike and loneliness. I had never expected to see the Red Planet again: five years skulking in claustrophobic corridors and ranging over sterile wastelands had more than satisfied my scientific curiosity and natural inquisitiveness. I had wanted no more of it.

"Isn't it a beautiful sight?"

The smooth, high-pitched voice, with the barest trace of New England accent, issued sibilantly from my headphones. I glanced at Linda Chapman, slender even in the exposure suit and bulky long johns. Two quivering, Earth-sky-blue eyes peered out of the wide plexiglass port. The rest of her face, from the tip of the nose down, was obscured by two breathing tubes and a bulbous diaphragm which supplied recycled air from a backpack unit.

"Impressive, perhaps, but far from beautiful." I viewed the scarred, scraggy, crater-pocked terrain. "It's as forlorn as the arctic tundra, and every bit as brutal."

Linda gazed wistfully over the shifting sands. "There's beauty in all nature if seen in the proper perspective. To a polar bear, the arctic tundra is as quaint as the Blue Ridge Mountains of Virginia are to you. To Martian eyes, this is a scene of splendor."

"Was. There haven't been any Martians here for millions of years. And it doesn't necessarily follow that they were enamored by their meager existence any more than Arabian Bedouins. Nomadic desert life is cruel and relentless, and the people are too busy trying to survive to enjoy it. They just happened to have been born there."

"Oh, Doug, your Earthly viewpoints have made you insensitive." Her voice was pleading. "For me, Mars holds an undying fascination, a refined elegance, a hidden glamour. She has so much to offer. If you would try to be more perceptive, more aware, perhaps even sentimental, you'd appreciate her fine qualities. You'll come to know and like her."

I saw this scant, otherworld outpost as anything but a rustic homestead. The ratlike existence in the domes and tubes and cubbyholes could never be anything but a hardship for the human psyche. I stared out over the barren wasteland, idly wondering if the Martians had ever had such luxuries as water and air and warmth. Certainly they could not have prospered on such an inhospitable planet.

Desolation extended as far as the eye could see. The

only lifelike break in the ocher beach was the sprouting community of Syrtis City. Two miles away and ten thousand feet below, the City lay close enough to the Western Plateau to offer protection from rampant windstorms prevailing from the west, yet far enough away so that boulders blown over the edge did not reach the domes.

From a height, Syrtis City looked alarmingly toylike and fragile. The Administration Dome, conspicuous by the huge retractable aerial over its shiny roof, was the central hub of the City. From there, the complex lives of some twelve hundred inhabitants were controlled and coordinated by a staff of quasi-military personnel.

Radiating outward like the spokes of a wheel, and interconnected by airtight tubes, were the four secondary domes which served and supported the City: nuclear power plant, hydroponics, laboratories, and garage. The tubes leading to them were merely hallways with rooms on both sides. In between the four main spokes were four shorter tubes which provided additional space for quarters and offices. For the most part, the spokes were either covered with a light layer of sand, or completely buried so that the four domes appeared to be independent of the central hub, the whole looking like dull-colored balls floating in an endless granular sea. If this protective coating were stripped away, the City would look like the web of some gargantuan spider.

Because of the tremendous windstorms that whipped across the open plain, most of the City, like an iceberg, lay hidden beneath the dunes. The tubes and dome roofs tapered to the ground to allow the wind to pass harmlessly by; they were, in fact, aerodynamic.

Further north, along the base of the Western Rim, the peaked walls of an ancient impact crater encircled the landing port, offering protection for the gantries and the space ships they tethered. I could barely make out the tip of the spindly shuttle that had landed me on Mars only a few hours ago.

Nowhere in that boundless desert were there permanent roads. Crawler paths meandered aimlessly, looking like worm tracks in the mud after a summer rain. But with the next storm, they would disappear under tons of raging sand, like a beach wiped clean by the rising tide.

This was the extent of life on Mars, all less than half a century old — unless one considered the indigenous lichen recently found hidden in dark crevices, and the remnants of the ancient race that once inhabited this ball of dust. I scoffed at Linda's prophecy.

"Where are the Caves? Can you see them from here?"

Linda raised a gauntleted arm, pointing south. "See that rocky outcrop that looks like a saw tooth? That's the Sasquatch Mountain Range. About half way between that and the Rim, and about fifty miles further south, is Ryans Rill. Another twenty miles past that is where three of the cities have been discovered, and where most of the excavating is going on now. It's a two day ride from here, mostly due to detouring crevasses and soil domes in the Rill area."

Distances are hard to distinguish on Mars, due partly to the lack of comparative objects, and partly to foreshortened horizon of a planet only slightly more than half the diameter of Earth. The uneven terrain, like a giant obstacle course, forced measurement in the form of time rather than in linear equivalents.

"How do people manage to work so far from the City? With such a large force concentrated on the excavations, living conditions must be insufferable."

"Emergency pods have been erected as temporary shelters, and many live, eat, and sleep right out of the crawlers, hotbunking. The work is so fascinating that no one seems to mind the temporary inconvenience. Besides, there's very little time for rest."

The discovery of the century, perhaps of man's entire history, was only months old. Now they were unearthing the ruins of a civilization that was dead and buried long before mankind had climbed down from the trees.

"Doug, I think we'd better start back for the crawler."

I rubbed my arm, still sore from Doc Reynolds' inoculation, turned from the alien panorama. "I was just beginning to enjoy the view."

Linda gestured toward the sky behind us. "I don't like those dark clouds on the horizon. There may be a sand storm on the way."

I blew condensation off my faceplate. "There was nothing like that noted in the weather report."

A warm hand gripped mine. "You've forgotten. It never pays to take chances."

There was more in those eyes than simple concern. Or was that my imagination? Or presumption? Or hope? "Of course, you're right. We'd better go."

We retraced our steps along the edge of the plateau to a broad gully. The fissure dropped steeply down a ramp of unearthly spear-pointed rocks. Linda led the way. "Be careful."

"The suit material is tough, and the sealant layer can repair anything short of a sword gash."

Linda picked a path through the geologic needles. "I know, but it never — "

" — pays to take chances. Sorry. Keep reminding me until I remember it."

Hopscotching down the slope in thirty-eight percent gravity was easy. The five hundred foot deep gully was equivalent to a golf divot on Earth, but the sharp protrusions created territory that even the steel-tracked crawlers could not traverse. Despite the miracles of modern technology, there was nothing better than the human frame for traveling on terrain where man's machines could not take him.

Sand whirled lightly around my face. I listened to the movement of grain-sized particles rasping against the rocks. The tenuous atmosphere tended to deaden sound so that I felt, rather than heard, the vibrations of the wind. The radio receiver added further distortion by detecting and magnifying the grating noise.

Linda raised her voice over the increasing interference. "We'd better pick up the pace. It looks like we're in for a real blow."

Jogging was not difficult considering that, even with all my life support systems, I weighed less than a hundred pounds. Even so, I turned up the oxygen supply to make up for my exertions. Internal pressure increased slightly. During the six-week journey from Earth, I had gradually acclimatized to the lower working pressure used in space and at the Colony.

The wind chased us down the gully with increasing speed. Great swirls of sand eddied around my feet, and spun dizzyingly past my helmet. Linda was only dimly visible in the sudden dusty maelstrom. I saw her leaping over the tilted ground, and dodging obstructions which never came to my attention until I either tripped over them or ran into them. It was uncanny the way she could move.

My suit radio crackled. "This is the way to the crawler. Let's run for it."

What have we been doing? "Okay," I said hoarsely.

The ghostly blue and red colors of Linda's suit faded entirely in the thick, dusty gloom, then became bright as I crashed into her oxygen cylinders.

"We go up here."

In normal gravity the hill would have been steep, but Mars has its own standards. I followed her obligingly up an almost vertical incline, clambering over large boulders. I recognized no distinguishing features. "Are you sure this is the way we came?"

After six weeks in zero gravity my condition had deteriorated. Aching legs strode forward with shortening steps. I increased the flow of oxygen to keep up with my demanding lungs. A sudden blast of wind almost knocked me off my feet. I teetered for a moment, then felt Linda's firm grip on my arm, holding me steady.

"We're at the top of the gully." Her voice was calm, her breathing controlled. "Keep close."

"I'm part of your backpack." I felt slightly dizzy. The swirling sand that grated past my faceplate was disorienting, moving in crazy circles that affected my sense of balance.

"It's not far now."

I nodded, forgetting for a moment that she could not see my head moving under the exposure hood. I tagged along obediently.

With the wind came the biting cold. The thermal underwear and heavily insulated exposure suit were sufficient for seasonal daytime temperatures: fifty below zero this time of year. And wind-chill is usually not a factor in vacuum, without molecules to conduct heat away from the body. It was the dust that sapped my energy reserves. With numbed fingers I turned on the auxiliary heater. Despite the thick padding in the soles of the boots, my feet soaked up the cold from the ground.

The reduced gravity that made running easier allowed phenomenal wind speeds to develop. Gusts of up to two hundred miles per hour were not uncommon when water vapor was migrating from the poles to the equator. Being hit by a handful of sand at that speed can have deleterious side effects. Even heavy crawlers had been overturned by such tremendous velocities.

The red and blue uniform, my only touch with reality, galloped ahead. I was amok in a spinning cacophony of debris that howled unmercifully, while clutching fingers tried to pull me to the ground. Sand and dust particles slammed into my faceplate, and hammered into my exposure suit like tiny bullets. Small rocks and stones rolled along the ground as if on a conveyor belt, seemingly aimed at my feet.

Visibility was nearly zero. Looking down I could not see my own knees.

The exotic, whirling sand was confusing, hypnotizing. I could have been on a lonely Caribbean beach, watching receding waves pull streamers of fluent sand past my feet.

I fell.

I was lost. Linda was gone, and I was alone. I stood up and moved in the direction of the prevailing wind, but sudden gusts came from unexpected bearings, knocking me off balance. The dizziness got worse. My arm burned frightfully.

I stumbled on. I no longer knew if Linda was in front of me, or behind me, or standing right beside me. I no longer knew if she even existed.

"Linda." I gasped into the suit radio, over the sound of the shrieking tempest. "Where are you?"

I waded waist deep in a river of sand, striding against the current. Pebbles and small stones were scooped up bodily, sweeping downstream. The reduced gravity did things which seemed impossible to one used to Earthly physics. But the momentum of that mass of sand was the same.

I leaned forward at an impossible angle, supported by a solid wall of air. Rocks floated effortlessly in the dusty blizzard. One giant boulder rolled past. The gust of wind carrying it hit me full force. Another blast, tangential, tackled me around the knees. I hit the ground with a thud, felt the whoosh of air from my lungs. An agonizing pain crept up from my ankle.

I lay there gasping, could see nothing but reddish, rushing sand on the other side of my faceplate. I was tumbled around like a swimmer in the surf. Because of the slight gravity, I could not distinguish up from down. I dug my fingers into the ground. I fought off nausea and the sensation of drowning. I leaned up and poked my head out of the flowing sand as if I were bobbing to the surface of an ocean.

I rotated my ankle, felt it throbbing. The wind howled in my ears, shouting my name like the temptress Siren. The stereophones put the sibilant calling right in my head. I refused to answer.

I felt a light touch on my arm, a helping hand under my shoulder. "Are you all right?" In the tumultuous storm, Linda's voice was orchestral music.

"I'm okay. I just lost my footing."

"We can't afford to become separated. Hold onto my hand. We're almost there."

The sand whirled about so thickly that Linda's lithe form was nearly obscured. With her faceplate only inches away from mine, I could hardly distinguish her features. She helped me to my feet, held onto my hand, led the way into the storm. We walked through a tank of black oil, the sun no longer in the sky. I followed blindly, leaning against her for support.

The suit heater was overworking, draining its batteries, warming the extremities through slender, imbedded filaments. But I grew increasingly colder. My fingers had long since ceased to have feeling. My feet were dead stalks. The intense pain in my forehead, like a sinus squeeze, hammered constantly. My upper arm itched sharply where needle had stabbed flesh.

Equilibrium gone, I stumbled to my knees, dragging Linda with me. "My ankle. I've twisted it."

"Hold on." Before I stopped groaning, Linda lifted me, cradled me in her arms as if I were a baby, and continued marching into the wind.

The blizzard grew fiercer by the minute. We would soon be frozen to death, or blown over the edge of the Western Rim by cyclonic forces. I dozed off lethargically, unknowing and uncaring. The Siren called my name. *Don't answer. Remember the fate of Odysseus' crew.* It called again, louder this time, but still obscured by the screeching whirlwind. It sounded almost real.

My body was being shaken violently. I opened my eyes and saw nothing but brownish-red sand. *I've been buried!* A strange face swam into view, was gone, came back again, hidden behind a spider web. I saw the name stenciled across the exposure hood.

"Doug, let go of me. I have to get the airlock open."

A metallic gleam rose over her shoulder, ten-foot-high flotation treads buffeted by the wind. I relaxed, and she struggled free of my grip. The splintered faceplate receded. I forgot the wind, the sand, the numbing cold. Linda dragged me up the steps and into the steel cocoon. Hydraulic pumps cycled and the door dosed, leaving outside the swirling sand and hurricane force winds.

Silence reigned.

I huddled in simple security, rubbed my aching

arm. Heat flowed into frostbitten limbs. I breathed deeply. The ragged edge of disaster had been narrowly averted.

"That was a close one."

I smiled weakly at Linda, strength returning. This was why I had left the Red Planet. One tour was enough on this cruel and infinite desert, this deadly wasteland, this arid and lonely strand.

"I don't think I like it here."

"You'll get used to it. Mars is different now. You're different. You'll see."

I shrugged. The fact that I was here offered proof of sufficient inducements to get me back. But for the moment, I could not recall them. My mind was a montage of recent events, jumbled out of order. Slowly, I started to sort them out, to put them into perspective. Something had convinced me to return to Mars. But what?

Chapter 2

"We have a problem on Mars."

Terrence Rogers, Chairman of the Mars Appropriations Committee, sat behind a plain, unadorned desk on which perched a computer terminal and a communication set, both switched off. Silver gray hair receded slightly over veined temples. Slate gray eyes stabbed sharply.

"Whether or not you accept this assignment, Mr. Martin, you are under the strictest secrecy concerning everything discussed in this room."

I tried to relax in the straight-backed, plastic chair. "I understand, sir."

Rogers continued without taking his eyes from mine. "I've called upon you because you are a valued and trusted member of this organization. Your past service, military as well as civilian, has been exemplary in all facets of duty performance. You've served well on Mars and possess the required experience to deal with problems which others, without your background, might find difficult, even impossible to solve. And I say this not to flatter you, but merely to state your qualifications."

I offered a perfunctory nod, took a moment to glance at the full color holographic mural behind him. The vermilion cliffs of the Western Rim dominated the scene, shot in the crystal clarity that can only exist on an almost airless world. The foreshortening effect of a long telephoto lens made the cliffs appear to touch the domes of Syrtis City in the foreground. Closer still, several exposure-suited figures entered a land crawler, a puff of dust showing the pneumatic door closing.

Rogers poised on his elbows as if ready to pounce. "I'll start by summarizing the latest events — priority classified information known only to the highest ranking officials of this Committee. About fifteen months ago, a geologic team was conducting preliminary ground mapping surveys in a heavily crevassed area south of Ryans Rill. Exposed strata analyses and mineralogical samples brought back to base indicated the region was one of the last in Mars' geologic history to have contained running water. Follow-up satellite scans showed previously unknown fault lines running for miles, as well as a large number of intersecting rills. Dr. Sanders organized a research party with the express purpose of descending into the deeper rills to search for fossil evidence that could be more recent than any previously found."

The Chairman neglected to mention that *he* had discovered the first fossils on Mars: imprints and bones that proved the theory of parallel evolution under similar conditions.

"A party of twelve took their crawlers a mile deep. Where the surface material had not collapsed, these rills continued underground through a vast network of caverns and tunnels. They split up, each taking a different route.

"Almost immediately they made a great find. Hidden in the dark recesses, away from the wind and constantly changing temperatures, Dr. Sanders discovered great masses of living lichen clinging to the walls. Life, Mr. Martin, not mere spores preserved for millions of years by a quirk of fate, but real, reproducing, thriving life."

I came halfway out of my chair. "But, that's — "

"This lichen thrives in the complete absence of light, relying on principles of chemosynthesis rather than chlorophyll and photosynthesis — somewhat like plants and animals existing in the extreme depths of the sea."

"Why haven't I heard — "

A heavily muscled arm waved me down. "Here me out, first. Soon they found mounds of geometrically shaped rocks — artificially worn, some even fitting together in an unmistakable tongue and groove fashion. Sanders deduced that it was the remains of a wall — an artificial wall — that had once sealed the cave entrance."

My heart pounded, my mouth was dry.

"Soon they found handmade artifacts, as well as the remnants of intelligently made structures. By the end of the day, they stumbled onto the almost completely buried ruins of an entire city."

Rogers jumped up out of his chair, presenting an athletic profile unslacked by the years. He paced behind his desk like a caged tiger. Thirty years after the first manned landing on Mars, he founded the first settlement. He watched it grow from a one room emergency pod to the sprawling city that it was today. The Mars Project that was his brainchild was now his ward.

"I . . . I can't . . . believe this . . . this . . . has happened in my lifetime. It's . . . "

Rogers put his weight on the computer console, held out a beckoning hand. "It's more than I could have hoped for. That we should uncover the remains of a civilization practically in our own back yard . . . and in the mere dawn of space exploration . . . "

He shook his shaggy head, resumed his pacing.

That life should be a common phenomenon in the universe was an accepted mathematical probability. Given infinite size and unlimited time, life was the inevitable culmination of molecular affinity for entering into more complex and eventually self-perpetuating chemical bonds. But the occurrence of self-awareness and cognitive thinking required billions of years of careful evolution and a rare combination of events.

The latest anthropological evidence placed man's beginnings on Earth five million years in the past: a mere one-thousandth of life's total inhabitancy on the planet. Individual communication filled only one ten-thousandth of this time. The consolidation of nomadic tribes into protective groups, the beginning of cooperative progress, reduced the fraction to one hundred-thousandth. Only one-millionth of the life span of the Earth could actually be accounted for by the farthest reaches of written history.

"And when I say city, Mr. Martin, I mean just that. I'm not talking about obscure bamboo huts, or

Amerindian cliff dwellings. I'm talking about multi-story buildings and paved streets and mechanized vehicles and — technology! Naturally, thousands of millennia have rusted the machinery almost beyond recognition. But think of it, the remnants of a civilization as great as, if not greater than, our own."

I followed the Chairman's peregrinations with bulging eyes. "It's all we've ever dreamt of, and more."

"Or, perhaps it's something we never *could* have dreamt of."

Rogers stared at the plexiglass cabinet that held his memorabilia: scaled-down replicas of a shuttlecraft, an unmanned long-range freighter, an asteroid roborocket, an early prototype Mars lander. Behind them were his personal photographs, a pictorial biography of his life in astronautics. He was portrayed in outmoded flight gear, variously posed with high-ranking government officials, and receiving unmentioned awards. One prominent enlargement showed him holding a fossil animal skull in one huge hand. His face was always adamantine.

"Sir, with all due respect, why wasn't I told this before? As Public Relations Officer, I — "

"Can you understand the implications if this news should be disseminated prematurely? Hear me out." Rogers reclaimed his chair, crouched forward. "Some mysterious malady soon gripped Dr. Sanders and the other three men of his crawler team. They managed to meet up with the rest of the exploration party, but by then they were raving maniacs. They died one by one, Dr. Sanders last. The men in the other two crawlers were unaffected, and brought the bodies back to the City."

"Wait a minute." I held up my hand. "Had the others been in contact with the lichen?"

"Sanders had brought back samples. They were in his crawler. It didn't affect the other crews. So you can see the problem. On the one hand, he had news of a stupendous nature and of immense portent to the human race, while on the other — well, the discoverers died as madmen. Was the city just a figment of insanity? Could we rely on the statements of dying lunatics? We were left with conjectures instead of facts, dreams instead of hope."

"Surely they had a video camera with them?"

"Too far away, too dark, vague shapes." Rogers shrugged. "I classified it top secret until we could study and evaluate the situation, until we had more conclusive proof. The Committee members did not all agree. But it was necessary. Can you imagine the cultural impact this might have? My god." Thick fingers dug into wavy hair. Rogers leaned back in his chair.

"Sir, I — You're right. There's no telling how the public might react. If the information isn't disseminated properly, in the right light, its reception could be confusing, antagonistic, even openly hostile. Putting people in their place in the universe . . . "

"On the other hand, we must protect the Project from unnecessary embarrassment if these — reports — are later found unsubstantiated."

"But, if all that was months ago, surely they've had time to verify the facts. An investigation would be routine."

Rogers stood up, walked to the other plastic case. He stared at the fossil impressions, fragments of bones, linked skeletons. Carbon based life always took the same path, from the lowest planarian to the highest vertebrate. The varieties evolved to suit local conditions, but the similarity on the biological scale was quintessential.

"After they came around the sun, and line of sight restored communications, intelligence has been infrequent and sporadic. What minimal radio contact _was_ established yielded no direct answers to our questions. We have received no updated reports of the archaeological excavations, no analyses of the lichen or the ruins or the Martians who built them."

I stood up, touched the front of the desk for support. "Do you mean that they are purposely withholding information of the greatest discovery in the history of the human race? How can they do that?"

Rogers turned slowly, the luster gone from his steely grays. "They can by simply ignoring our questions. Of course, we still receive automatic telemetering information from orbital tracking satellites and ground-based data pods. It's the direct verbal reports that have been lacking. We haven't lost the means of communication, but the common grounds of understanding. They simply refuse to respond."

"Why, that's mutiny. It sounds as if the Colony is waging open rebellion."

"That is subject to interpretation. Let's just say that it's a scientific experiment temporarily out of control."

"Out of *our* control, or out of *their* own control as well?"

Rogers' broad shoulders sagged. "That, Mr. Martin, is what I want you to find out."

My eyebrows arched sharply.

"You are in a unique position, a knowledgeable position. You are intimate with the workings of the Appropriations Committee. You understand the Earth's economic dependency on the space program. You are acutely aware of the ramifications that the Mars Project has on the future of mankind — especially in light of recent developments.

"At the same time, you have a deep perception of the function and management of Syrtis City. You know how it operates, you know its needs and weaknesses. But most importantly, you know the people. You've worked with them, you've talked with them, you've lived with them, you've dreamt with them. They are your friends. I believe that if you were to return to Mars as an emissary of this Committee, an ambassador if you will, you could learn what we have been unable to ascertain."

My pause was long. "Why not interrogate the returnees."

"Because there won't be any."

"*What?*" I nearly screamed.

"Every one of the approximately six hundred people

due for rotation this opposition has elected to extend for another tour. *Every* one, without exception."

"Why, that's unheard of."

Rogers flung out a wayward hand. "Hell, I'd have stayed there too if this had happened during my tour. And you don't know how much I want to go back. But I can't leave now. There's too much at stake."

I shook my head slowly. "This is going to throw the recruiting program way out of kilter. What are we going to do with all the trainees? We have obligations to them."

"Major Tarkington has requested that all personnel slated for duty on Mars be transported anyway."

"But, that's ridiculous. Where will they put them? How will they feed them? Where will they get the air to breath? How can they support six hundred extra bodies unless . . . "

Rogers gripped me with his penetrating stare. "Exactly. Unless many more have died. I don't know." He threw his hands in the air, jumped up, found his pacing path, stuck his hands in his pockets. "Major Tarkington swears there is no cause for alarm, that the additional personnel are needed to help excavate and study the ruins. He swears there have been no further fatalities, but he's been so evasive in other ways that I'd like to be a little more informed on the situation before I sentence six hundred souls to some unknown fate."

He stabbed his finger on the desk. "Don't misunderstand me. I trust Tarkington implicitly and value his judgment. Despite his flamboyant devil-may-care front, he's a conscientious man dedicated to his job. I picked him for those very qualities. He gets along with people. But whatever is happening on Mars makes me doubt everyone's sanity."

"So what's their answer?" I ticked off facts on my fingers. "We know the hydroponics farm can supply only so much food. The permafrost layer can yield only limited amounts of water. Minerals having water of hydration require a considerable expenditure of energy for reclamation — and limonite doesn't grow on trees.

Besides, they need that energy for life support functions. And as for radioactive fuels, well, it'll be a long time before they can even consider implementing the technology to extract and refine their own."

Rogers ticked back. "They propound extreme conservation, improved recycling techniques, new discoveries in natural resources. In fact, they're almost blatantly saying that they can get along without us. Now, I'm not willing to concede that as a possibility. Not yet, anyway. But I do know that we can't live without them. Our whole economy hinges on the space program. To disrupt the exchange of materials and ideas between Earth and Mars would disrupt the continuity of our entire planet. It doesn't sound plausible that a mere twelve hundred people millions of miles away can have such an effect, but the political harmony brought about by the space program, of which the Mars Project is the largest part, is the only thing keeping this planet from blowing itself apart at the seams. They are the key to international cooperation.

"There's a change taking place on Mars, Mr. Martin. The Colony is no longer a mere scientific outpost — it has become a culture unto itself. But that change is not necessarily a bad one." Rogers sat down again, worked his hands nervously. "The Colony is evolving its own psychology. What we on Earth construe as abnormal or unstable may no longer be valid for a group of people segregated from the mainstream of humanity, and living under unnatural conditions and pressures. It could be that a psychological wall has been erected to hold back their incipient fears and the implications of what they've found; or, it may be a natural adaptation to an alien environment and a new way, an altogether different plane, of thinking.

"The people on Mars are not just numbers in an experiment, they are human beings. They are my friends. Dr. Sanders was a great man, and I would like to know that he and the others died for a good cause. If they've found something so exciting, so overreaching, that it's inaugurated such protective measures, I respect their caution. But I need to know what it is.

"And in order to find out what I need to know, so I can make the proper judgments and decisions from this Chair, I need a more intimate knowledge of the circumstances. I need a representative who has been a part of the Colony, one who can think as they think, who can understand their wants and special needs, who can work for the Project as they work for it, who can feel for it as they feel for it. I want to find out about the people: why are they different, how have they changed, what are their goals, what makes them tick?"

I saw Rogers as an anxious father, worried about his progeny, and asking simply: how are my children doing? If the Colony had decided to strike out on its own, he wanted to know only that it was for their own good. Nothing mattered other than the Project having every chance of success, that man continue in his expansion. And he was willing to back them to the limits of his position, his name, his life.

The vein on his temple throbbed visibly. "You don't have to stay. Just conduct an investigation, gather all pertinent data, and bring it back. If not on this shuttle, then the next. And they've agreed to hold an inquiry and give a full briefing — if I send someone there. No one there wants to leave Mars."

I took a deep breath, held it for a moment. "This is really quite unexpected, Mr. Rogers. To see the wonders of an ancient, alien civilization, to be in the forefront of mankind's greatest discovery. I have the feeling that we're about to be vaulted into the next higher plane of existence. But — " I paused, diverting my eyes. "But, there are personal considerations . . . "

"Mr. Martin, I don't like being manipulative. I am when it's necessary. I have to be. It's my job. So, perhaps you weren't paying attention when I said that *everyone* was extending — without exception."

My eyes widened, a chill ran down my spine.

"Lieutenant Chapman won't be coming back either. At least, not now. Perhaps later. I don't know. You might be able to convince her."

At what point do two people agree that they have been apart for too long, that they have grown away from each other too far for reconciliation, that they have had such widely divergent experiences that they no longer think alike, dream alike, feel alike? When does one admit that personal communication has ended?

I took another deep breath. "I'll do my best, Mr. Rogers."

For the first time in all the years I had known him, during all the time I had worked with him, I saw the glimmer of a smile touch his stern lips.

It was a smile not of triumph, but of hope.

Chapter 3

"Passengers will please return to their seats and don helmets and chestpacks."

With exaggerated motion, I looked over my shoulder at the rows of empty acceleration couches behind me. (Or below me, or above me. Orientation in space is purely subjective.) *Who're they trying to kid? I'm the only passenger aboard.* After six weeks on this stinking tub, the crew could at least be a little less formal.

"Suit umbilical oxygen supply must be engaged during reentry procedures."

I swallowed two zero-gee pills (puking into your faceplate can be messy), pulled the helmet down from its cubical, and clamped it onto my breastplate. A half turn of the intake knob was followed by the faint hiss of oxygen. I squeezed into the gloves and sealed the rubber gaskets.

The chessboard on the computer screen dissolved as I pushed the monitor up and out of the way. I detached the chestpack from the forward bulkhead, attached the hoses and safety locks. When I repositioned the viewscreen, the ocher orb of Mars hung motionless in the center of the three-dimensional reflector plate, lending a dioramic symmetry that was both divine and austere.

Conspicuous by its absence was the flurry of neophyte comments: "It's not red at all," or, "It doesn't look any different than the moon," or, "What a frightfully desolate place." The "oohs" and "ahs" were loud by their omission.

From this altitude I saw the straight, crisscrossing lines — often mistaken for canals — which were mountain ranges and fault lines and deep, wide rills, all of which were either dissolved into obscurity from a more distant viewpoint or brought into resolution during closer approach. Atmospheric swirls of dark brown, laced with delicate traces of yellow, were strung gossamerlike across the face of the planet. The surface seemed peaceful and aloof. But the appearance of serenity was misleading, for much of Mars was a churning maelstrom of wind and dust and sand: an inhospitable welcome at best.

As we descended, the horizon curves were forced out of view and the pockmarked surface filled the screen. Craters survived the ravages of time only slightly worse than their lunar analogues. Unlike the Moon, time moved inexorably onward — although at a pace much slower than Earthly geologists are used to observing. Crater rims were rounded, beaten down by wind erosion, and trapped sand lay deep in their interiors. Great crevices sometimes bisected the older, antediluvian craters, evidence of the violent quakes and tectonic plate slippage that had shaken this desiccated world in its not-too-distant past.

Within the ship, heterodyning vibrations roared like a base fiddle: powerful retrorockets were fired for our entry into the thin atmosphere. At this height, the rarified atmosphere did not yet offer the resistance of friction. Wind would not be encountered until we were practically on the ground. The ship strained from internal stress.

The forces of gravity in space were almost nonexistent, and structures which did not have to fight the heavy gravity of Earth were designed with less load criteria: mainly that of acceleration and deceleration. The whine of overworking engines was the only sound in the lonely cabin, although I could feel the disturbing creaking and groaning of metal fatigue.

The rough, rocky ground passed by with ever-quickening speed. Excitement tingled my spine; the lump in my throat almost choked me. It was like coming home after a long absence.

The screen suddenly went dead. A voice on the intercom stated flatly, "We are now entering the Martian atmosphere. For reasons of safety, all cameras and external instruments, except those of the command module, will be withdrawn into the body of the ship until landing is effected. Please do not leave your seat for any reason, and do not — I repeat — do not remove your helmet or disengage your umbilical, in case of accidental depressurization. If you experience any equipment malfunctions, press the emergency button on the couch console and we will abort the landing. Thank you."

I laughed. A complicated system of limit switches, pressure switches, and float switches would automatically register any malfunctions on the pilot's central control board. Every movement in the ship, either mechanical or human, was constantly monitored. They knew more about what I was doing than I did.

I may as well have closed my eyes and gone to sleep. There was nothing to see, nothing to hear, nothing to do. I felt cheated. In poor resignation, I relaxed in the cushioned acceleration couch and waited for the final spiral to begin. I swallowed, wondering when the zero-gee pills would begin to work.

In a way, the landing was a disappointment: it was smooth and almost carefree. There was some mild buffeting in the lower atmosphere, but for the most part we glided in and touched down gently, the final jar not even hard enough to spill a glass of water. I applauded to the empty compartment but refrained, in my isolation, from cheering. Despite their coldness and lack of pomp, these astronauts were true professionals.

The viewscreen flashed on and the intercom crackled.

"We have effected landing in Dobbins Crater at zero-nine-two-seven local time. Visibility is in excess of fifty miles, the wind is northwesterly at five to ten miles per hour, the temperature is ranging in the low thirties — below zero, of course. Do not leave your seat or disengage your suit oxygen supply system until instructed to do so, as the cabin is being depressurized for unfreighting."

First I was treated as an animal in a zoo, then I was to be unloaded like a parcel of luggage. But then, I was the most expensive cargo this bucket ever carried. This was the only passenger shuttle that ever arrived with only one paying customer.

I released the decel-straps, happy to find that Martian gravity was enough to keep me from floating out of my seat, but light enough so I did not feel overburdened with weight. The viewscreen was switched on. As the dust settled around the landing strip, the outside landscape took on an oddly familiar ring. The miserable, flat sandbox that was Dobbins Crater was broken only by the low structures of the spaceport — a loose conglomeration of pressurized Quonset huts that had served as the first beachhead before Syrtis City was built.

The sky was dull orange, shading more toward the pink near the horizon, and contrasted sharply with the harsh reddish soil which stood out boldly in the midmorning sun. High crater walls surrounded the entire landing zone and support buildings, a natural protection against the ravages of wind. The only motion was the rotating aerial atop the command building, its sweeping radar beam sensitive enough to detect the approach of dust clouds and sand storms.

An orange cloud erupted to the right of the screen. A huge tractor strained under the massive weight of the gleaming gantries employed to tether the ship to the ground. Slowly the tracked vehicle clanked toward the ship, leaving great gouges in the sand.

Behind the tractor, a crawler sped across the field, a churning cloud of dust in its wake. It seemed small in comparison, but Martian sand crawlers were much bigger than army tanks, and even in Mars' gravity weighed nearly as much.

The airtight hatch on the forward bulkhead of the passenger compartment was undogged and opened, and a spacesuited figure climbed down the ladder. "There's a crawler coming for you, Mr. Martin."

"Thanks, Lieutenant." Except for a slightly twisted nose, the navigator's face was handsome and expressionless. Adams was the more personal of the three-man crew. "Aren't you eager to get your feet on the ground?"

"We'll be several hours getting the ship shut down and checked over, but you can disembark immediately." He disconnected the umbilical and let it slide into its compartment. "You've already got your chestpack hoses in place."

"I'm not altogether helpless, except when it comes to chess. Do you know where I can pick up a good book on opening moves?"

Practiced hands checked the oxygen bottle and carbon dioxide scrubber. "Not on Mars. But you might ask Major Tarkington for a few pointers. He's a skilled logician and a good strategist."

"Just like you — always thinking ten moves ahead."

"Chess is nothing more than an intellectual sequence of perceptive anticipations, bold advances, wise retreats, and deliberate counterplays. Your opponent has no real advantage except in knowing what he himself intends to do. As long as you logically deduce his moves, you can predict where he will strike next." Blandly, he switched off the monitor and stowed it. "As soon as the gantry is in place, you may leave by the freight lock. The all-clear lights will be flashing green."

I pushed myself up to a sitting position and swung my legs over the edge of the couch. "Thanks for helping me to wile away the time."

Lieutenant Adams nodded perfunctorily, and was gone.

The ship rested on its broad tail and, with the return of gravity, the other couches were, in truth, below me. I climbed down the inset rungs and jumped lightly to the aft bulkhead. The pressure suit had a resistance all its own as I bent down awkwardly to undog the hatch.

I descended through three cargo holds until I stood on the loading deck. Below me, the nuclear reactor throbbed dully like a beating heart. The suit stiffened as air was pumped out of the compartment. Clear lights flashed over the loading bay.

The suit radio squawked. "You may remove the mechanical overrides, Mr. Martin."

The enormous door was unsealed, cranked into the room, and slid on rollers into a hidden recess by the gentle sucking action of a hydraulic pump.

The cold hit me like a bolt. As a natural byproduct of atomic energy, heat was constantly recycled throughout the ship, providing comfort as well as a margin of safety for delicate computer circuits. The auxiliary bioregulators attached to the suit power-pack whined into action.

The engine cowling spread out below me. Wider than the cargo, passenger, and command modules, it offered a wide lip that surrounded the cone-shaped ship like an all-around, unroofed portico. I easily scampered down the exposed rungs and leaped outward, floating down, and landing with a puff of dust on the reddish sand.

It was as strange an experience now as it had been when I first touched Martian soil seven years earlier. Lasting impressions of that long-past day were vivid in my memory: the sky was just as orange, the sand just as soft and grainy, and the spaceport just as bleak and dismal. But then, I had been accompanied by fifty fellow colonists, all as thrilled and eager as I.

The gantry was in position, the ship safely tethered, and the tractor retreating. A hundred yards away a crawler squatted in the sand. Picture a steamship's boiler: cylindrical, forty feet in length, ten feet in diameter. Place it on a rectangular skid on which an atomic motor block ran the length of the undercarriage. Surround it with oxygen cylinders and dozens of aerials, sensors, and cameras. Straddle it with ten-foot-high tank treads, place a plexiglass bubble at one end, and an armored airlock hatch at the other.

When the door swung down and became a ramp, I had the impression of a giant grasshopper extending its ovipositor. A blue and red egg dropped to the ground, turned and became a slim figure dressed in a typical Martian exposure suit. A waving hand caught my attention. My heart skipped a beat as I recognized the flowing feminine motion. On all of Mars, there was but one woman this could be. The cold forgotten, I bounded toward the still figure.

Five feet away from her I stopped. Inside the glass of the protective hood, curly golden locks framed a pure white face. Dimpled cheeks puffed, blue eyes glistened. The bleakness of the terrain, the utter solitude and loneliness of this strange and alien planet, were swept away by that waving hand and smiling face.

Silently, we stared at each other for a full minute. I had dreamt of this moment for the past two months, and now that it had arrived, I was drained of all emotion except a warm and overpowering relief. She reached out with two gauntleted hands. I responded by raising my arms and lightly cradling her fingers in my open palms.

"I've been expecting you, Doug."

"It's been a long time, Linda."

"It might have been longer if you hadn't come back."

But don't you remember? You were supposed to come back to me. She did not appear like the Linda Chapman I had left behind so long ago.

I had dreamt and rehearsed this meeting a hundred times, and now that it was happening I had forgotten my lines. It was not going the way I had imagined. "Yes, it's a good thing I did."

Two tiny, iridescent pearls fell from her lovely eyes and rolled down her cheeks, to disappear behind the breathing diaphragm. "Oh, Doug."

We leaped forward at the same time, and fell into each other's arms. It was a strange hug, she in her exposure suit, I in my spacesuit, and with my awkward chestpack between us.

She cried softly. I tried to rub her back, but her own life support system was in the way. Many moments later she pushed me away, laughing. "Well, let's not stand out here talking about it. Let's get inside where we can get out of these damned suits. I want to *touch* you."

"And I want to kiss you."

Linda took my hand firmly and led me to the rear

hatch of the crawler.

We climbed into the narrow confines of the airlock, and she closed the outer door. She started the repressurization cycle. With a hiss, the small chamber filled with oxygen. When the ready light flicked on, she pushed open the inner door.

A huge, bearlike fist wrapped around my gloved hand, squeezed the blood out of it, and pulled me into the main compartment. A deep voice boomed, "Welcome home, son."

There was no mistaking that fine western drawl. I looked up into the gritty face of Thomas Tarkington and was instantly speared by two dazzling blue eyes that had a life and awareness all their own. Hoodless and gloveless, his burly form filled out his exposure suit like a padded football player. After all these years in the dimness of Mars, he still retained his dark, Texan complexion. If he had been wearing a ten-gallon hat, it would not have looked out of place.

"Hello, Major." I retrieved my hand and stretched the fingers; miraculously, they still worked. Numbly, I unsnapped the safety buckles from the breastplate. The Major lifted the stainless steel and plexiglass dome off my shoulders and placed it on a bunk. "It's good to be back, although I didn't expect a welcoming committee."

"Nonsense, my boy. We were tickled pink when we heard about your little visit. They could have sent some stuffed shirt who doesn't know air from oxygen. Nice to have one of the scattered sheep return to the flock."

"Flattery will get you everywhere."

Linda doffed her exposure hood and fluffed up her hair. Her eyes were still damp when she wrapped her arms around my neck and kissed me on the lips. "Did you ever know the Major to flatter when he didn't mean it?"

"I never knew him to flatter at all. And you did all the time. But then, you had ulterior motives."

"Oh, you." She pushed me away playfully.

"Bah." The Major scowled in mock anger. He plopped down in one of the front seats and started the engine. "In case you've forgotten how rough these babies ride, you'd better sit down and strap yourself in."

"You can ride shotgun." Linda sat behind the Major and pushed me into the copilot's seat. The machine lurched forward just as I cinched down the safety harness. With a twist of the steering wheel, the crawler veered toward the low buildings near the crater wall.

The landing zone had been groomed for touchdown, and the flotation treads carried us along smoothly. But when we reached the edge of the graded field, the hillocks and moguls took on the guise of a poorly designed ski slope. Like an off-road racecourse, we followed a line of flagpoles stuck upright in the ground.

"Things have really changed since you left," Linda said enthusiastically.

"Yes, we've entered a new era of exploration and colonization." Major Tarkington bunched his fleshy cheeks as the crawler crashed hard over the peak of a dune. "I venture to say the next decade on Mars will offer more challenge and enlightenment than all of man's past history."

The bounce took my breath away. "Let me be the first to offer personal congratulations from the Committee. Needless to say, we're all excited about it — at least, those of us with a need to know. We're keeping it classified until we can ascertain the facts and assess the best way of gaining public approval."

"Loosen up, son. You sound like a government announcement. With the new digging tools in this shipment, we can practically double our productivity. Keppert's got a big crew working day and night, uncovering more all the time. We'll show you the whole operation when we get out there."

"There's enough time for business later." The crawler slewed sideways, straining Linda against her straps. "How was your flight? You must have had the run of the ship."

I swallowed my stomach. "Well, you know how those military blokes are. They treated me like any other passenger, making sure I kept within the specifications of standard operating procedure. They stayed up in their cubbyhole most of the time, although Adams played chess with me through the terminal. Those guys hardly ever talk, and when they do they sound like a recording. You know, I used to wonder why they don't replace space crews with computers. Now I know: they replaced them years ago, they just haven't told anyone yet —."

The crawler took a sudden dip, clipping off my conversation.

"Sorry about that. I should have warned you." The Major slowed the crawler to a gallop. "You'd better keep your tongue in your mouth if you don't want to lose it."

Through the six-foot-diameter viewing port, I saw the low domes of the spaceport. Prevailing winds created a shadow effect, with one side of each structure covered to the very roof with drifts of sand, while the other side was bare. No attempt was made to change this natural order; in addition to insulating against heat loss, the dunes offered protection from windblown debris. The crawler slipped into the deep depression on the downstream side.

"Somebody hand me a bag. There's something else I'm going to lose."

Chapter 4

"All ashore that's going ashore," announced the Major in his gruff, stentorian voice.

With the garage doors closed and air pressure pumped into the cubicle, there was no reason to don our headgear. We filed through a set of double airlock doors and entered the main corridor of the spaceport.

I parked my helmet on the dressing shelf alongside a row of exposure hoods. The names stenciled on the forehead were not so much for sizing, but because from a distance, practically everyone looked alike.

"I hate to run off like this, but I want to check with the loading crew. Linda will get you squared away with a suit, and I'll meet you a little later for lunch." Major Tarkington waved off and hurried along the corridor.

I shook my head. "Doesn't he ever slow down?"

"Only in his sleep, and then it's only to half speed."

The Major bumped into someone a head shorter and considerably slighter, emerging from a side passage. The two faced each other, exchanged words, and separated after the Major pounded him on the shoulder and gave a hearty laugh.

The man turned our way. He wore the ubiquitous beige uniform whose dense pile lining doubled as thermal protection. He moved quickly and flamboyantly, and carried a black leather bag in his left hand.

Linda tapped me with an elbow. "Uh-oh. You're in for it now."

Before I could ask why, the man stretched out his hand and picked up mine. "Hello, Doug. Long time no see. Welcome back to our humble community."

"Doc! I didn't recognize you without the beard."

"I had to shave it off in 'professional interest' when I became the senior local practitioner."

"So, you finally made the big time."

"Who in their right mind would have made me the head of anything on Earth? I had to travel fifty million miles before I could find an opening. Now they call me the Syrtis City Healer."

Linda nudged me. "We call him 'Heal' for short, but we usually spell it with two e's. He gives very penetrating examinations. Ask any of the girls."

Aloysius Reynolds pushed a shock of thick black hair off his long forehead. "Hey, cut it out. You'll give me a bad rep."

"It can't get any worse." To me, "Don't get into any arguments with him. As chirurgeon and chief necromancer, he'd rather change your body than your mind."

"Doug, you'd better watch this gal. She may be warm and toasty on the outside, but where it counts — " He thumped his chest with a finely manicured hand. " — she doesn't have a human heart."

Linda feinted with her left. "You'd better watch yourself, Mr. Doctor, or I'll give you a medicinal nightcap — on your chin."

"She screeches like a tigress, but you should have heard her meow when she heard you were coming." Linda pouted and flashed dagger eyes at Doc Reynolds. He winked at her. "Seriously, Doug, it's good to see you again. How do you feel?"

"Was that asked in a professional capacity, or do you really care."

"Both."

"Well, aside from a confused equilibrium, I might consider challenging you in arm wrestling."

"No fair. You've still got your Earthbound muscles, while I've been wallowing under one-third gravity for half a decade." Under that shapeless uniform was the broad chest and narrow waist of a weight lifter.

"This might be my only chance to beat you. Why the little black bag?"

"Regulations. With the discovery of a new life form, we've decided to take precautions. We no longer live in a sterile environment, and we don't want anyone infecting our little world. From now on, all incoming personnel get complete physicals and a series of immunization shots."

I tried to peer through Doc Reynolds' perpetual off-beat grin. "Has — there been any more contamination?"

"There hasn't been *any*, and I aim to see that it stays that way. Now, I hate to pry you two apart so soon, but I need to see Doug's body before you do."

"I can take a hint." Linda gave me a peck on the cheek and a sturdy hug. "I'll make myself scarce, and meet you two in the cafeteria."

Doc Reynolds called after her as she pattered away, "And the next time you want to hold a private conversation outside, keep your radios on low power. You had me in tears."

"Voyeur!"

"Hey, it wasn't just me — we piped it over the intercom." She rounded a corner, and Doc Reynolds grabbed me by the arm. "Right this way, said the spider to the fly. I've got a dispensary and sick bay all set up, so I can handle the new recruits when they start arriving — assuming you give the go ahead. The spaceport is going to be our quarantine before we let anyone into the City."

He led me into a closet crammed with medical supplies, surgical equipment, and oxygen storage cylinders. The furniture consisted of a metal cabinet stocked with a wide assortment of pills, lotions, and medications; a low couch with a crank-up foot and headrest; and a swivel stool.

"The first thing you can do is take off your clothes."

After six weeks without a change of underwear, I was happy to shed the spacesuit. "Your bedside manner alone will cure the ill."

"But it won't get me a raise." Doc Reynolds took a gallon bottle from the bottom shelf and poured a greenish liquid into a basin.

"I've already had my antifreeze checked, and I'm cold enough."

"Keep your shorts on." The doctor handed me a washcloth. "Scrub yourself down with this and let it evaporate. You'll be chilly at first, but just put up with it. I'll get you some thermals. Use some of this paste on your hair; it'll get most of the grease out."

"Doc, you forget, I've done this before."

"Sure, but I need the practice. I' m going to have to go through this routine another six hundred times."

After he left, I performed all the vigorous motions of a sponge bath, shivering from the cold as the alcohol evaporated. After five minutes I felt completely refreshed, and smelled like an Avon saleslady. I was shaking apart by the time he returned. "Hey, my goose bumps have goose bumps."

The good doctor handed over the one-piece thermals. "Put these on right away. I can conduct most of the exam through the zippers and up the sleeves."

After thirty minutes of oral medical history, I protested, "Doc, all that's in my files."

"Just testing your memory."

The physical was designed to cause discomfort to the patient. I was poked and prodded in every conceivable location, private and otherwise; all my orifices were thoroughly looked into; I was given a complete gamut of electronic tests. I was checked for hearing, sight, and skin sensitivity. I was x-rayed, electroencephalographed, blood sampled (more than once), breathalyzed, and urinanalized. From under the examination couch, he pulled every kind of instrument except the kitchen sink — that he left in place in order to wash.

"You're the picture of health. A little out of focus around the edges, but otherwise printable."

"'I'll take two copies."

"How's the nausea?"

I wobbled my hand.

"Roll up your sleeve." He rummaged through his medical cabinet and brought out a clear plastic bottle containing a dark amber liquid. He removed the sterile covering from a long, ominous looking hypodermic syringe, filled it from the bottle. "This will only hurt for a little while."

"'I'm a man, Doc, not a horse. What is that stuff?"

"This," he intoned, "is Dr. Reynolds' panacea for frostbite, dehydration, oxygen starvation, acclimatization, and all related Martian maladies, including the common cold. It's an old family recipe made from rare Martian herbs."

He dabbed an alcohol-soaked cotton puff on my upper arm and stabbed me in a delicate, almost feminine way. The prick stung mildly at first. Then a growing pain, like a wasp sting, grew around the needle point before he pulled it out. It left a dull, throbbing sensation.

"It might itch a little, but try not to irritate it by rubbing or scratching. And if you feel slightly lightheaded for a few hours, it will be a normal reaction."

I rolled down my sleeve, squeezed the swelling. "It hurts like the devil."

"Only the first one. The rest won't be so bad."

"You mean there're more?"

"At least half a dozen. If I gave them to you all at once, you'd run out of here screaming like a maniac. I'll give you one a day for the next several days. Stop in my office whenever you get a chance and I'll take care of you."

I climbed to my feet and slipped into a pair of insulated slippers. "That's what I'm afraid of. Hey, what's that?"

On a shelf by the door stood a beautifully crafted glass vase with a wide, thick lip. It was filled with reddish sand streaked with tan, producing a curious design that cascaded concentrically around the crystalline perimeter. Topping the arenaceous decoration was a brownish substance that resembled animal fur, or bread mold.

"Areolichen."

"Huhn." I hunched a little closer, squinting.

"Areo — of Mars. Lichen — a composite plant. Areolichen, plant of Mars. It's a sample from the Caves."

It was oddly attractive, almost captivating. Yet, it was such an ugly thing. A chill coursed along my spine as I drew nearer, sensing its uniqueness, it aliveness, its utter alienage.

Abruptly, I jerked my head back. A violent wave of

nausea overcame me. My stomach wretched and my throat gagged. I nearly vomited. The lichen stank with putrescence that was uncommonly strong and savagely emetic.

Doc Reynolds placed a hand on my shoulder, gripped tightly. "The flavor's a little rank till you get used to it."

"Rank isn't the word." I swallowed, and slowly regained my composure. "I'm surprised the first settlers didn't smell it out."

The doctor laughed. "It's hard to smell from inside an exposure suit."

Still a little queasy from that first whiff, I examined the lichen from a distance. Out of olfactory range, I again felt a warm adduction.

Doc Reynolds stole a glance at his wristwatch, grabbed his middle. "I knew my stomach was trying to tell me something. Let's hightail it to the cafeteria and fill our breadboxes. And don't rub that arm."

I pulled my hand away guiltily. "Sorry, I didn't even know I was doing it. It's still throbbing, like a dull ache."

"A little coffee'll make it go away." I backed over the sill while the doctor bent down to store the breathalyzer mask and close the oxygen valves.

A loud report was followed by a thunderous roar of air. Three clangs like the ringing of a bell tolled so close together as to seem simultaneous. A dent appeared in the bulkhead in front of my eyes, and I caught a fleeting glimpse of something shiny flying around the room, ricocheting off the panels and ceiling like a madly flying racket ball. The object narrowly missed the cabinet of glassware, and slammed onto the floor, spinning madly. The roaring went on and on.

In an instant, half a dozen people filled the narrow corridor. Since there had been no pressure drop, the hydraulically-operated airtight bulkhead doors had not closed automatically, but already two female technicians had stationed themselves at the ends of the corridor. One released the backup hydraulic cylinder and snapped the door shut; the other cranked furiously at the manual closing valve. A short, muscular man opened the emergency oxygen station, slung a tank over his broad shoulder, and, donning a mask, dispensed units to nearby personnel.

Someone slapped a mask over my face and pulled the straps over my head. I stopped him. "It's okay! It's okay!"

Doc Reynolds stepped out of the dispensary, his hair windblown. "It's all right, folks. Just another defective valve."

Calmly, the rebreathers were replaced in their niche, the bulkhead doors were opened, people returned to their duties. By the time the oxygen tank was empty and the noise was gone, the hallway was as deserted as if nothing had happened.

"What's all the fuss about?" Linda clutched my arm, looked up with her pretty blues. "I couldn't get in because the pressure doors were locked."

Doc Reynolds showed her the valve. "The threads stripped off the base and the tank pressure blew it around the room like a billiard ball. That's the third one that's gone blooey. I'm afraid we'll have to check every one that came in with that last shipment. And we'll have to do it right away before any real damage is done. Doug almost became a casualty, and it wouldn't look too good to the Committee if their special envoy got zapped as soon as he got here."

"Thanks for your concern over my safety," I scowled mockingly. To Linda, "It was the lichen that saved me. It smelled so bad that I was backing away from it when the valve let loose."

Doc Reynolds fingered the creased paneling. "Put a nice dent in the wall where his head had been."

"It's going to be quite a job tracing down all the valves in that batch." Linda squinted, staring up at the ceiling. "I think they came in about three months ago, on a freighter. They've been installed all over the City as replacements. Maintenance will really have their hands full for the next few days."

"I just want to occupy the next half hour feeding my face." Doc Reynolds pushed me along the corridor, led Linda by the hand. "We'll call Maintenance later."

"Shouldn't we do it right away?" I said.

"Technically, yes. But I'm sure they've had half a dozen reports in the last five minutes. So we'll wait a while and give them a reminder."

When we charged into the cafeteria, Linda took her hand back. "Remember, Doug, this is just an everyday occurrence on Mars."

"Grab a seat, folks." Doc Reynolds ushered us into chairs, and slipped into a pronounced French accent. "Today I am maitre d', waiter supreme, and chef magnifique. What is your pleasure, madame? Monsieur?"

"*Mademoiselle*, s'il vous plait."

"Ah, par*don*. I anticipate."

Linda licked her lips sensuously. "Well, I'm simply ravenous. I'll start out with New England clam chowder, spinach salad with Russian dressing, Swiss steak, Chantilly potatoes, Chinese vegetables, French bread, and for dessert, Boston cream pie."

"A truly international meal." Doc Reynolds slipped a plastic tray under Linda's nose, let the microwaved steam assail her nostrils. The variously colored items made the tray look like a painter's palette. "But today's special comes highly recommended. A local dish I think you'll enjoy."

"I had the luncheon special yesterday," she groaned. "The trouble with your menu is that it has no imagination. The least you could do is dress it up with something from hydroponics."

Doc Reynolds set another sectional tray in front of me. "This stuff is practically fresh, guaranteed not to be frozen more than five years."

I stuck a plastic spoon into the blue section. "It certainly can't be worse than those pasty liquids I've been sucking out of tubes for the past month and a half." The instant meal was good, if a little musty. All the flavors had the consistency of pudding, without crunch or chewable chunks.

The doctor set steaming plastic cups in front of us, slid into a chair. "Wash it down with some of this."

I took a sip and almost gagged. "Oh, god." I placed my hand over my mouth to prevent spitting the dark fluid all over the table. "This is the worst coffee I've ever tasted. What did you put in it — poison?"

"Don't let Phyllis hear you say that." Linda swallowed half a cup. "She blends fresh grown ingredients from her garden with the normally bland freeze-dried mix. You're just too used to that prepackaged shipboard alloy to appreciate it."

I pushed the cup her way. "You can have mine. I'll settle for a glass of distilled water — with no additives."

"All right. Plain H2O it is." Doc Reynolds filled a clean cup from the dispenser. "But eventually you'll acquire a taste for our brand. Like a lot of things on Mars, it grows on you."

I sipped the water approvingly. "I don't doubt your sincerity, only your veracity." The coffee left a bitter aftertaste in my mouth which the water did little to dispel. It was a pungency that lingered not only on the tongue, but on the mind. "Well, enough small talk. Tell me about the ruins. I know only as much as the Committee, and they haven't been very well informed."

Doc Reynolds chowed down. "Well, you can understand why. We have to be careful with what we say over the air — anyone can intercept radio waves. The cultural shock to the average mind could be devastating. You know yourself that in public relations bad news can be mitigated by the way it's given. People need to be conditioned to accept great truths, great changes. And this is the greatest — of both."

"Come on, Doc, stop patronizing me. When you withhold information from the Committee, you're leaning over the edge of mutiny. The Mars Project is essentially a military operation, in that it's supported by grants from the defense departments of the participating nations. The role of the scientific staff is to conform to policy determined by the Committee, and the military staff must enforce such conformity. Any misdirection is strictly accountable by court-martial."

Linda said, "Doug, there is no question of mutiny, but a discovery like this is not the kind of thing that can be shouted from every street corner."

"The Committee never asked to have it broadcast. They just want what they're entitled to have: a simple, straightforward, and accurate report, not the garbled nonsense they've been getting. Mars may be on the fringe of Earthside administration, but Project members are not beyond the pale of its jurisdiction."

"Let's not pass judgment before all the evidence is in." Doc Reynolds pushed aside his tray. "We just can't afford to have this information leaked the wrong way. We need to publish a complete and unbiased report of our findings, and I think Linda will agree that you are exactly the person to help us do it. But you do need to reserve an open mind, and let us show you in our own way the wonders of Martian civilization."

"If it's an open mind you want, you've got it. I want to see success here as much as you do. But we've got some influential countries backing this Project, and the whole of Earth's economy supporting it. They have a right to have answers to their questions."

My index finger was sore where I had been pounding it into the table. I bent and flexed it and gulped down my water.

"And answers you'll get, son. I promise you." Major Tarkington burst into the room, scooped up a cup from the counter, half filled it with steaming black brew, and still managed to spill some of it as he galloped towards the table and seated himself opposite me, sitting backward in the chair. "In fact, I'll guarantee that we've got more answers than you'll be able to think up questions for."

"That remains to be — "

He held up a halting palm. "I know. Rogers is chafing at the bit, but you have to understand this is a unique situation in the history of man. We've never been faced with a discovery of this nature, of this profound importance, with such an unforeseeable impact on the human race. We have to be sure of our ground before we go shooting our mouths off, or we might end up sticking a Martian foot in it.

"Now, I want you to have time to settle in. Take is easy for now, get around and meet some of the folks, and get the spacehives out of your system. Tomorrow afternoon we'll have a debriefing session and break you in. Keppert will show you some slides of the ruins, and fill you in on the background. But for today, for god's sake, don't fritter yourself about it. When you pour water out of a jug, it doesn't all come out at once. Linda, take a crawler. Just the two of you. Take the high road back to the City. Doug, I promise by the end of the week you'll have complete disclosure of the situation. But I'm going to do it my way."

Chapter 5

The massive crawler rocked gently in the twice-hurricane-force winds. Sand gritted and rocks pinged on the thick steel walls — but softly, the sound deadened by ample insulation between the inner and outer hulls. All sight of the raging storm was hidden: external camerascopes were withdrawn, and the viewport nestled under the protection of its opaque plastic shield. We were safe from the elements in our artificial iron womb.

My head cleared slowly after the waves of vertigo that I had experienced outside, but my arm still throbbed where Doc Reynolds had stabbed me with his infernal needle. I shivered uncontrollably for several minutes, to raise my body temperature, and I flexed my fingers to restore circulation in the partially numbed joints. Oddly, Linda seemed only mildly discomforted.

"Syrtis City. Syrtis City. This is crawler number seventeen. Come in please." Linda reiterated the plaintive message in a calm, even monotone.

Abruptly, she turned off the transmitter. "Damn. The storm must have fouled our antenna."

Sitting in the command seats, we faced a complicated array of switches, dials, annunciator lights, digital readouts, and monitors. Together we tested the various mechanical and electronic functions. After five minutes, it seemed certain that everything was in working order — everything, that is, except the radio. All other aerials and external sensors responded to test modes. But the antenna retract button failed to actuate.

"It must have been blown away, or twisted out of shape, so it no longer fits the housing."

I familiarized myself with the controls. "What's the wind speed?" Linda glanced at the anemometer. "One seventy."

I whistled. "I've seen worse, but always from the safe side of the viewport. That came on rather suddenly, didn't it?"

"We should have been warned. Base always broadcasts storm watches on the automatic emergency frequency. I don't understand what could have happened."

"Could our receiver be broken? We haven't used it at all, so we would have no way of knowing."

She studied the readouts. "I don't think so. The Major radioed the ship when you arrived. Damn it, they should have warned us before we left. We have weather stations a hundred miles away." She slunk down and stared emptily at the blanked viewport.

There was nothing to do but sit tight like a turtle in its shell and wait out the tempest. "I think your Irish anger is aroused."

Her faced cracked. Linda forced a half smile, patted the back of my hand. "I'm sorry. How about something to eat?" She pushed her steering wheel against the sidewall and swiveled around in her seat.

"Sure, I could use something warm."

The buslike interior stretched for twenty-five feet between rear passenger seats and inner airlock. Encased in the magnesium steel shell was a dazzling assortment of scientific instruments, equipment racks, and portable testing gear, all of which could be exchanged or removed to suit the needs of the particular exploring party. Fitted into all this were four bunks, a kitchenette, a chemical toilet, and water tanks. (Water froze if stored outside.) Filling up every available nook and cranny were small closets and drawers packed with food, clothes, air mattresses and sleeping bags for outside use, pressure tents, emergency signal and survival gear, and the million and one items that were essential on a Martian "camping" trip.

Slung under the pressure hull, the atomic motor and drive train were exposed to the cold natural environment. The single uranium slug would power the vehicle for years without a core change. And as long as we started out with a new set of CO_2 scrubbers, the oxygen supply would last for weeks.

Linda returned from the kitchen console with two

steaming mugs of thick soup. "Speaking off the record, and aside from the objectionable secrecy, how do you view our situation?"

I cupped my hands around the insulated plastic, and blew away steam. "That's rather a broad question, don't you think? There's a lot more at stake than the cultural ramifications. If this city is all it's cracked up to be, there could be widespread technological advancements — deciphering some of the Martian's achievements. But since I don't have all the data, it's impossible to say."

"Well, speaking in general terms, what I mean is — is the Committee still behind us? Despite the — insubordination — have they turned against us, or are they willing to go along with us, with our work and recommendations? Do they still have faith in us?"

I thought cautiously before answering. "In general, I would say yes. Rogers is behind you one hundred percent. So are some others. But there are several members who think that staff actions have not been in the best interests of the Project — or, at least, of those who support the Project. You've been in liaison long enough to know that an organization must function as a body, as a single unit, not as two discordant branches working against each other. Just as an army *must* take orders from its command post."

Linda gulped down her soup, put the empty mug on the console. "There was never any thought of working against Earth's best interests, or the dictums of the Committee. Our actions were those of *dis*cretion rather than *trans*gression. Sometimes decisions are made in the field that those in their offices are not in a position to see or understand."

"But how can you expect them to understand if you don't give them the facts? The Committee wants nothing more — nor expects any less — than full cooperation. They can't make decisions of protocol without information. They have a right to know the score."

"Can they accept a change in the basic tenet of the Project?"

I rolled my eyes, put down the soup that was still too hot for me to sip. "Accepting change is inherent in any scientific investigation. The *idea* of establishing a colony is to open new avenues for discovery and exploration — and to adapt to them."

"But this is adaptation to the nth degree." She paused, tilted her head. "Do you think you can face up to sharing the universe?"

"I wasn't aware that we were going to have to share it, unless — did you find any living Martians in the Caves?"

"No, of course not. There hasn't been a Martian soul alive for five million years. I meant intellectually. The Martians achieved technological heights rivaling our own present state of development. It's even conceivable that those ancient Martians visited the Earth in our dim beginnings. It's a notion that could really set mankind back on his haunches — not just a change of attitude, but a complete reassessment of his station in the scheme of life."

"Linda, the Committee is made up of progressive and imaginative people. They're handpicked men and women, capable of comprehending man's position in life and well versed in the vagaries of human understanding. They can accept change, and they can help ease that change throughout the world."

"And are you yourself willing to adapt?"

"I hope I'm sensitive and broadminded enough to accept whatever I find." Linda's eyes glazed. Her face softened and the sharp set of her lips relaxed. "Doug, did you ask to come back?"

"Off the record?"

She nodded slowly.

It took a minute to collect my thoughts. "Linda, I was selected because I had the necessary experience, position, and prior knowledge. But I *accepted* for a variety of reasons, some of which I'm still not sure of. With no mail, with such secrecy, I had no idea you — or anyone else — were not coming back on the shuttles. It came as a shock. Intellectually, I suppose, I'm here out of scientific interest and intense curiosity. But emotion-ally . . . "

Linda placed her hand on mine, tenderly. "Doug, I want you to understand that some things have changed. I'm not the same woman I was two and a half years ago. And you aren't the same man. But I still feel for you now as I did then. Our relationship means as much. But try to understand what it was like to be here when word broke out that a civilization, an actual humanoid civilization millions of years old, had been found. Try to understand the clamor it raised, and how deeply involved we all felt. We were all swept up in the tide of events. It wasn't just another discovery; it was the *ultimate* discovery. It was so important that no one could possibly let personal matters interfere. So, it doesn't mean that I have any less feeling for you, just that for right now, at this moment, the Project is the most important thing in my life. And I simply *have* to stay and see it through."

I shrugged. "Careers have dissolved more than one love affair."

"Oh, Doug, that's not fair."

"Sorry." I squeezed her hand, leaned forward and looked deep into her eyes. "I guess I'm overreacting. I came here with a deep sense of distrust, and nothing has happened yet to dispel that distrust. But I'm still an active participant in the Project, and I have as much concern for its success as anyone else." I threw up my hands. "I guess — I have — to respect your decision to remain here just as you respected mine to rotate to Earth. But it's not easy to be understanding when the shoe is on the other foot. Oh, I'm sure you weighed the circumstances carefully, based your decision on reason and sound judgment. And I guess if you had acted dif-ferently, you wouldn't have been the same woman I knew and loved. But it still *hurts*."

"Just like it hurt me before."

I glanced away, but her hand pulled my chin back. A lone tear, a glistening pendant pearl, hung tenacious-ly from one shimmering eye.

"I'm sorry. I didn't mean that. And thank you for your honesty. You couldn't have said it any better. And you, too, have lived up to my expectations. I just knew that you . . . you . . . "

With the back of her hand, she wiped the solitary tear from her calcimine cheek. She smiled broadly and cried at the same time, in a way that only a woman can do. She threw her arms around my neck and hugged me wildly, shaking me from side to side. Her kisses were long and deep.

How does one get reacquainted with a lover after an absence of years? We clung together for many minutes, not knowing how to start. Time passed unnoticed as we found solace in each other's embrace. I sensed a feeling of relief that was warm and flowing and desperately pleasant.

When it happened, it happened naturally, demurely, unpretentiously. We gave of ourselves what we had, and accepted what each of us needed.

*   *   *   *   *

" . . . number seventeen . . . *crackle* . . . please . . . "

I didn't remember falling asleep, but the static pulled me out of dreamland. I squinted my eyes, trying to focus on something — on anything. I did not feel the warm sensation of safety that I should have felt: my head throbbed vacuously with a dull pain; my arm ached.

"Crawler number seventeen, come in please." The emergency relay had been tripped by the priority transmission, and for that one instant came through crystal clear.

Linda slid out from beside me, leaving in her wake an uncomfortable coldness. She scooped up the microphone and calibrated the gain. "Seventeen to base. We read you. Come in please."

" . . . glad to hear from you. We were worried . . . " The rest was lost in an almost continuous burst of static.

After the noise abated, Linda continued. "Why the hell didn't you warn us there was a storm on the way?

We damn near got stranded away from the crawler."

. . . *crackle* . . . experiencing malfunction from weather stat . . . *crackle* . . . *crackle* . . . suggest you return immediately as we . . . *crackle* . . . *crackle* . . . "

"Thanks a heap, base. We're on our way. Seventeen out." Linda flipped the switch and leaned against the seat. "I guess it's not their fault. They got caught just like we did."

I burst into gales of laughter.

Linda turned to face me, a quizzical expression on her face. "What's so funny?"

"You. Standing there nude, and so casual. I like it."

"Oh, you." She tramped back to the bunk, bent over, and buried her lips in my neck. "I'm glad you still like it." She pulled her one-piece long-johns out from under me and twisted around on the edge of the bunk. I did my best to keep her out of them. "Doug!" She hobbled across to the opposite bunk, plopped down, and slipped into the thermals. "You're impossible. Now get dressed."

"Hey, how come you didn't remind me that it never pays to take chances?"

She wagged a finger at me. "You're stretching your envelope. Now get up."

"What? So soon?" She ignored me. Slowly, my head still thick, I rolled up to a sitting position. "What's it like outside?"

Linda hastily checked the gauges, then activated the motor that operated the viewport shield. Like a slowly blinking eye, the viewport expanded its iris until the bleak landscape was entirely visible. Ambient light flooded the compartment as if spring had suddenly bloomed.

The wind had died down as quickly as it had begun. Sunlight glinted off suspended dust particles as they settled lazily in the thin Martian atmosphere. The pale pink sky reappeared in its near perfect clarity, sharply defined above the rocky horizon. The russet colored sun permeated the veil of dust-laden clouds, reflecting softly off each tiny grain of dehydrated sand. It was Mars' equivalent of a dry rainbow.

"Come look at this, Doug. It's beautiful."

Still buttoning my thermals, I sidled alongside her. "This time, I'll agree with you. I think my perspective is changing already."

She gave me a peck on the cheek, picked up the soup mugs. "As long as you think it's so nice, how about going outside and replacing the antenna."

"Even on Mars, the men put out the trash and the women do the dishes." I pecked her back, and shuffled to the bunk. I pulled on the rubbery exposure suit - like a big pair of kiddy pajamas complete with feet - fixed the neck seal and sleeves, and closed the chest with an airtight zipper. I squinted my eyes at the hood with my name stenciled above the wraparound faceplate. " 'Dug up a Martian.' "

"Stop being silly." Linda handed me a life-support pack. "Try out the equipment and make sure it still works. It never — "

"Pays to take chances. I know. You only remind me when it's to your advantage." I donned the hood, slipped on the backpack, made all the appropriate connections and linkages. "If I'm not back in ten minutes, send out the cavalry."

Linda rummaged through an overhead storage compartment, unpacked a spare antenna. "It's a universal screw adapter with — "

I snatched it playfully out of her hand. "I think I can figure it out." I pressurized the suit, listened for leaks, picked up a tool kit, stepped into the airlock, and cycled the pump. The suit expanded as the air was siphoned from the chamber. With all systems go I opened the outer door and passed into the cold beyond.

I took a minute to appreciate the tranquility which a short time ago had been a seething sand blizzard. Mars is a planet of quick change: a demon in its fury, an enchantress in its calm.

"Linda, can you hear me all right?"

"Loud and clear."

"The starboard side of the crawler is buried right up

to the roof." I climbed up the sand dune, found the tangled mess that had once been an aerial, unscrewed the base with a wrench. The spare slipped in easily. "Okay, hit the retrieval switch."

Slowly, the antenna folded up and withdrew into the protection of the outer hull, then worked its way back out again. I squirted some oil onto the shaft. "Try it again." This time, it operated quicker and more smoothly. "Okay, I'm coming in."

"Works like a charm," Linda said, as I stepped into the warm interior. I peeled off the hood and her voice became louder. "I checked with base and they read us loud and clear. The motor is revved up and ready to go."

I sat in front of the viewport and strapped myself in. "I'm ready when you are."

Linda applied power to the starboard track. Nothing happened at first, until she rocked the vehicle gently back and forth. Then it broke free of the encrusting sand. She equalized power, spun the crawler within its length, and peeled off. "Nothing stops these babies."

Mars is the geologist's dream and the explorer's ecstasy. It is also the traveler's nightmare. My fillings rattled in my teeth as we fought over the primitive land, climbing hillocks and spanning fifteen-foot trenches. Linda pushed the indomitable crawler to its limits, traversing sixty-degree slopes, speeding fifty miles per hour over flat terrain, bumping over dunes like an armored personnel carrier on war patrol.

"Okay, I admit it. The crawler is tougher than I am. I'm still feeling a bit queasy."

Linda smiled as we rolled along the high plateau. I studied the rear camera screen, saw the dusty rooster tail as rocks and sand were crunched and spit out by the wide flotation treads. Even as I looked, sand settled into the tracks with graceful languor.

"Hold on. This is where it gets rough."

I gripped the armrests as we cascaded over a brink and wound down a snakelike trail that switched back and forth over loose talus. Losing altitude rapidly, Linda deftly turned the big machine first one way, then the other, descending drastically. We leveled out on a smooth escarpment several hundred feet above the ancient seabed, then slid down the last, steep embankment like an out-of-control roller coaster.

No longer was the ground as flat and perfect as it had appeared from the bluff above. The convoluted surface was rough and craggy. From the base of the cliff, fluted fissures reached out like bony fingers. Water never shaped those antediluvian crevices: wind storms had gouged them out over the course of millions of years, long after the sea of Syrtis Major had been absorbed by the greedy sand.

For all its weight, the crawler handled the steep incline deceptively easily. Because of the balanced hydraulic systems, it responded well to turns.

Although its forty tons of Earth weight was now reduced to fourteen, its momentum was still forty tons. Mass and momentum do not change with gravity — less gravity meant only less friction to stop forward motion. When bringing the vehicle to a halt, one often had the feeling that it was running ahead of itself, like a car sliding on an icy road. On Mars, a skid was three times longer than on Earth.

"We'll make it just before dark," Linda confirmed.

The westering sun had already sunk behind the Western Rim so that we were in its shadow. The sky overhead was still bright, but darkness would come quickly in the thin atmosphere, almost as if a shade were drawn across the heavens. There was little appreciable afterglow.

Again pain welled up in my arm, and waves of dizziness swept fleetingly through my head. "Doc Reynolds is a quack."

"Don't rub it. You'll get used to it. I did."

"You mean everyone else got immunized, too?"

"Sure, it's the only way. Hey, it looks like they really did get caught flatfooted."

In the still settling dust, faint blue and red figures faded in and out of obscurity. A work party pushed against the bulk of an overturned sand buggy: a two person excursion vehicle with four balloon tires, each independently powered, and a protective but unpressurized hull. With its wheels in the air, it looked like a weird dead insect. They rocked it from side to side on the roll bar until it rolled upright.

Another crew wielded shovels and air hoses, clearing entranceways that had been piled high with sand during the storm. The anemometer registered fifty miles per hour: a mild breeze by Martian standards.

Linda halted the crawler in front of the garage and activated the remote control opener. Compressed air blew sand off the sliding door track. Billowing clouds of dust reduced viewport visibility to nothing. I shifted my attention to the five camera screens on the forward console. Stars were already visible in the overhead fisheye lens.

Movement in the port camera caught my eye. The dust was thick all around, but I thought I saw a tall, blanched shape duck behind the hydroponics dome. I blinked, rubbed my aching arm, and it was gone. The spindly mirage was wiped from my mind by a sudden twinge. I saw stars behind closed lids. *That damned injection.*

"Well, Doug, we're almost home."

Grimacing, I forced back tears. "Wake me when it's over."

Chapter 6

The jungle was hot and steamy; it wreaked of rotten bark, dampness, and crushed underbrush. Tall lianas crept up huge boles, plaited with moss and soft green leaves, reaching for the faraway canopy that shielded the matted, moldy floor from the yellow sun. Many-legged insects swarmed in the tepid air, alighted on crusty-barked trees, squirmed and slithered on the soggy soil or under rocks and logs.

The air was inspired with the sights and sounds of life. Brown furred monkeys screamed raucously as they leaped from tree to tree. Bright plumaged birds took flight before their onslaught, chirping wildly as they flittered through the convoluted upper branches. On the ground, a saber-toothed tiger growled in anger at the sudden commotion as the prey it was stalking sprang away from the jungle's edge and dashed across the open veldt.

The prong-horned antelope was not the only animal to come charging out of the wooden enclosure: the untimely growl had alerted a creature that stood on two legs, with forepaws that hung long and ponderous at its sides, reaching almost to its knees. It walked with a stooped, rambling gait. The body was covered from head to foot with thick, coarse hair. The face was naked, brutal, atavistic. Gleaming white teeth lined a large mouth that drooled saliva. The pig nose sported flared nostrils. Bulging supraorbitals crowned dark, deep-set eyes.

The tiger stepped out of cover, stood exposed on the grassy plain. It spotted the nearby troglodyte, and was itself spotted at the same time. From a crouched position, the tiger glared, tail flicking nervously. It prepared to pounce.

The grass rustled behind the cave man, and yet another creature came into view. Bipedal too, he was taller and more refined than the hulking beast which could have been his long lost ancestor. The head was overlarge, but proportioned on a smaller scale. His body, while strong for its size, was thinner and slighter. He represented a very unlikely suspect to challenge the supremacy of a hunger-maddened cat.

But he had two things that neither of his opponents on the field possessed. In one hand he wielded the jaw-bone of an antelope, the teeth honed to a razor-sharp edge. And behind the soft and delicate eyes there glimmered a heritage of quiet emotion, hidden intelligence, and utter fearlessness.

In the middle, the cave man reacted instinctively: he dashed away howling and flailing, and disappeared into the obscurity of lush vegetation.

Two actors were left on the scene. Their eyes met for a long moment; neither dared to move. The tiger snarled. The man moved forward, shaking his club. Then, the tiger leaped up and bounded off into the seclusion of the jungle.

For a brief moment, in triumph, silence reigned.

*   *   *   *   *   *

I awoke with a start, lost.

I found myself gasping for air; my body was cold and clammy. When I tried to move, I discovered that my muscles had stiffened: they ached in every joint. I felt as if I had been sorely beaten by a gang of thugs and left in a gutter to die.

The room was dark: in the portal-less cubicle, no early morning light shone through the windows to caress my face. I could as easily have been lying in a closet, a crypt, a coffin.

Fear ran rampant through my mind, and I gripped the sides of the bed assaulted by waves of vertigo. My body seemed to soar through space, pitching and yawing as a returning shuttlecraft flying down the maw of a cyclone.

I reminded myself that I was on Mars, that I had been here less than twenty-four hours. I tried to recall all that had occurred since that gentle touchdown, to attach reality to an otherwise unreal and dreamy fantasy.

Instead, dark shadows crept through my mind, like slender tendrils wafting in a summer breeze. Vaguely, I recalled the phantasmagoria that had occupied my sleeping hours. Spasmodic contractions coursed along my spine as I perceived indistinct prehistoric shapes, nearly tangible and fantastic animal odors, screaming, chirping, growling sounds, the feel of grass under my naked feet.

Ridiculous, I thought.

I rolled over and reached out for the nightlight — I hardly had the strength to flip the switch. Five-thirty was much too early to arise. But at the same time, I was afraid to close my eyes, afraid that sleep might return, afraid that I might see — what?

I threw aside the electric comforter and swung my feet out of bed. My head swam, and I fell back to the security of a horizontal posture. When my vision cleared, I rose more slowly. Despite the pain in my joints, I jumped up and down in my tiny quarters and shook out my cramped limbs, aided by the reduced gravity. My head continued to throb, and the chills that racked my body were real, not left over from silly dreams. My arm ached abominably where Doc Reynolds had pricked me with his syringe. Rubbing only made it worse.

I bent over the washbasin, opened the tap, tossed cold water on my face, and rubbed the gritty particles of sleep from my eyes. I stripped off my thermal-lined pajamas and ran a chemical cloth over my body, goose bumps rising in protest as the alcohol evaporated. Gradually, the cobwebs retreated from my mind. I donned a thermal uniform.

The intercom beeped while my mouth was still full of chemical paste. I spat in the sink. "Do you know what time it is?"

"Up an' at 'em, Doug. Day's a wastin'."

"Doc, the roosters aren't even up yet. What the hell's the idea?"

"Just wanted to find out how you slept. You looked a little green around the gills last night."

"I could sure use a new body, if you have one lying around. I twisted and turned all night, and now my muscles feel like they've been through the decathlon."

"I thought as much. Listen, how about stopping off at my office first thing. I'd like to check you over."

"I'm on my way."

"Do you remember how to find it?"

"Do you remember how to ride a bicycle?"

"Good. See you soon. Out."

I was still shivering, so I threw on an extra thermal vest. I unlatched the airlock door and stepped out of my cubicle, taking in at a glance the barely lit corridor, bare beams, exposed plumbing, explosion-proof electrical conduits, instruments, valves, levers, and gauges. Every available space not otherwise utilized was filled with leafy plants in their nutrient solutions: organic machines for producing oxygen and scrubbing carbon dioxide, and for giving an Earthlike fragrance and appearance.

The corridors were already crowded. Most people seemed to know who I was, nodding and smiling and sometimes addressing me by name. I threaded my way through the maze of offices, leaned against the jamb of the hospital cubicle.

"Is the doctor in?"

Doc Reynolds had his back toward me, engrossed in filling chemical bottles from a bulk dispenser. He jerked a thumb at the opposite door. "There she is." The Medwife was a medical analogue computer that could examine, diagnose, and prescribe without a human monitor. The program was simple enough that anyone could follow the prompts. "All I do is turn her on."

"That seems to be your primary occupation."

"Don't let the buttlescutt fool you." He turned around slowly, a smile already planted on his cleanly shaven face. "You didn't waste any time getting here."

"I was afraid I might die if I waited too long."

Doc Reynolds put down his bottles and syringes and approached me professionally. Holding my cheeks firmly in his strong hands, he peered into my eyes with

profound penetration. "Your eyeballs look like an inter-
state road map — in Technicolor. Were you stepping
out on the town last night?"

I rubbed the stubble on my chin. "I wish I had. At
least I'd have some fond memories for my misery."

"The party was too much for you, huhn? Well, have
a seat."

I climbed onto the Medwife's examination couch,
looked around at the dials and digital readouts. "I was
unbelievably tired, so I left early."

He attached some skin probes and typed data on
the keyboard. The viewscreen lit up with my medical
history. He took a stethoscope out of the freezer and
dragged the cold diaphragm across my bare chest.
When he had the thermometer firmly implanted in my
mouth, he began asking questions.

"Do you feel tense?"

"Uhm hmn."

"Do you have a headache?"

"Uhm hmn."

"Do you feel sick to your stomach, and on the verge
of vomiting?"

"Uhm hmn."

"Do you feel shortness of breath?"

"Uhm hmn."

"Do you have chills, or feel abnormally cold?"

"Uhm hmn."

"Do you feel weak, or are you suffering from lassi-
tude?"

"Uhm hmn. Uhm hmn."

"Do you feel sleeplessness? Dizziness? Loss of
appetite?"

"Uhm hmn. Uhm hmn. Uhm hmn."

"Hmmnn," he said meditatively, pulling the thermometer out of my mouth. He studied it carefully, then
put all his instruments away. The viewscreen scrolled.
"Hmmnn."

"Doc, what was that injection you gave me yesterday? Could that have anything to do with the way I
feel? My arm's been hurting ever since."

He rummaged through some bottles in a wall-mounted cabinet, picked one out.

"You seem to have expected something. Am I having an allergic reaction?"

He located two glasses, filled them with water. "I did expect something. Or more correctly, I suspected something." He indicated the viewscreen. "What you have is acute mountain sickness. Forgive me for not thinking of it sooner, or I might have saved you a great deal of suffering as well as a good night's sleep."

"But how could I . . . ?"

The doctor plopped an orange pill into each glass, shook them both. "Let me explain. I noticed last night you looked a little pale. You started out at dinner by eating everything but the faucets off the kitchen sink. Then, suddenly, you quit and rubbed your temples. When you stood up, you lost your balance several times, but wouldn't let Linda help you. I registered all these impressions, but it just never clicked with me. After you had gone, Linda told us about the close call you both had up on the Western Rim. She said that during the worst of it, you acted strange, were slow to respond, became easily disoriented, fell down." He spread his hands and hunched his shoulders.

"Come on, Doc. You know what it's like in a sand storm. Two-hundred-mile-per-hour winds can do funny things to your equilibrium. If you hadn't stabbed me with that needle . . . "

"Wait a minute, Doug." He handed me one of the glasses. "Have some of this."

The tablets had dissolved. I looked at the orange liquid askance. "What is it?"

The doctor drank half a glass, swilled some in his mouth. "Orange juice. I always have six ounces before breakfast."

I sniffed. It smelled like orange juice. I drank it down. "Not bad."

"Doug, things have changed in Syrtis City since you've been gone. In the interest of economy, we've cut back on a lot of extravagances. For example, our coffee is partially home grown. Our food, you may have noticed, has overtones of unfamiliar additives. And that vest you're wearing is not needed because of any infectious internal disorder. The temperature in the City has been lowered."

"But why? What's it all for? And what does it all mean?"

Doc Reynolds sat on his examination stool, ran his tongue under his upper lip. "It may mean freedom. Economic freedom. The more we can save, the less we have to borrow. The more self-sufficient we can be, the less subservient we become. It's all part of a big plan to stand up on our own two feet: not to cut our ties with Earth — because we're part of Earth, and we want to keep it that way — but to have the inner strength, the confidence, and the assurance that we can live on our own. We've never felt this way before, not when you were here, nor any time previous. But this discovery has given us the impetus and the promise of being more than an outpost. We are entertaining the possibility of becoming an independent autonomy."

"When do you plan to secede?"

He showed me a palm. "Set your mind at ease. We have no intentions of seceding, now or ever. We only want to do what we have to. The discovery of life — of intelligent creatures — is not covered by the book. We have no preplanned operating procedures to guide us. To be blunt, we want the latitude to be allowed to handle the situation as we see fit — only because we're in a better position to understand it."

"So you set yourselves up as owners and administrators of the greatest discovery since the invention of the wheel."

"No, merely as arbitrators. We need time to study the Martian civilization and to learn what long-term effect it may have on humanity. And those on Earth need time to ascertain what impact this knowledge will have on human culture."

"Doc, don't you think cultural impact is a thing of the past? Science fiction writers worked out all the possible scenarios back in the twentieth century. Today we're enlightened. The exploration of space and the search for intelligent life is a soap opera plot."

"So was invasion from Mars — as long as it was fiction. But when people thought it was real because of the way it was broadcast over the radio, by Orson Welles in 1938, they panicked. So sure, we've been talking about life in the universe for a couple hundred years, but this time it's for real. People may be thrilled, or they may be scared. The stock market may leap all out of bounds, or it may crash. The space program may find itself involved in uncontrolled expansion, or it may collapse.

"There's no predicting public reaction. We can study an individual, learn his likes and dislikes and innermost fears, and we can anticipate his response to certain stimuli with a fair amount of accuracy. But no one yet knows how to predict mob reaction, or explain why a person's temperament will change when surrounded by his fellow men."

I pulled off the skin probes, leaned forward out of the niche. "The Committee certainly never could have predicted the way Project members have reacted."

"There you go."

"Covering up a find of such importance is one thing, but hushing up the death of a fellow worker is another."

Doc Reynolds recoiled. "Whoa. That's a serious accusation."

"Doc, let's face facts. I knew Dr. Sanders well. I worked closely with him. He was as cool as a cucumber and not given to mad flights of fancy. For that matter, all Project members are specifically trained, scientifically oriented, psychologically tested, and emotionally fit. Just like you, and just like me. We're essentially stable elements. Sure, we all have the right to display surprise, concern, shock, even fear. But not hysteria, and certainly not death. What happened to Dr. Sanders that's such a big secret? What did he die from? What did he see?"

The doctor's green eyes danced around the room. "Doug, I really can't talk about it."

"Can't, or won't?"

"Doug, please listen to me. Don't jump the gun. Everything will be explained in time."

"The time is now."

"The time will begin at the debriefing session. Trust me. Everything will be presented in a concise and orderly manner. Then you'll understand."

"I would prefer to conduct this investigation my own way."

The doctor shook his head. "You'd just be led astray by your preconceived notions. It won't make sense if you get your facts jumbled around."

"So far, nothing makes sense anyway. And you are going to have a tough time making me believe that drivel you sent to Earth about Dr. Sander's death: 'The terrific stress and psychological impact of an unprecedented nature on a striving scientific mind'."

Doc Reynolds got off his stool, placed his hands on my shoulders, spoke with sincerity. "Doug, you and I are old buddies, and I wouldn't try to deceive you. But take my word for it." He pumped his fingers with friendly informality. "Keep an open mind, and an open heart. And you will learn."

"That's what I keep hearing. It's just that — "

"It's just that you have mountain sickness and your thinking is a little muddled." He released me, hung his hands at his sides.

I remembered my headache. "Yeah, what's all this crap about mountain sickness?"

"Well, as I started to tell you before, in the interests of economy, we have made some major changes. One of them has been to lower the total atmospheric pressure while increasing the partial pressure of the breathing medium."

"I don't think I understand."

"All right, I'll remind you of some elementary physics. The Earth's sea level pressure of fourteen point seven pounds per square inch is too wasteful in space. On shuttles, and here in the City, we operate on nine p.s.i., the pressure equivalent to an altitude of fifteen thousand feet above sea level. That's S.O.P. What *we've* done is to further reduce our ambient pressure to six p.s.i."

I closed one eye, concentrating. "That's something like twenty-four thousand feet."

"Which is why you have mountain sickness."

"But, it's never been done before."

"Which doesn't mean it *can't* be done. In any case, I don't make the rules, I just prescribe medicine. As medical officer, I approved the change on an experimental basis, as long as there were no indications of poor health or other ill effects. So far, there have been none. Pressure was reduced so gradually that most people were hardly aware that depressurization was taking place. You, on the other hand, are experiencing all the grim symptoms of altitude sickness because you haven't had time to acclimatize.

"And this is just the beginning. If our people remain physically and mentally stable, I will recommend that we continue to decrease pressure to five p.s.i., and perhaps even lower."

"Why, not even the mountain Sherpas of Nepal can live at that altitude, simulated or not."

I don't know where it came from, but suddenly Doc Reynolds had a long, ugly looking hypodermic syringe in his hand. "Man has an amazing body and an even more amazing mind, and both can endure much more change than is commonly accepted."

I backed away. "Well, what can I do? How long will it take to acclimatize?"

He rolled up my sleeve and daubed my arm with alcohol. "It could take weeks, but a man in your condition should feel better in a few days. And I have just the thing here to fix you up." He stabbed me with the elephant gun. "People change naturally over time, but this will help you adjust to conditions. It also contains a mild sedative that will dull your sensitivity to pain."

I winced as he withdrew the needle. "Don't make me

too dull. I have a full day ahead of me and I need to be alert — so the Major doesn't pull anything over on me."

He laughed. "Don't worry about that. This isn't intended to put you to sleep, only to make your day more bearable."

I rolled down my sleeve and jumped off the couch. Except for the dull throbbing in my arm, I felt better already. "Yeah, well, thanks for the advice, Doc — all of it."

He grinned warmly. "You'll come to appreciate what I've done for you. In the mean time, drink plenty of liquids. And if you can stand it, try the coffee."

Chapter 7

"Instinct, Mr. Martin, is quite a fascinating field of study. Despite the fact that very little can be said to be known about it with any amount of certainty, the subject embraces many interesting ideologies, and throughout the centuries has been the cause of unremitting debate."

Dr. Henri Malle ran a wizened hand through the dark, curly hair that topped his dapper, five-foot-tall frame. The goggle-eyed Frenchman hid behind a pair of thick, horn-rimmed lenses held implacably in place by a bulbous nose and long, oversized ears. His small mouth and weak chin made him an unlikely-looking suspect as one of the most brilliant minds in his field.

His patent ideas in the study of evolution and genetic survival had long since vaulted him to the emeritus of professional standards. His renown in the field of the biological sciences was as prominent as that of Charles Darwin. Yet, in the middle of a venerable career, when he could have retired with distinction and leaned on his laurels, he turned over his Earthly studies to his subordinates, pulled up his roots, and planted them deeply into Martian soil. Having seen five oppositions from the Red Planet, he now had more time on world than Terrence Rogers.

"Although the study of evolution goes back only as far as the middle of the nineteenth century, animal behavior as a science is at least as old as the Greeks. Perhaps you, too, may have wondered what causes birds to build nests, bears to hibernate, rabbits to care for their young. All these phenomena can be summed up in a single word.

"We can define instinct within certain parameters." He stuffed his hands into his immaculate white lab coat. "But a definition, by definition, is merely a brief description. Instinct, however, has a wide range of interpretations. In a rather broad sense, we can state that instinct is the opposite of individuality. It is the governing factor that makes all of one species respond in the same way to a given stimulus. Rabbits, as a species, will react to a certain situation according to precise inborn tendencies. Given the same set of circumstances again, they will react the same way — time and time again.

"In a narrower perspective, instinct can be defined as an inherited behavioral process, an innate impulse, an automatic response that exists totally without reason. In the so-called lower animals, we term this a blind compulsion. In the case of an intelligent species, such as man, we term this a subconscious effort, a subliminal sensitivity, or plain common sense.

"However, they are all manifestations of one and the same. The fact that animals of the same species, widely separated and living in different environments, act consistently in an identical fashion, would indicate that their basic behavior patterns are predetermined and governed by heredity, rather than by learning or experience."

I followed Dr. Malle as he strolled along the aisle of the biology laboratory. The room was filled with glass cages and wire enclosures. An assortment of animals occupied various niches in this artificial ecology: the real experimenters in this tangle of habitats. The odor was not unlike that of a poorly-tended kennel.

Several assistants hovered about, attending the many chores. A large, oversized man dropped food pellets into a fish tank. An equally tall, dark-haired, fair-skinned woman took notes on an arm-held pad. She stood in front of a maze, perfunctorily putting a gerbil through the paces for a simple reward of food. In an adjacent aisle, an intent young man was oblivious to our approach as he studiously placed his camera on a tripod in front of a glass-encased spider web, in the process of being spun by an adept arachnid.

"You seem to have quite a menagerie. Didn't this used to be the frog cage?"

"Your memory is unimpaired by time, Mr. Martin. I

had frozen eggs flown out by freighter several years ago, obviously when you were still here. Unfortunately, they could not adapt to the gravity, and kept leaping into the ceilings of their cages. Most died from concussion. You see, they had not the ability to learn."

The tall woman looked up from her pad and uttered a how-do-you-do. I smiled as we squeezed past her. The man with the fish pellets nodded in my direction but quickly glanced away, his face a mask. A sudden bright burst of light indicated a discharging electronic strobe.

I wondered if the spider, too, had been temporarily blinded. I pointed to the eight-legged creature. "How has life on Mars affected the instincts of the other animals?"

"It hasn't affected them at all."

"But I can see some differences myself. That spider web isn't like one built on Earth."

"That is quite true. What you see are not differences in instinct, but only that part of its instinct which its present environment permits it to act out. If that species of spider were to live on Mars for a thousand generations and then returned to Earth, its offspring would go about their daily routine in no way different from members of the same species which had spent that intervening time Earthbound. The spider does not have the mental capability of change — its size and physiology limit its intelligence simply because there is no room in its 'brain' for a large stored memory. It has no space for feedback, and consequently cannot learn.

"Instead, it uses genes much as a computer uses chips. When a spider is born it comes alive as an adult and must act accordingly — and immediately. There is no time for it to learn appropriate responses. Everything it needs to know in order to carry on its survival must already be programmed. Its behavior is rigidly monitored."

I stared at the distorted web. "But somewhere along the line some spider, or its ancestors, must have learned something."

"Which came first, the chicken or the egg? Ah, you

think I jest, but I do not. It is true that sometime in the past a change must have occurred, but nothing that a creature experiences during its lifetime can cause that change. The alteration must occur in the programming. The genetic structure must be altered by what we call 'mutation.'

"In answer to my purely rhetorical question, we can safely assume that the egg came first, but it was laid by a bird which was not quite a chicken. In the case of our spider, some genetic misprinting caused it to be born with the innate knowledge of web spinning — a knowledge which its progenitors did not possess. We can deduce from this line of reasoning that instinct is a kind of progressive racial memory. But you must beware that for every mutation that developed into a response that became a survival factor — in this case, an increased ability to snare prey — there were a thousand others that resulted in the death of the offspring."

In a darkened corner of the room, we stopped in front of an eight-foot-high picture window. It was filled to within a foot of the top with ocher native sand. In the reddish glow of infrared lamps, I could see small tunnels along the panes, and the excited motion of scurrying insects.

"Modification of the behavior of an individual is called intelligence. Modification of the behavior of a species is called evolution. Take these fellows, for instance."

The tiny red ants dashed back and forth along their glass-lined corridors, carrying eggs from one chamber to another, transferring food from mouth to mouth, living a fishbowl existence, yet moving with world-wise knowledge.

"Ants have populated the Earth for over fifty million years. Specimens preserved in amber reveal that in all that time, they have remained essentially unchanged. In the world today, there are about fifteen thousand species. They are the most widely ranging animal known to science, and can be found virtually everywhere: in all climates, at all altitudes.

"These busy little creatures, seemingly charging about in a random fashion, are actually performing in a strict, premeditated pattern, foreordained by a code of ethics indelibly imprinted by a specific twist of DNA molecules. Like actors in a play, they do what they do not by reason, not by experience, but by ancestral rote."

The biologist picked up a glass jar which held several large, energetic black ants. "Let me expend one of our abundant harvesting ants in a simple demonstration." He removed the lid and carefully withdrew one of the creatures. It squirmed frightfully in the air, but its thorax was held firmly in the grip of the padded forceps. Dr. Malle dropped it into a test tube where it repeatedly tried to run up the sides of the slippery enclosure.

"Climb up onto the platform with me, Mr. Martin, where you can see into the top of this colony of fungus-growing ants."

From above, I saw a miniature Martian desert, complete with dunes. Ant holes dotted the surface like craters on the plain of Syrtis Major. Nowhere was there any movement. The gentle sucking noise of a compressor, which aerated the sealed glass cage, was the only sound.

Dr. Malle attached the test tube containing the squiggling black ant to a siphon tube and clamped a rubber seal around it. When he pulled a plunger, which protruded at a right angle to the tube, the ant was sucked into the large chamber and deposited onto the reddish sand.

"Now watch what happens."

For several seconds, the black ant showed complete disorientation. It ran around in circles, gesticulating wildly with its antennae. Gradually it moved farther and farther away from its initial landing spot; but always it returned to the location as if it were searching for the entranceway into this strange new world. On one of its farthest journeys, it came upon a hole. Tentatively, it half crouched at the opening, antennae vibrating.

A red ant, half its size, emerged from the craterlike aperture and inspected the intruder. The ants touched antennae, and for a moment the two pairs of slender threads intertwined; then they separated and increased to a rapid-fire motion, tips touching. The red ant scurried into the hole while the black ant quickly retreated to its original landing zone.

Soon a stream of red ants erupted from the mound, milled around for several seconds with gyrating antennae, then took off in a straight line in the direction the larger ant had taken. The black ant saw them coming and frantically ran around in circles, but it would not leave the area of direct flight: it did not know where to go. The charging red army surrounded it and attacked from all sides. Daunted by uncertain odds and paralyzed with fear, the black ant was dispatched with very little effort. Its dismembered body was carried into the bowels of the red ants' domain.

"Fascinating." I climbed back down to the floor.

"Also predictable. Even though these ants all stem from one queen who was hatched here on Mars, and who never had any contact with another of her species, their reactions were identical to those observed in their Earthborn relatives. A simple experiment, but it proves that whatever compulsion caused them to kill the intruding ant could not have been learned or reasoned or based on past experience.

"The black ant, by the same token, could not break out of its genetic mold even to save its own life. Both were acting out the automatic response that governs their lives — what we call, for lack of a better term, instinct. And that very instinct that is a survival factor for one colony of ants proved to be the undoing of another simply because instinct does not allow the latitude of change when necessary."

Dr. Malle fidgeted nervously. After some obvious facial contortions, he continued almost childishly. "Let me explain the nature of our experiments in adaptation." He tapped the thick glass with a gnarled knuckle. "The infrared lamps that you see here are to keep the ants in the dark. They cannot see very well at the red end of the spectrum, and since their breeding chambers must be away from light, it allows us to observe them without their knowing.

"In this particular tank we have a colony of fungus-growing ants. They are found only in the New World, and were tilling the land there long before the advent of Indian agriculture. Their only form of sustenance is a specific fungus which they cultivate in their subterranean gardens. Each species of ant generally grows its own brand. Indeed, some forms of fungus no longer exist in the wild state: they continue to flourish only through the agency of their hosts. The trick is to get them to change their brand of food. On Earth, they do this very reluctantly, often starving to death rather than adapting to new sources of nourishment. Here, the difficulty has been aggravated in that we are trying to adapt them to a food source which is not only different, but alien — and with a slightly different chemistry. I speak, of course, of areolichen.

"I cannot tell you how much the discovery of this native plant life meant to me and my colleagues, for it gave us a definite direction towards which to work. We have found that by introducing small quantities of lichen along with their normal food supply, they have been able to accept it as food, especially when we kill off some of their natural supply. Eventually, we hope to be able to switch them completely to a diet of Martian lichen."

I whistled. "That sounds like quite a task. I'm surprised they can even stand the smell. Or do ants even have the ability to smell?"

The biologist adjusted his glasses. "Fungus ants rely heavily on their olfactory senses, and it is quite acute, as you saw when they tracked the invading black ant to its death. On the other hand, the harvesting ant has a poor sense of smell — it relies more on sight."

We moved on to an adjacent glass tank. Here, too, infrared lamps dimly illuminated the small black inhabitants.

"These ants are quite different from their red cousins. If we would label the fungus ant as living in an agricultural society, we would call the harvesting ant a hunting society. On Earth they are desert dwellers, inhabiting drylands the world over. Odor plays only a minor part in their lives simply because windy desert conditions quickly cover odor trails. They forage for food, subsisting mainly on seeds, but will accept little pieces of meat and dead insects when available. Here, of course, we feed them.

"Insects, because of the simplicity of their design, can survive in a variety of niches. This simplicity also offers a wide assortment of pre-adaptations: structures and behavior patterns suited to one environment which may have an even greater viability in another, or which may become useful in the event of changing conditions. This accounts for the wide proliferation of insects on Earth.

"In this tank, we are purposely altering the environment. Gradually, we are changing the atmosphere and pressure, seeking new strains of ants. Essentially, it is a hit or miss situation, but we hasten the process of evolution by inducing genetic mutation through radiation treatments."

I scratched my head. "That smacks of Lamarckism, or Lysenkoism, if I remember my biology correctly. Are you saying that you believe that ants will someday populate the Martian desert?"

"No, Mr. Martin. Ants, I am afraid, will never live on Mars. In all their millions of years of existence, there has never been a need to cope with this kind of environment. There is no past experience to guide them, there is no hereditary factor to program their actions. They must of necessity die out."

"But you just said . . . "

Dr. Malle transfixed me with brown eyes distorted through thick lenses. "I just said that ants will die out, and so they will. But they can evolve into an animal that is not quite an ant. Like the chicken from the egg, this new form of life will be something new and unique.

It will be governed by a different set of rules, react in its own fashion to given stimuli, will be guided by its own instincts. It will be a great boon to science — and it will be a greater boon to the expansion of the human race and the colonization of Mars. What I hope to achieve is to bring life back to a dead world for humankind to enjoy and utilize."

"And how long will this take, Dr. Malle?"

"Time does not matter in science. If I do not accomplish this feat in my lifetime, there will be many eager colleagues to carry on the effort."

I shrugged my shoulders. "But, where does it go from here? Will you alter man's genetic future next, enable him to live on this planet?"

Dr. Malle looked at me whimsically. "That is beyond Earth science — at least in its present state of technology and scientific understanding. But it is not inconceivable. Man, the most adaptable of creatures, can change much more easily than the ant because he has a quality that the lowly insects do not have: he can learn.

"Each generation of man can be reprogrammed by society. He is not an immutable statue, but soft clay that can be molded. He is a personality that can be shaped from without and actuated from within.

"Every day parts of our bodies — dead cells and waste products — are disposed of and replaced by young cells and new energy: life from the food we ingest. And every day our horizons are enlarged, our minds expanded, our selves permuted by what we see, what we hear, what we learn. We are in a continual state of change, for we are like patterns that perpetuate themselves from moment to moment. We can become something different — if we choose."

I recalled the fate of the ants. "And does that mean that man must die out in order to spawn a new race?"

Dr. Malle knitted his brows, paused overlong before replying. "It means only that we must realize when it is our turn to retire, and to let our progeny take over for us. There is no pain in that, for we teach and train and love our children for just such a purpose. We want them to have what we did not. That is progress, Mr. Martin. The other path is evolutionary stagnation. There is no standing still in the stream of life, there is only advancement — or death."

Chapter 8

The Hydroponics Dome was the largest enclosure in the Colony, and a dome only in the figurative sense. It was shaped like a half cylinder bisected longitudinally, and broken up into four self-sufficient airtight segments, each offering a breadth of openness otherwise unknown in the City.

Vegetation grew at a prodigious rate and to tremendous proportions in nutrient solution and low gravity. Fluorescent lights aided photosynthesis in the absence of sun, since cosmic ray shielding that was transparent to light had not yet been invented, and the heat loss through glass was extravagantly expensive.

Dr. Phyllis Trimble was bent over a dirt-filled box, injecting the base of a tomato plant with a fat syringe. Even as she stooped, she lost none of her straight-backed posture, her well-trimmed figure, her heraldic bearing. Once brunette hair was streaked with gray, and efficiently pulled back and tied in a bun. Rather than showing her age, it accentuated her striking appearance.

Although she had been widowed early in life, she could have passed equally well as a grandmother of many or a spinster school marm.

"Got a sick plant?"

She leaned back and stood to her full height, not in a jerk but in simple surprise. Wide shimmering eyes matched the emerald green of unripe tomatoes. She wiped her hand on her white smock and offered it to me. "Captain Martin. I didn't expect to see you until this afternoon. It's so good to have you with us again."

"Thank you, Phyllis. It's good to be back." I held onto her hand. "But I've been demoted to civilian for reasons of diplomacy. Now it's just plain Doug."

She laughed merrily, like the chirping of a bird. "You'll never be just plain Doug."

Our hands parted. I praised her body with a practiced eye. "Mars has been good to you. You haven't aged a day or put on a pound."

"Still the eternal flatterer, aren't you, Douglas?" She pronounced my name with maternal carriage.

"It's the key to my success, and I see no reason to change now."

The tiered shelving behind her rose all the way to the arched ceiling. "I don't think I would want you to change — at least, not your brand of humor. You should never lose that."

"I promise, as long as you promise not to lose that marvelous British accent."

"It's a deal. And I'll let you in on a little secret: the gravity is great for your diet. You can gain three pounds and count only one."

I glanced around at the luxuriant foliage abounding in fruit. "Mars still produces the nicest tomatoes."

She pulled a bright red one from her apron. "Want to taste one?"

The firm fruit filled my hand. I sunk my teeth into it greedily. "Tastes a little musty, but since it's the first fresh food I've had in weeks, it'll do".

"It's a cherry tomato. Beefstakes grow as large as watermelons, and can still stay off the ground thanks to the gravity."

I made short shrift of the wet pulp, licking my lips and fingers after it was inhaled. I indicated the hypodermic needle. "Were you giving or taking."

An aquiline nose perched above thin lips set in a perpetual smile. "Actually, I was injecting the soil with an experimental serum. Plants can't be inoculated like animals because they don't have the same kind of cen tral nervous system. In order to get anything into a vegetable you must go through channels, so to speak. By suffusing the roots with sera, the plant will absorb the solution along with water and other chemicals through their canal system. It's not quite as efficient as the animal circulatory system, and it reacts slower, but it works."

I pulled out a compact drawer, sniffed the petals of

a dandelion. "It doesn't look like there's room to grow any more. You're running out of space."

"Actually, we don't want it to grow any taller, we want it to bear more fruit. Equally as important as supplying nutrients to stimulate growth is conditioning depauperate native soil with organic material. Most of Mars' desert is regolithic in quality, but loamy in capacity."

I closed the drawer, blocking out the backlit fluorescents, and held up a hand. "If you're going to give me a botany lesson, you'd better start from the ground up."

Smiling, the chief agronomist slipped into her best professional manner. "Very well. We'll do just that." Besides her work, Phyllis Trimble's favorite pastime was talking about her work.

"Regolith is the forerunner of soil. It's essentially rock debris, and ultimately comes from pure rock that's broken into fine particles by alternating temperature variations, mechanical processes such as wind and water erosion, natural chemical solvents, and oxidation. But it's not soil.

"There is no soil without life, and no life without soil. Soil, to be differentiated from a loose collection of minerals, must contain organic matter. The distinction between a swamp and a desert is the content of this organic matter: some peaty soils of Florida are almost wholly organic, whereas the soils of deserts of the American southwest are only a fraction of one percent organic. On Mars, the surface soil is silicon dioxide, like beach sand, enriched with iron oxides which give it its reddish color. But the amount of organic matter is only between one ten thousandth and one millionth of one percent — and that, all dead.

"Extensive coal deposits and fossil evidence prove irrefutably that at one time Mars had an intricate and widespread ecosystem. This Colony is built on the bed of a vast sea, a cradle in the formation of life. Yet today there is not enough organic material in the soil to support even the most fundamental life forms. The living microbial spores discovered by Terrence Rogers had been waiting for millions of years for the right conditions which would awaken them and start new life — and might well have waited until eternity."

"Why couldn't they survive in the ecosystem of the Caves where the, uh, areolichen was discovered?"

"They can. And do."

I raised my eyebrows.

"A diversity of microbial life was found. But, if you'll allow me to digress for a moment, I can tell you about areolichen first, then tie it in with our discussion of soils."

I laughed. "You must have been reading my mind."

We ambled along the narrow aisles, the smell of freshness in the air. Although the bulk of vegetation were oxygen-fixing varieties, some served as additional sources of nourishment — a needed break in the routine of frozen dinners. The biggest crop was soybean, whose meal and oil found numerous uses in food and industrial products.

"What you must first understand, Douglas, is that lichen — any lichen — is not a simple life form. It represents the culmination of an evolutionary process rather than the bare beginnings of one. By way of analogy, consider the whale: an animal perfectly adapted to its environment.

"It's streamlined for efficient travel through a liquid medium, its musculature enables it to move at tremendous speeds, it has stabilizing fins that keep it upright, its eyes have a covering so it can see clearly in the water, and it finds itself unrivaled in its particular food niche. But, unlike other marine animals, it is warm-blooded and must supply itself with a heavy layer of blubber to maintain that warmth; it breathes air instead of taking its oxygen directly from the water; it must nurse and protect its young, a task involving great time and care. And, like other creatures of the sea, it will die out of water, not from suffocation, but from the drying out of its skin. In short, the whale is a paradoxical creature that could never have evolved in the ocean — it represents a further step in land evolution.

"By the same criteria, areolichen could never have evolved on the dry, desiccated planet that Mars is today. It had its beginnings at a time when conditions were much different, and since then, it's adapted to the changing environment. It symbolizes the end of evolutionary development because it contains elements of function necessary to its survival that were brought about under completely different conditions."

She stepped over an airlock sill into an adjoining section. Powerful hydraulic hinges were ready to seal off the separate chambers in the event of an emergency.

"It's often been said that long after man has been dead and forgotten, the lowly insects will remain and rule the Earth. The same is true here: long after the Martian civilization has been buried by the sands of time, and their machines and buildings crumbled into the ground, the lichen has survived.

"Mars has long since reached a stage in its geology in which a swamp is more barren than Earth's driest desert. Yet somehow, areolichen has maintained a foothold — not because of its simplicity, but because of its complexity. It's a unique and manifold biological phenomenon, a symbiotic relationship much more complicated than the simple coexistence of fungi and algae thriving on Earth. It's a three-way symbiosis in which the fungus provides shelter, the alga furnishes food, and the bacterium catalyzes byproducts and fertilizers by means of chemosynthesis. Furthermore, besides being a mere biological curiosity, it may provide us with the solution for adapting cultures that can live on Mars."

I ducked under overhanging branches, brushed aside leaves pouring off trellises. Foliage spilled out into the aisles like thick copse along a jungle path. Burgeoning fruits and vegetables lay hidden beneath the lush, green growth.

"That sounds like what Dr. Malle expects to do with his ants: controlled mutation, recombinant DNA, turning his ants into not-quite-ants . . . "

"Oh, yes, we're working in the same vein. Actually, we have some of Henri's animals right here."

"Does he know that?"

"Yes. You see, all animals are parasitic upon plant life. But some help to stimulate plant growth while supporting themselves."

I shook my head. "You've got me there."

"Earthworms are one of nature's humus factories. They are little more than living machines which manufacture fertilizer — and at a prodigious rate for their size. Into one end go particles of mineral and organic matter, out of the other end come castings: a blend of chemicals with the larger soil particles strained out, rich in nutrients, high in phosphorus, nitrogen, and potassium — in a word, topsoil. In addition, their tunnels help aerate the soil and increase the depth of its profile. They're great little workers."

"How does the worm union feel about all this?"

"They couldn't be happier," Phyllis laughed. "Actually, they wouldn't have it any other way. The humus supplied by the worms makes the plants grow bigger so when they die there is more food for the worms."

"Sounds sort of like perpetual motion."

Two wisps of grayish hair had been pulled out of her bun by protruding twigs, and framed her narrow face. "Of course, it's much more complicated than that. Worms can't live in barren ground. There must be vegetation there to begin with. And certain other conditions must be met. Earthworms need moisture as well as specific minerals and a digestible food source."

"Do they get all that here?"

"They do as long as we continue to add what's missing. Now, with the supplemental benefits derived from areolichen, we hope to reach a point at which the process will become self-perpetuating. Did Henri show you his fungus growing ants?"

"Every one of them."

"Then you know what he's already accomplished. We're doing much better with earthworms because they're much more easily switched to a new diet. Actually, cave lichen supplies most of their basic needs. And by keeping it on their list of victuals they process through their bodies and return to the soil an enriched combination of natural fertilizer and endemic chemical compounds to which our plants, like that tomato you so heartily consumed, are becoming accustomed."

We crossed into the third pressure chamber. Hydroponics was, in reality, a misnomer since the liquid nutrients had long since been phased out, except in the corridors where piping fluids through copper tubes offered the most maintenance-free method of horticulture. Here in the dome, a dry system using natural sand and rock chips, with the nutrients supplied in powder form, served as a basis of plant rooting. It no longer qualified as soil-less agriculture, but the name has stuck.

"Life is an intricately woven pattern of chemical checks and balances, and each life form has its tolerance of deviation. Many of our plants — and worms and ants as well — have died because too high a concentration of areolichen-derived chemicals have been fostered upon them. But we've had our successes, too."

Phyllis Trimble paused in her monologue, cocked her head slightly. "Now that you know all about it, how would you like to see a sample culture of areolichen?"

"That's my main purpose in coming here. Although," I was hasty to add, "your cultivation was a big attraction."

"You never give up, do you, Douglas?" She laughed out loud. "Come on back to Room Four and I'll give you a close-up view."

"Now we're getting somewhere." I followed her over the sill into the last room. The crowded garden was an agricultural nightmare, with wild plants and weeds of every variety. "You know, I've already had a whiff of that stuff, and I don't care to repeat the experience. The odor is strong enough to walk, and that's being kind."

Dr. Trimble smiled. "Have you ever smelled cave fungus back on Earth, Douglas?"

"Well, now that you mention it, I don't believe the

opportunity ever presented itself."

"You'd find they differ not as much as you might think."

"A fungus by any other name would smell as foul?"

At the end of the room stood a small laboratory and workbench. Bent over a Bunsen burner over which boiled a beaker of dark, soupy liquid, a tall man with wavy, brown hair and a thick, handlebar mustache was so intent upon his purpose that he failed to hear our approach. He looked up wearily when Dr. Trimble placed a hand on his white-smocked shoulder, then perked up quickly.

"You're working too hard, Dana."

"Not too hard." His voice was thick and slow. He turned off the Bunsen burner and poured the contents of the beaker into a mug. "Just too long. I've reheated this coffee four times this morning."

"Livingston Dana, this is Captain — I mean — Douglas Martin, the Committeeman from Earth."

"I'm not a Committeeman yet. Unofficially, I'm still listed as Public Relations Officer — officially without rank."

Dana extended a hand. "Glad to meet you, Mr. Martin."

"Most of my assistants are at the Caves setting up another greenhouse, leaving just the two of us to mind the store. Dana has been on duty since last night."

"Oh, I don't mind."

"You always say that, but your eyes speak differently. Now, Douglas wants to participate in an experiment. Would you mind getting the atmosphere chamber out of the ice box, please?"

"Sure thing, Phyl." He checked the gauges, undogged the emergency airlock door.

"Oh, and take out another tray of specimens for Dr. Malle."

"Okay." He entered the airlock and sealed it behind him.

"What's in there?"

Phyllis leaned against the bench. "Oh, we've had a

little addition built outside the dome so we can keep our lichen cultures under simulated cavelike conditions. They don't like the light." She took apart the syringe she had been carrying all this time and washed it out in the laboratory sink. "And while they can exist quite comfortably in what we call normal temperatures, they don't reproduce well outside their natural environment."

Dana pushed open the airlock door with his hip, and stepped out with a tray full of lichen in one hand and a cumbersome metal and glass box in the other.

"Here, let me help you." I took the box, sniffing carefully.

Phyllis dried her hands on a towel. "Put it on the table, Douglas. Over there."

"This thing is like dry ice." I dropped it hastily with a loud clunk, and inspected the skin on my palms.

Dana laughed. "Oh, you get used to it after a while."

I rubbed my hands vigorously to take out the chill. "That's what people keep telling me."

"Dana, I want you to take the afternoon off and get some rest. Just leave that tray with Henri on your way through."

"Thanks." Dana dogged the airlock door. "I'll do that, and come back later. Mr. Martin, be seeing you around."

"Sure."

He scooped up his mug, and left carrying the tray in one hand over his shoulder like a well-trained waiter.

Dr. Trimble spun the box to expose the side with a glass window. "The lens is convex so what you see is slightly magnified."

I bent over and peered into the box. Inside, I saw a tangle of filaments which looked like something you might see on a slice of damp bread left in a jar under the kitchen sink. The soft, furry mat that filled the confines of the box appeared to be nothing but common mold.

"Without the aid of a microscope, you really can't discern the individual plants. But what I really want you to see is how it looks in its own environment. These areolichens grow in the absolute darkness of the Caves, and they've developed a peculiar kind of bioluminescence. The outer bacterial cells are covered with a lens-like structure, while the cells beneath the lens secrete a luminous substance. The result is breathtaking."

She dimmed the lights and drew a curtain around us. Then, she took a heavy cloak off a hook and draped it over the box. She motioned for me to get underneath the cloak.

I stuck my head under the black shroud. "I feel like an old time photographer." The only thing missing was the squeeze ball and the birdie sitting on the pole.

The inside of the box assumed a faint glow. As if someone were cranking up a rheostat, each individual component of the dull, brown lichen erupted into a scintillating design of thousands of beckoning beacons. Myriads of stars glistened like a globular galaxy, flooding the miniature universe with cool, green light, and bathing the interior walls with a wild, artificial aura. The stagnant crusty-looking mold came alive in a dancing, prismatic pageant, twinkling like stars viewed from a peaceful suburban lawn on a warm summer's night.

It became more than a formless, amorphous mass. Odd, but strangely familiar shapes took form — like a child's puzzle in which a series of dots connected with thin pencil lines silhouetted a picture. But the pictures I saw were nothing mundane, nothing natural, nothing — real. At the same time, I was both fascinated and horrified, enraptured and agonized, drawn and repulsed.

I was hypnotized by the auroral display. I stared into it for an eternity, until the light touch on my shoulder became a fervent tug. Mustering all my will power, I still could not pull myself away from that spectacular tableau. I was enveloped by a power that was beyond my experience.

The hood was thrown back and I was forcibly wrenched away. My eyes — my brain — could not adjust to the stark reality: the curtain was gone and the lights in the room fully lit. The interior of the box was dark, cold, and lifeless, its ephemeral beauty destroyed by the onslaught of overhead fluorescence. Urgently, I wanted to dash out those invading lights, to bring back the elegant splendor of that alien being, to be enthralled by that hypnotic embrace. Suddenly, I wanted to cry.

Blindly, I felt myself spun around, felt stinging slaps on my face, felt the chilling return of reality. I stared into the anxious face of Phyllis Trimble. Her eyes were as big as dinner plates.

"I — I'm sorry, Douglas. I should have warned you, but I didn't know that you would take it so — strongly. Are you all right?"

I shook the phantoms out of my brain, and placed a quaking hand on my forehead. I brought it away drenched with sweat. "Yes, I'm — okay. I — I wasn't prepared — for that. It's a powerful force."

"It's a unifying force. Since its discovery, and the excavation of the Martian city, all of us have felt a common bond much stronger than we ever felt before. We have been infused with a purpose and direction — and a common identity."

My head was still swimming with strange images.

"It has given us a platform from which we hope to launch a new world, a new civilization. You can join us, Douglas. You can be a great help to us. We need you."

Chapter 9

I stood alone on the Observation Deck, far above the room where the debriefing session was to be held. The only structure above me was the antenna motor room — and above that, the rotating antenna locked in on the satellite relay station. I shoved the recorder in my pocket while I gathered my thoughts for the report.

Syrtis City was in the midst of a great change. If I could believe it, half the personnel were working at the Caves. That accounted for the abandoned cubicles, the empty corridors. Entire strands of the City web had been sealed off, lying fallow. Portions of research facilities and resource reclamation machinery had been dismantled, transported, and reassembled at the site of the Martian ruins. I witnessed cannibalism of crucial equipment and irreplaceable scientific paraphernalia, occurring at a frenzied pace.

This did not necessarily mean the end of the Colony, merely the relocation of its parts. Syrtis City was nothing more than the bearer of the torch: mankind was the flame. The spirit still ran free.

The Observation Deck was a closet-sized room, a nipple on the breast of the Administration Dome. The only furnishing was the central ladder wrapped around the retractile antenna housing. The room was unique in that it was the only cubicle in the City with windows.

A flip of a switch opened the protective diaphragms that covered the four round portholes, like an iris opening the aperture of a camera lens. Each port beheld a different quarter of the compass. Through the west-facing glass, I looked over the laboratory domes where were housed most of the experimental centers as well as the bulk of the geology stores. Beyond that and far, far above, the two-mile-high wall of the Western Rim reached toward the sky: I felt like an ant at the bottom of the Grand Canyon.

Slightly to the north rose the huge breakdown

where Linda and I had yesterday brought the crawler down from the storm-swept plateau. Shifting my gaze to the north port, from where the talus was still visible, the spaceport was hidden by Mars' curvature, out of sight over the foreshortened horizon. I thought I caught a glint of sunlight off what might have been the tip of the spaceship hanging in its gantry.

At the end of the northern spoke was the main crawler garage. Outside, in the clear, near vacuum, men and women were busily loading trailers with crates and packages that in heavier gravity would have been unwieldy. Between the garage and the entrance to the Administration Dome squatted a series of small, interconnected domes, like a cluster of polyps, housing the main stores, water extraction plants, and various mechanical and repair shops.

Eastward lay the nuclear power plant and generating station. The wild, wintry wind was funneled into cooling chambers surrounding the core and, with perfect flow-through ventilation, was discharged into the atmosphere. Layers of screen mesh filtered out the sand, while electronic crackers did away with smaller particulates and dust. Power plant personnel jokingly claimed that their main worry was not overheating or meltdown of the core, but freezing of the electromagnetic field in the generator.

Overhead, the late morning sun beat down on a desert that was larger, grander, drier, and more spectacular than the Sahara — the main induction center and training ground for potential Mars colonists.

A light wind was blowing, not hard enough to be troublesome but gusting violently every now and then. Red grit danced in spurts, rippling like the orange coat of a stalking lion. Sound travels poorly in near vacuum, so the lion's roar was reduced to a faint high-pitched whine like the humming of bees. The anemometer needle fluctuated silently in a world in which windows did not rattle and walls did not creak.

To the south, I strained to see the Sasquatch Mountains, but their pointed tips were obscured by atmospheric haze. Nearby, the small biology dome was a frog sticking the tip of its nose through the sand, as if for a sniff of air. Farther away, the taller Hydroponics Dome stood out in high relief as the harsh sunlight sparkled off its sandblasted aluminum exterior.

This was the extent of the colonist's world: five years in a pressure hull. The pall of claustrophobia hammered at my temples.

Lock up a person in a closet all day long, day after day, year after year, and his sanity would be in doubt. Strap a person in a chair, wedge him in between walls so tightly that his elbows rub the sides and only inches separate his nose from a wall, and death could be the result. Yet, an elevator operator spent his working life in a cage, and a truck driver steered for long dreary hours behind the wheel. Both have one thing in common: sensory input.

The elevator operator sees different floors, different faces, different personalities. The truck driver sees miles of rolling landscape pass under his wheels. The imprisonment of the body is counteracted by the freedom of the mind.

But for a colonist, there was no coffee break, no stretch stop, no bailing out. The next opposition, after two and a half years, would bring new faces, and a change in direction from trainee to trainer. But there was no going home until the second opposition. Life in a submarine goes on. The only opportunity for change lay outside.

The human mind needs line of sight. Inside, I could *feel* the infringement of the walls. I needed to get out in the air, in the open, to walk without purpose, to wander without aim, to think freely without pressure. I glanced at my watch. There was time before the meeting. An instant later, I was on my way down the ladder and through the corridors to my room.

I donned my exposure suit and backpack, found the nearest airlock, stepped inside, sealed the hood and attached the hoses, cycled the chamber. Hidden pumps silently sucked out the oxygen. The ready light blinked on and I pushed open the door, the last bit of oxygen that could not be siphoned out helping to break the seal. I stepped into the dust snorkel, then out into the glowing sunlight.

The atmosphere was crisp and clear: my suit thermometer registered twenty below — warm by Martian standards. A light breeze played around my feet and kicked up a cloud of sand. I took a deep breath, surveyed my surroundings. Light filtered through the portholes on the Observation Deck. I had forgotten to close the protective diaphragms, a breach of economy. But I was not going back inside now.

My room was close to the central hub, in the northwestern auxiliary spoke. From here I could see workers loading the trailers. Seeking solitude, I walked along the spoke and rounded the end so that the Western Rim rose on my right.

I threaded my way around the shallow dunes, first heading away from the City, then turning and coming back on the south side of the western spoke. Hardly any of the auxiliary southwestern spoke was visible: the shifting sand had buried everything except the personnel airlock, kept clear by periodic checks.

I walked right up onto the spoke as if it were a dune. Under my feet the personnel quarters were quiet and empty. Should I give the go-ahead to have them refilled?

At the crest, I leaned forward to compensate for the wind, put out my foot for stability, and felt the bottom slip out from under me. I tumbled down the other side, shaken but unhurt. I jumped up and looked around foolishly, half afraid that someone might have seen my idiotic fall. I checked over my suit and its life support systems, found no malfunctions.

Sand was blowing in plumes over the top of the tube and, like a snow cornice on an Earthly mountain, had built a bridge of sand out over the air. Only in Mars' low gravity could such a sand cornice exist.

Nowhere did I see signs of outside activity at the southern end of the City. When I reached the spoke that was the tunnel leading to the Hydroponics Dome, I crossed over between it and the biology laboratory. This time I was careful as I scampered over the top and down the lee side. A violent gust howled after me like all the hounds of hell, but was gone in an instant, as if it had never existed.

In the relative calm, I circled the broad dome. I pictured Phyllis Trimble inside, standing perhaps not more than ten feet away, yet separated by a gulf that might well have been the Great Wall of China.

A sleek and recently erected aluminum bubble was attached to the emergency airlock. Its metal exterior was smooth and unpitted. But this "little addition" attached to the dome, like an oversized remora on a prowling shark, was almost the height and width of its attendant dome — and over fifty feet in length. When I stood at the end of it, the tall profile of the Hydroponics Dome prevented me from seeing the Observation Deck.

A long line of shallow depressions led away from the extended airlock canopy. The wind blew lightly around the dome, and a fine layer of sand kicked up a small cloud of dust just above the ground. I kneeled down to inspect one of the depressions. It was long and narrow, and sunk into the soft sand about the same distance as my own boots. One end of the hollow was narrow and rounded, while the other broadened and split into five elongated parts.

It had an uncanny resemblance to an oversized caricature of a naked human footprint.

Even as I watched, the sides of the shallow pit caved in, and windblown sand settled into it. It melted from sight. The wind had already obliterated the other depressions; as if they had never existed. And perhaps they did not, except in my imagination. The shifting sand, the colored minerals, the freaky atmosphere could play tricks on the human mind.

I shrugged it off, and studied the airlock door to which those evanescent toes had pointed. The sand had recently been swept clean from the opening. I actuated the release mechanism, felt compressed oxygen clearing the seals, entered the chamber, locked myself in.

The ready light blinked, I pushed open the inner door. The interior was shrouded in utter darkness as the red glow from the airlock chamber filtered dimly past me. My own shadow lurched into the gloom. My eyes danced with a blackness that was somehow not black. The unnatural cold of the room gripped me, colder than the outside temperature. I was aware of a faraway effervescent glow.

In the feeble light, I groped around on the wall for a switch, found none in the standardized places. When my eyes accustomed themselves to the darkness, I began to discern vague shapes in the unreality. I saw a desk and a laboratory table, strewn with books and assorted glassware, and an incandescent lamp mounted on flexible tubing. I switched it on and, in the light of its twenty-five watts, stepped back to the airlock and pulled the door shut.

On the desk were a diskette reader/recorder, and a computer terminal. The row of books on the overhead shelf, like most of those on Mars, were not paper and cloth but chips and disks. One textbook drew my attention, titled, "An Historic and Progressive Study of Indigenous Lichen, with Respect to Location, Chemistry, and Function." It was transcribed by Dr. Phyllis Trimble, with additional feasibility studies and analyses on human compatibility by Dr. Aloysius Reynolds.

I powered on the user terminal, snapped in the disk, bulk loaded the document. The screen immediately flashed "Protected Information. Please Input Password." I hit the "proceed" key, but the prompt remained on the monitor. I switched off the computer, replaced the disk.

As my eyes adjusted to the dim light, I turned around to see what else the room had to offer. I saw shelving, row after row of it, stacked floor to ceiling. The narrow aisles were bordered by tiers only three inches high, allowing tens of thousands of square feet of storage.

And every bit of available space on every shelf was

filled with that foul, brown, curly-leafed lichen.

I stepped back so sharply that I banged into the table and knocked over a rack of test tubes. The noise was deafening in that surly, eerie silence. Overcoming my initial shock, I moved closer to the botanical specimens. They were in various stages of growth, from a furry covering to tall stems scraping the bottoms of the drawers above.

I heard the grating of the connecting airlock. Quickly, I switched off the light, ducked under the desk, pulled a chair in front of me.

I felt secure in the darkness for only a moment, for the blackness disintegrated into an enhancing, coruscating green glow. From every corner, from every shelf in every aisle, bioluminescent shadows melted together into a wondrous montage of emerald shimmering, bursting forth like a silent explosion, a green solar prominence.

And into this fantastic aurora walked Dr. Trimble's mustachioed assistant, still garbed in his white smock and carrying a shallow, plastic tray.

I felt as exposed as if I were standing in the beam of a spot light. I crouched lower, scarcely breathing.

Livingston Dana sauntered up the middle aisle. I caught only partial glimpses of him through the narrow shelving. He stopped several times, and I heard the sliding of trays. He inspected them, then slid them back. So bright was the combined light from the thousands of plants that every detail in the room was distinguishable to me. I fought off that hypnotizing, paralyzing effect by forcing my eyes closed every few seconds, and remembering that foul odor. If only I had doffed my exposure hood, the rank smell would have helped me retain my sanity. Despite the chill of the room and the cold of fear, I sweated profusely.

Slowly, Dana picked his way along the aisle. When he reached the end near the outer airlock, I could hear his breathing. He was within two arms reach of me, but facing the other way. If he turned, I knew I would be discovered.

But I have every right to be here. I am conducting an official investigation.

Dana found a tray of lichen that suited him. He pulled it out, cradled it in his arm, and replaced it with the empty tray that he had carried in. He made a half turn. I shrank. Limned in the pervading green radiance, his coarse features wavered in a weird, horrific way, like a face lighted by a flashlight held upward under the chin.

He fingered the lichen lightly with one finger, his attention held solidly - I thought, by that unexplainable hypnotic effect which was putting such a strain on my own concentration. He pinched off a glowing green nugget, held it in front of his eyes.

And popped it into his mouth!

Still chewing the ugly morsel, he turned and retraced his steps along the aisle, exited through the airlock, and slammed the door behind him.

I burst out from my hiding place, fingered the light switch, wrenched the hoses from my mask, ripped the hood off my face, and vomited raucously into the sink next to the laboratory table.

The odor exuded by the roomful of lichen fouled the atmosphere with the stench of rotting flesh. As soon as I could, I replaced the hood, plugged in the hoses, increased the oxygen flow. Even when I was again self-contained, the effluvium lingered inside my suit. I purged the oxygen valves several times to change the air. I was still sick.

I had to get out of there, away from that mass of ugly lichen that was now, in the dim glow of the desk lamp, a mass of curly, brown smudges. Whether the foul smell was real or psychosomatic did not matter. I felt weak, dizzy, confined, and cold. I needed to get into the open.

Quickly, I cleaned the mess in the sink. Everything was washed down the drain and pumped into a reclamation chamber. All liquids were recycled: water was too precious to waste. I might be redrinking it tomorrow. I scraped the broken glassware into a waste receptacle.

I did not switch off the desk lamp until I had the inner airlock open — I could not stand the momentary darkness which would allow the lichen's bioluminescent cells to come to life.

Once outside, I stood in the breeze and breathed in the sky and the sun, and my bottled oxygen. It was warmer than I remembered. I felt free — freer than I had ever felt in my life. A childish exuberance overcame me, and I felt like running barefoot through the sand, rejoicing in the wind.

Almost without realizing it, I found my hands gripping the rebreather hoses, pulling them out. The pressure relief valve saved me.

Am I mad? A cold shiver of fear bristled my hair as I grasped the impact of what I had been about to do. In a moment of weakness, of incaution, of utter depravity, I had allowed myself to think that I had no need of such mechanical encumbrances as a pressure suit and stored oxygen. I was shaken by the mental impulse that had almost overtaken me.

What would Rogers think of such an urge? Was it insanity? Infection? Contagion? In my imagination, I could see him sneering at me. I could sense him watching me. But I was alone out here; no one was in sight. I looked up at the Observation Deck.

The viewing ports had been shut and sealed.

Chapter 10

Department heads, administrative personnel, and interested spectators filed into the large meeting room in accordance with the planned debriefing session. Colonists existed in all sizes and shapes and colors and creeds, but they had one thing in common: the love of their work and the good of the Project. As they stepped over the reinforced sill, they exhibited a step that was bouncy and airy: a graceful blend of exuberance and low gravity.

I greeted those I knew and remembered. Linda introduced previous opposition arrivals with requisite formality. "Mr. Martin, this is Dr. Phillip Keppert, Chief Geologist."

I thrust out my hand. "Nice to meet you, Doctor."

He took it grudgingly. "Areologist, if you please. And I'd prefer to be working instead of wasting valuable time giving interviews. There's nothing I can tell you that the Major can't say just as well."

"Yes, well — " I glanced at Linda. She shrugged. "Uh, the Major seems to have his own ideas about things, Doctor, and has demonstrated some reticence about discussing certain aspects of your work."

"We differ in our opinions. He thinks we need to be diplomatic. I don't. Furthermore, I don't care."

He scowled as he brushed by, claimed a seat at the long table next to Major Thomas Tarkington at the head, and folded his gangling body into a chair. He plopped his briefcase on the simulated wood-grain plastic, pulled out a sheaf of notes.

"He's not always like that," Doc Reynolds whispered from over my shoulder. "Usually he's worse. But don't worry. He warms up as he gets to know you. Besides that, he's brilliant, and genius will have its quirks."

"What's *your* excuse?" Linda smiled.

The doctor pointed a finger at her. "Don't get sassy, or I'll take it out on your hide." To me, "Don't let Keppert worry you. Treat him like a geologist and take him for granite."

Linda groaned.

I turned, pulled the doctor away from the oxygen gauges. "If you're finished with your adjustments, you can get out of here. I'm trying to maintain an image of righteous anger and justified animosity. I can't do it if I'm laughing."

"But the Major told me to keep you off balance."

I stared at him, hard.

"Okay, I can take a hint." He picked up his emergency bag and found a seat.

Linda found my hand. "Doug, don't be too serious."

"Someone has to be."

"You know what I mean."

"No, I'm not sure I do. Especially when you wouldn't let me come to your cube last night."

"I told you, I had work to do — to prepare for this meeting. Doug, just — "

I held up my hand. "Forget it. We'll talk about it later." Although I would not admit it to her, I realized I was at fault - for putting my personal life before my professional one.

The room was filled almost to capacity, and latecomers brought their own chairs from the mess hall. Linda turned away, pouting.

"Well, hello Adams." I shook hands with the shuttle navigator while pilot Hodges-Smith and co-pilot Anderson sneaked by. "I didn't expect to see you fly boys here."

"Mr. Martin." He nodded perfunctorily. "We're just as interested in this as anybody, I guess. Passes the time better than chess. Have you been playing?"

"Quite a bit, but without a board." I smiled at his pinched eyebrows. "As you said, the Major plays quite a game. How's the arm?"

"Huhn?"

"The arm." I rolled my shoulder. "You know, the shots?"

"What shots?"

"Hasn't Doc Reynolds been giving you inoculations?"

He shook his head slowly.

"Uh, any problem with, you know, getting used to the air?" I shrugged. "The pressure?"

Adams shook his head again.

"Well, never mind. It's not important. Listen, I'd better sit down before someone claims my chair."

I slipped through the crowd to my reserved seat, sat at the opposite head of the table that doubled as a Ping-Pong board (an interesting game in low gravity). The din of voices was like the cadence of a beehive. I heard the soft whoosh of overworking circulators. Judging by the relaxed smiles and joking, the meeting seemed to be more like a social gathering than a debriefing session.

Major Tarkington rose from his chair, leaned forward on bruiser knuckles, and drawled in his ordinary booming voice, "All right, we all know why we're here, but for the record — Arty, is that recorder on?"

Arthur Kimball touched the electronic boxes in front of him. "Both of them."

I put my own recorder on the table, checked to make sure I had inserted a fresh tape.

"Good. For the record, I will state that the Mars Appropriation Committee has sent Douglas Martin as a special appointee — as, let's say as a sort of emissary. For those of you who have not met Mr. Martin previously, you should be aware that he served as our Administrative Secretary for the five years before Arty took over. Since then, he's been acting in our behalf Earthside as Public Relations Officer. So, as far as we're concerned, he's still a member of the Project.

"Now, he's here to make a full report of our findings which he will deliver, along with our recommendations, to the Committee. If you haven't already been instructed to do so, let me say now that he is to receive your full cooperation in all aspects of his investigation. I know that you're all tired and overworked, and I knew what kind of pressure you've been laboring under these past months. We all feel the same way, maybe a little irrita-

ble when we shouldn't be, a little short in our explanations when we should strive for detail and accuracy.
Mr. Martin must be made aware of all the facts that we
have uncovered, all the implications they may have, the
importance of each facet of our work, and the reasons
for our change in operational procedures, so he can
form his own conclusions about our methodology and
the necessity of its unhampered continuance — conclusions which we hope will coincide with our own. Doug,
would you like to say a few words before we start?"

The Major sat down. There was general applause as
I stood up awkwardly and glanced around the room. I
adjusted the recorder's volume control.

"Thank you, Major. First of all, I would like to
extend sincere congratulations from the Committee on
your discoveries, and to express gratitude to all of you
for having chosen, in this great moment in man's history, to remain beyond your time in order to see
through this period of intense learning and expansion
of knowledge.

"But I must also express deep concern over of the
lack of cooperation between this outpost and its bene-
factors, due to the paucity of information released to
the Committee, and because of the virtually rebellious
manner in which requests for clarification have gone
unacknowledged. The seriousness of this matter can be
realized when you accept the possibility of a military
rebuke. Should my findings be unfavorable, the next
shuttle may be full of arresting soldiers.

"On the other hand, we hold no one person responsible, nor will any prejudgments be made until all the
facts are known and have been weighed. I'll do my best
to understand the situation from your point of view, but
you should be aware that the Committee, while maintaining faith and confidence of success, is less than
satisfied with the performance of its members. I sin-
cerely hope, both personally and as a dignitary, that
the reasons for your . . . ah . . . discretion have been
valid, and that your continued loyalty to the Project can
be counted on. Please proceed."

The short applause that followed was strained. People talked in hushed tones behind cupped hands, and enigmatic expressions were exchanged.

My arm continued to annoy me, the itch waxing and waning, but the muscle aches were bearable. My temples throbbed only mildly.

Major Tarkington rose again and the noise subsided. "Thank you, Mr. Martin. On behalf of the Colony, too, I'd like to thank you for your trust and show of confidence. Now, I'd like to get right into the meat of the matter, so without further ado, I'll turn the floor over to Dr. Keppert. He can offer some historical perspective, and fill you in on the theoretical and geological background. Dr. Keppert?"

The leanness of the geologist's body was hardly disguised by the thick, foam-padded uniform, for it showed through in the hollows of his cheeks, in the sunken, fathomless eyes, in the narrow, aquiline nose. His thin, receding black hair and pointed goatee gave a devilish look to an otherwise sour expression.

"Yes, thank you, Major. First, I'd like no interruptions so I can get through the basics quickly. No questions until after I'm through."

Dr. Keppert's nervousness was evident through obvious displacement activity: he continually ran through a sequence of reaching up with his right hand to pull his ear lobe, scratch his nose, and pinch his chin under the goatee, after which he gave a sharp intake of breath through flared nostrils. He stared down at the table as he talked.

"Mars, as you may already know, once had an atmosphere much denser than it now possesses, and capable of holding water in great quantities. Nothing in comparison to the choking atmosphere of Earth, to be sure, but as far as the forces necessary to form life it was more than adequate. Life began on Mars much in the same way it began on Earth, and much, we suspect, in the way it begins on any suitable planet. Life also evolved in the same manner as life on Earth, carbon based, forming the same basic orders of plants and animals, but varying according to local conditions. Fossil evidence has long since proven this.

"Then, some millions of years ago, the planetary crust underwent a traumatic event, an unaccounted for upheaval which drained away oceans, upthrust mountains, and set continent against continent. This did not happen overnight. In fact, one living on Mars at the time would scarcely have been aware of any change. Areologic processes work in time spans on a different scale than that by which human generations are measured.

"As a consequence of this long-term seismic activity, the atmosphere began to dissipate, to leak away, not so much into space but rather absorbed by the very soil, forced into chemical combination with the rocks, converted, so to speak, into solid matter. Along with the lessening atmospheric pressure, free liquid became an ever-decreasing commodity until today, it is virtually nonexistent, and survives only in minute quantities frozen out of the ground near the polar ice caps.

"But at one time water was plentiful, forming vast oceans and huge, rushing rivers that carved the Martian surface into miles-deep fissures. The force of this water also created a complicated water table and dug enormous subarean chambers. This underground system is similar to the famous Blue Holes of Earth, and the numerous fumaroles found at the ocean bottoms. It was through this subsurface network that Mars' water flowed when it first began to recede, until it disappeared from the surface altogether.

"Because of this extensive undercutting due to water erosion, in many places the surface we find today is weak. While seismic tremors are rare due to subsequent stabilization of the crust, surface collapse is common. Crevasses, such as are formed in the ice of glacial moraines, abound. They are bridged by thin veneers of loose rock, waiting to collapse should the proper pressure be applied. The weight of a passing crawler is sometimes sufficient to break through the unstable covering, which is why they are equipped with gravimeters that can detect the hollows underneath, and — "

"Excuse me, Dr. Keppert, but can we skip the basics?" My voice was louder than I intended, and coarser. "This isn't a high school class."

Keppert glanced quickly around the room, returned his gaze to the table, and went through his nervous gestures: touching ear lobe, nose, and chin. The slight inhale of breath was clearly audible in the strained silence. "Major, must I go on with this nonsense? I don't really need — "

"Come on, Phil. Loosen up." Major Tarkington shook pudgy cheeks. "Just get on with the technical data. Art, you want to get the projectors ready?"

Kimball activated the multiple projectors in the corners of the room, and fumbled with the dials. A control image appearing above the center of the table was brought into focus.

I felt a warm hand on my shoulder. Linda, standing behind me, flashed a bright smile and squeezed twice — our old 'I love you' code. "Try not to be so analytical. Just sit back and watch the show."

From across the table, Doc Reynolds made a megaphone out of his hands, and whispered, "The slides, not Keppert."

I shook my head at the doctor while reaching up and returning Linda's squeeze. "It doesn't pay to take chances."

The room darkened, the hubbub died down. The hologram appeared to be facing me, but it was facing every other viewer as well. "General Survey Number 1107. Location: Syrtis Major south, area Ryans Rill. Coordinates — " The following series of numbers were based on the arbitrary Greenwich meridian.

"It's all yours, Dr. Keppert." Kimball slid the pocket-sized remote control box across the table. "Just push the black button to advance the slides. Red for reverse."

Keppert touched his ear lobe, nose, and chin. He picked up the slide changer, practiced on the controls. The first slide dissolved and another appeared in its place, an aerial photograph taken, as subtitled, from an orbiting survey probe.

With the sun close to the horizon, contrasting elevations were clearly delineated by dark shadows. Craters of various sizes dotted the landscape like large drops of water from a heavy rainstorm plunging into a thick, muddy puddle. A long, grayish gash sliced across the picture, traversing in its path several craters and ridges, and intersecting with other, fainter gashes, lending the impression of a patchwork quilt with holes in it. The ground was tinted carmine.

"The rills on Mars," started Dr. Keppert, pinching his ear, scratching his nose, and squeezing his chin, "are identical to their lunar counterparts: rectilinear fracture zones caused by uneven cooling and massive shrinkage of the planetary crust. Being smaller than Earth, these tectonic processes occurred much sooner and are but a warning of the eventual fate of the Earth. Am I being too elemental for you, Mr. Martin?"

"Yes, but go ahead. If you have to indoctrinate another six hundred people, you'll need the practice."

Dr. Keppert picked up a lighted pointer and indicated the faint gash. "This view from space shows Ryans Rill as a very prominent feature, although sometimes, such as when the sun is at its zenith or when the aerial distance is increased, it cannot be seen at all. This is because rills are seen not by the depression they cause, but by the shadows they create. Ryans Rill, which is twenty-five hundred feet deep (relatively shallow as rills go) is five miles wide and extends for over one hundred fifty miles.

"You will notice faint lines perpendicular to the main rill. With the sun at an oblique angle, we can determine that these superficial surface features are minor fractures which have not separated enough to cause roof collapse. In the evolution of the planet, these might one day become rills. But, because of Mars' crustal stability, they are likely to remain as they are for many millions of years.

"Now, despite this stability, a mild tremor was recorded two years ago, causing some local damage in this area." The green dot circled a spot that was only a smudge that could have been mistaken for dust on the slide. "It did little more than draw our attention. A follow-up study revealed a fracture zone at least as long as Ryans Rill, and which had previously been overlooked. Not only is it extremely narrow, but it is open only in a few places. It is, in fact, a fracture zone still in the process of collapse, a rill in the building."

Dr. Keppert glanced at me. I nodded noncommittally. The slide dissolved and another appeared. Taken from ground level, the left half showed gentle, fluid dunes and small, rocky outcrops; the right side dropped off into an infinite abyss. The reddish hue of the sand and rock stood out in sharp relief against the pale pink background of the sky. The clarity of an almost airless world and the three-dimensional quality of the hologram added a stark sense of reality.

"This is the edge of what has since been named Sanders Rill. Here is one of the few places along the fracture zone where the surface has collapsed. This picture was taken nine months later, when a survey team explored this previously ignored region south of Ryans Rill. As you can see, descent is impossible at this point due to the sheer walls. But after a diligent search, a way was found down to the bottom. I might mention that, although Sanders Rill is only a quarter mile wide, it is over five thousand feet deep."

The next slide put us right inside the rill. The fisheye lens distorted the perspective but was necessary to show the extent of the mile-high walls. The sheer cliffs seemed to have been chipped off, as if by some Cyclopean chisel.

Ear, nose, chin. "Only for a few minutes on either side of high noon does the sun penetrate to the bottom of Sanders Rill. Now we recognize the major difference between the rills of Mars and those of the Moon. Here we have a planet that once sported great oceans. As the sea level dropped, these rills became the main watercourses, adding to the already extensive undercutting. It follows that all life on Mars concentrated itself around these rectilinear oases: where water was available, there was a profusion of vegetation and the animals which fed upon it. Elsewhere was barren and completely devoid of life.

"It was upon this declining scene that intelligence chanced to rear its inquisitive head above the dull swarm of common life, and to build for itself a civilization."

Waxing poetic, I thought. The silence in the room was absolute: no one scraped a chair, or moved a foot, or cleared a throat. Dr. Keppert had somehow gotten off on a theological tangent that sent shivers down my spine. If, until, now I had viewed the finding of an alien civilization somewhat distantly, even disbelievingly, his statements brought the truth of the matter into proper perspective. What had once been merely theory had now become an actuality.

While everyone's eyes were glued to the hologram, Keppert pierced me with a cold stare. I tried to fathom what thoughts passed through his scientific mind, but his face was an inscrutable mask that released no secrets, hinted at no subterfuges. It was blank, and if anything, oddly frank.

By way of signaling that our eye-staring contest was over, the geologist changed slides. Formed in spectacular realism were the distinguishable features of hand-hewn rock and carved boulders, molded together to form statuesque colonnades.

Without concern for dramatization, the slides dissolved and appeared in quick rotation. Keppert did not pause to dwell on any one scene, but maintained a running commentary.

"Here you see a city which, if constructed by man in the constantly changing atmosphere of Earth, with its wide ranges of temperature and the blight of humidity, its airborne chemicals and acids, its geologically unstable conditions, and scores of other processes which tend to wear away, etch, and erode, would have crumbled into unrecognizable dust eons ago. But here on Mars, we have a living museum carved out of stone, the very building blocks of the universe, and I daresay that it could stand to the end of time.

"This may seem crude by our Earthly standards. Our cities of steel and concrete and plastic and other short-term materials may seem more modern, but they need constant maintenance and offer very little in the way of endurance. The Martians, throughout the long lifespan of their kind, continued to make their homes out of rock, and without the aid of artificial cements. They relied on the tongue-and-groove method in which each stone is carved so that it interlocks perfectly with another. By the time a structure was completed and the key stone put in place, there was no possible way the building could come apart."

Doc Reynolds held up a pad on the top sheet of which was scrawled, "They don't build houses like they used to."

Ear, nose, chin. "The area around Sanders Rill is a vast and complicated network of underground passageways, of which the rill system is but a small external part. The Martians utilized these tunnels and caverns as an underground highway and as protection for their important industrial centers. Their cities, however, are always placed at the entrances."

Eerie, alien structures now dominated the scenes — a city built on the edge of a towering cavern that was hundreds of feet high and thousands wide. Tall spires reached toward the cave roof, some topped with globular stones of bright colors, others terminating with sharpened points like a giant's pickaxe. These attracted my attention but were by no means predominant. Most of the buildings were rectangular — Martian artistry did not lend itself to curved architecture. The multiple-story dwellings were sectioned into rooms or apartments whose doors faced outside and were accessible either by ramps or pegged ladders.

Most fantastic and seemingly unnatural of all was the way they had used stone for roofing and flooring and overhanging porches — all unsupported except at their edges. Even longer spans of extreme thinness, stone sliced like bread, adjoined the buildings at roof level, creating a maze of elevated sidewalks. It was not until I remembered Mars' low gravity that I realized how this kind of architecture was possible. My earthbound physics no longer held true.

Interiors were mostly empty and unfurnished, but a collection of artifacts was displayed by the hologram. An assortment of kitchenware had been preserved, such as clay bowls and dishes: some rare crockery had been found intact, but most had been pieced together from shards.

Scores of workers had unearthed hundreds of metallic items that could have been purely ornamental jewelry or simple machine parts. Scraps of metal had been analyzed and tagged as to constituent materials (mostly copper, bronze, and brass) but their intended uses or purposes had been left open to conjecture.

"Artifacts buried in silt or dust have been protected fairly well from the worst enemy of erosion — time. There is much, much more, enough to keep hundreds of archaeologists occupied for decades to come. In the few short hours we have today, I can't begin to show you everything we have found. Nor do I want to. For the rest, Mr. Martin, I suggest you come and see for yourself."

The hologram dissolved, the room lights brightened, and Dr. Keppert sat down. I did not want it to stop. I wanted to see more of the Martian cities, more of their wonders. I had a million questions to ask, but could not think of one.

A din of chatter started immediately, as if these people had seen these pictures for the first time. How long, I wondered, would it take for a revelation of this magnitude, of this preponderance, to become commonplace?

Too often, once an impossible task has been accomplished, or a great discovery has been made, or a long-sought goal has been achieved, it is promptly forgotten. Too quickly, once the novelty wears off, the impossible becomes the banal.

For the members of the Colony, that time had not

yet come. Nor, judging by their actions, was it even near. All around me was excitement. Linda and Doc were both vying for my attention, but I was numb to their entreaties.

Finally, all conversation was belayed by the Major's booming voice. "That ends the formal presentation. We'll adjourn to the mess hall for refreshments and a more casual discussion. And for those of you to whom this applies, get a good night's rest. We leave in the morning for the Caves."

Chapter 11

Terrence Rogers was right on target when he said that Syrtis City had become a culture unto itself. Exactly where the colonists veered off the track was hard to say. The people looked and acted much as I remembered them. Their personalities and idiosyncrasies had not changed at all. Yet somehow they *felt* different. I was not yet able, as Rogers put it, to think like they think. But some of their experience was rubbing off on me, and I was certain that I was getting closer to them.

I shuffled through a stack of plastic cassettes and computer disks, picked the one I had requested from Phyllis Trimble, and shoved it into the viewer. The title that appeared on the screen was simply, "Lichen," and subtitled, "Notes." No mention was made of Doc Reynolds. What followed was a fairly exhaustive study of its life cycle, growth patterns, reproduction rates, nutrient requirements, and evolutionary history.

The fungus constituent was the fort, providing physical protection as well as retaining water and minerals. The algae was the cook, and did the actual work of synthesizing useful foodstuffs through a chemical reaction catalyzed by bacteria living within the fluid portion of their cells. I did not understand the physiology of chemosynthesis, but the fundamental elements of symbiosis were clear: the whole was greater than the sum of its parts, and neither component could survive on its own.

The bioluminescent glow oscillated by cellular contraction, and by some agency located the exact frequency of the electrical circuits of the human brain. The unposed question was, since each person's brain wave patterns were different, how could the lichen have the same effect on everyone? Did it function on a feedback system? And if so, why?

It almost seemed as if the lichen had a purpose in human terms. Dr. Malle would undoubtedly scoff it off as random pre-adaptation, coinciding only by chance with the human mental process. But was there a connection between areolichen and Dr. Sanders' death? Or worse, could the entire Colony be infected with synchronous delusions?

Is this what happened to the Martians?

A chill coursed along my spine. I fingered another disk, one that I had lifted from the infirmary. It was titled, "Physiological Responses to Pressure Change," and, according to the author, there were a few things about altitude sickness that the good doctor forgot to tell me.

For instance: degenerative changes leading to weight loss, muscular wasting, and deterioration of the liver and other organs.

For instance: high altitude pulmonary edema, in which the lungs become flooded with liquid, as in pneumonia. The symptoms were weakness, shortness of breath, sore throat and coughing. Coma and death could ensue.

For instance: cerebral edema, a direct attack on the brain. It was symptomized by severe headache, hallucinations, weakness, a staggering gait. The eyes should be examined for retinal hemorrhage and excessive intra-ocular pressure. The victim might survive, but permanent brain damage was possible.

Drugs and steroids could alleviate symptoms, but in all cases there was only one known cure: the increase of external atmospheric pressure. A mountain climber would descend the mountain.

Doc Reynolds was known to drag a person into isolation if he cleared his throat twice. In a confined environment, the simplest ailment could quickly reach epidemic proportions. The doctor I used to know was too cautious, too observant, too skilled to let anything pass by him. He was right about only one thing: something did not click.

The colonists were in a bizarre mood, with something on their minds other than ancient Martians. Lichen had been planted alongside hydroponic vegetation in the corridors, secreted in odd corners, and adorned as centerpieces on tables and in cubicles. It was everywhere. It was omniscient. And if it held contagion, it was already widespread.

A soft knock came from the door.

I threw the pilfered cassette into a drawer and stacked the others up neatly on the desk. I ran a hand through my hair, hoisted up my long johns, and pulled open the hatch.

Linda poised coyly at the opening, holding two glasses and a bottle. "I can use some company. How about you?"

I nodded slowly, expressionlessly. "Sure. Come on in."

She stepped over the sill. "You sneaked away right after dinner, but I wasn't hurt. I made allowances for the fact that you might be tired after a long day at the office."

I dogged the door. The cubicle was so small that when I turned around I could feel her breathing on my face. "Sorry, I had a lot on my mind."

She kissed me on the cheek, clinked the glasses together. "So have I. How about if we discuss some of them over a drink?"

I nodded, smiling faintly. "I guess I haven't been myself lately." I gave her a peck on the cheek. When I pulled back, she grabbed my head and held it in place for a return kiss — a long one.

We broke for air. "That's more like it, Doug."

"You rat." The old term of endearment slipped out before I could catch it. "Have a seat and start pouring."

Linda made herself comfortable on the bed, sequestered carefully between the built-in bureau and the bulkhead. She spun around so that one foot was on the floor and the other bent up to her chin. She leaned back. "Will you do the honors?"

I adopted the same attitude opposite her, my extended leg touching hers. I took the bottle, popped the plastic stopper. "Is this a local brew?"

"Yes, Doc Reynolds distills it for medicinal purposes."

I sniffed the cork. "Smells good. What is it?"

Linda held out her glass. "I don't know. I doubt if it has a name."

I half filled her glass, poured two fingers into my own. "Hmmnn, it has a slightly musty flavor, but not too bad. What's it extracted from, butyl mercaptan?"

She frowned at my allusion to the chemical that was responsible for a skunk's odor. "Don't. You're beginning to sound like Doc Reynolds. Let's keep this between you and me."

"Uh, oh. Sounds like something serious." I wiped off my smirk, and said solemnly, "What's wrong, Linda?"

"Off the record?"

I thought for a long moment before answering. "Linda, there is no off the record. Not any more."

"But this is just about the two of us."

I ran my tongue over my teeth. "Okay, off the record." I pulled the recorder out of my breast pocket, switched it off, set it on the desk.

"Doug, after this is all over, I still want to marry you."

I sucked in a breath. I peered into deep, ocean blue eyes. My throat was suddenly dry, but swallowing did not relieve the lump.

Linda put her free hand on mine. "I didn't mean to sound so harsh — in the crawler, that is. It's just that, well, I've had time to think it over since then. Not that I didn't think about it before, but when the Martian city was found, we all sort of got swept up with it. No one had any time for personal considerations. This was something that was too big to miss. It harbored all my thoughts, every waking moment."

She flattened out her leg, tucked in her heel, took a hefty draft.

"I'm sorry if this sounds repetitious. I'm sure you've heard the same thing from everyone else. But it *is* important." She paused. Her eyes glittered, overflowing with warmth. "You're important to me, too, Doug. I don't know how this whole mess is going to turn out, but whatever happens, whatever you have to do, for what it's worth, I do love you."

"Well, I hardly — "

"Wait, let me finish. God, I should have the whole speech memorized. I've said it to myself a thousand times since yesterday, but I'm afraid I won't say it right. First, don't think you have to comment, or commit yourself. I'm not asking for that. I just want you to understand how I feel." She squeezed my hand. "I love you just as much as I did before, just as I always have since we first . . . met, when I first came to Mars and worked for you. And I want you to have no doubt about my feelings for you. They'll never change.

"But we each have our jobs to do. We each have obligations to fulfill. There's a lot to be done yet. The Major, and I, and everyone, want you — need you — to handle this . . . uh . . . release of information to the Committee and to the people of Earth. But we're afraid, honestly afraid, of the effect it may have on the human race. There's so much at stake, so much you don't understand yet. It's got to be doled out in just the right way — you know, like in advertising. We just can't give you a Martian body to take back to Earth and say, 'Look what we found.' You have to see it in context."

My heart skipped a beat. "Have you found any actual Martian remains?"

Linda took a deep breath. "Yes, we have."

I blinked at her.

"Doug, I'm sorry. We wanted you to see them in place, in the Caves."

My voice thundered. "What the hell do you want to do? Wrap it up like a Christmas package so I can find it under the tree? What kind of game are you people playing?"

Linda withdrew her hand, held it up protectively. "Doug, that's not the way it is. We don't want you to go the way Sanders went. Too much knowledge, too fast, killed him. If you absorb everything piecemeal, you can assimilate it the same way we did."

"Linda, I'm going to start blowing some fuses if people don't quit treating me like a child."

"Doug, it's like reading a book, a mystery. You can't start chapter two complaining that you weren't told about material in chapter one. There's only room in chapter one for one chapter. You have to read it through. All we're doing is arranging the order of the chapters. Please try to understand." She squeezed my knee.

I leaned back, my head against the bulkhead, my eyes staring at the overhead. "All right, I'm sorry. I didn't mean to explode — not at you. But I'm tired of being pushed around like a pawn on a chessboard. I'm not here to play find-the-Martian. I want facts. I want truth. And I want it now."

Linda stared hard at me, her face open and innocent.

I stopped grinding my teeth. "So, tell me more about the Martians. What do they look like?"

"They look . . . like us. That is, they're taller, they're thinner, they had less weight to support. We don't know what they're like inside, of course. But they're bipedal, they have five fingers on each hand, five toes on each foot. They could almost be caricatures of us — or we of them."

"Parallel evolution."

"Just like all the other plant and animal fossils we've found. They have some environmental adaptations, but their musculature is designed much the same way as ours. They breathe through nostrils, eat through a mouth, hear through an enormous set of ears, make love — "

"And when was I supposed to be given this little tidbit of information?"

"Tomorrow, I guess. I don't know. We were talking about it tonight. Doug, we've been working twenty-five hours a day, fourteen days a week." The standard joke because of Mars' slightly longer day and vastly longer year. "Ever since the ruins were discovered. All that data can't be compressed into a five hour meeting."

"The highlights could have, and the details could

have been filled in later. Look, I don't want to argue with you. I had a long talk with the Major, to our mutual dissatisfaction. I don't like the way the situation has been handled right from the start. This damned secrecy has got the Committee in a bind. What I would like to have is some straight answers."

Linda placed her hand against her chest. "Please don't put me in the middle. I'm honor bound not to interfere with agreed-upon policy, especially since I helped to make that policy. I slipped, and I'm sorry, and there'll be hell to pay. I just can't say any more about it. But believe me, Major Tarkington's heart and soul are in the Project just like everyone else's — "

"Linda, you don't have to defend either the Major or the Project. I'm not making accusations about honor or integrity or devotion to duty. I'm talking about the way this whole situation has been hushed up so that I had to be sent here on a special shuttle to find out what the hell is going on, so we know what to do with six hundred replacements sitting on hold, and with six hundred soldiers waiting to take their places."

"I understand that. But we're not on opposite sides of the fence. We're just looking from different angles. It's a delicate situation, and we have the opportunity to make something out of it. This is a chance for Syrtis City to become more than a Project. This could well emancipate our colony status."

I put down my glass, the drink forgotten. "So the cat's out of the bag. You're using this discovery as a bargaining point to achieve independence."

"No, that's not true at all, Doug. We're a part of humanity, and want to remain that way. Look what we've got here. We live in barless cages, fragile shells that have to be oxygenated, pressurized, heated, powered, lighted, insulated. We can't even step outside without cosmic ray shielding in our suits. Artificial habitats are costly to build and expensive to maintain, and will forever be contingent upon Earth technology and manpower. Mars can never be conformed to fit man's needs. Doug, we're a naked animal who takes his own environment with him — but at great expense."

"So what? We've been carrying our own environment with us ever since the first cave man donned an animal pelt. That upset the balance of nature, because he was no longer bound to one prescribed niche. Once he learned to make clothing and fire, he was on the road to the conquest of the stars. Carrying an envelope of air into the depths of space was nothing more than an extension of protecting himself from the ice age. Both kept him safe from attacking elements. Who's to say that the next step in his evolution is not enclosing himself for his entire lifetime in a metal cocoon? This Project could be the very conditioning necessary to prepare man to wrap himself in a starship and set out to explore the universe. This may be the dawn in the next phase of the evolution of mankind."

Linda finished her drink, put the glass on the deck. "That much I'm sure is true. But all philosophical considerations aside, it's historically known that colonization eventually leads to independence. But independence is a two-sided coin, since it implies self-sufficiency. We're not ready for that. In fact, we're a long way from it. We'd need a hundred thousand people on Mars before we could meet minimum requirements to provide the services and products needed to run an autonomous commonwealth. Let's face it: most of the Mars Project is carried out right on Earth.

"Business accounts, bookkeeping, inventory control, purchasing, personnel recruitment, machinery, parts, raw materials: we don't do any of that. Without monthly deliveries from long-range freighters, we'd fall apart. Highly technological and specialized services such as medicine, higher education, and those branches of science and engineering not used in day-to-day living still have to come from Earth. As well as cultural variety. Doug, we just can't manage all that — not now. And we can't pay for it. What do you think we're going to do, sell Martian antiques?"

I stared at her grimly. "So what do you want?"

"Just time. We need the impetus for growth and

expansion. We're like a snowball on the edge of a hill, and this could give us the push we need to start rolling."

"You've almost got me believing you."

Linda looked at me brightly. "If I can't convince you with logic, I can always try charming you."

"You've done that already." I forced a smile. "So what does all this have to do with marriage?"

She blushed beautifully, and lowered her eyes. Silently, she slid across the bed and, pressing me up against the bureau, gave me a long and sensuous kiss. "I meant it. I meant everything I've said."

"But you forgot to tell me never to take chances."

She kissed me again. "That's because I'm the biggest chance you'll ever take."

"You also said that I didn't have to commit myself."

"I've changed my mind. Now I want to know."

I forced her away from me, looked deeply into her eyes. "I'm sorry, Linda. But, I'm so confused about — everything. I — I can't think straight."

She sat back slightly. "I didn't mean to press you. I guess I'm being too forward."

I snickered. "Well, at least that hasn't changed."

She hit me playfully.

"Linda, you said, when you first came in here, 'when this is all over.' When will it all be over?"

"It'll never be over, Doug. From here on, there are only new horizons."

"Then, how will I know when the time for us has arrived?"

"I'll tell you."

"You sound so sure of yourself."

"One of us has to be."

"And suppose, then, I change my mind."

"Oh, your mind will change — about a lot of things. But not about us. If I wasn't sure of that, I never would have asked you."

I drew her closer, ran my fingers through her silky tresses. I shook my head slowly. "I do — feel — very close to you. Perhaps so close that it's clouding my judgment. So, for now at least, I'm treading water, waiting to see which way the current takes me. Please don't be hurt, Linda. But I just can't make any promises yet."

"I understand. And I'm not ready now anyway. When the time is right for us, we'll both know it."

I held her tight until my arms ached with tension. Then, we wriggled out of our thermal uniforms, tossed them aside, and huddled under the comforter. Her muscles were firm and taut as she arched against me. We made love slowly and tenderly, and late into the night.

Two and a half years and thirty millions miles were as nothing. For this woman, I would wait an eternity and cross the universe.

Chapter 12

Three strange, ghostly phantoms glided through the still, clear air. They were tall and lean and moved on stiltlike legs with flowing grace over the sloping dunes. Their pace was quick, but not a run — almost casual, if one can run casually. Their emaciated bodies belied the hidden strength of sinew and muscle, and were only partially covered by close fitting shorts and bloused, rust-colored tunics cinched tightly at their waspish waists. Their skin was sleek, marmoreal, of the purest white texture, but firm and unyielding to the touch.

One, the male, stopped. In reverent contemplation, he gazed fixedly into the faded pink sky at the golden fireball that was the sun.

His face was a pale, ashen mask: sad, lonely, forlorn. The deep-set, melancholy eyes were like pearls set in limpid pools of the faintest amethyst; they whimpered lachrymally, but the rare fluid refused to run. The elongated nose flared in time with the short, rapid-fire gasps. The mouth twitched but stayed shut: a grim line, a barrier, stemming the tide of precious water held within. The ears were overlarge, hanging like limp pennants. The forehead was furrowed all the way to the middle of the hairless scalp.

The slender body bent at the waist, bent almost double, as he buried one flat, splayed hand deep into the ground. Scooping up a palmful of dry, ocher sand, he rose to his full, proud height. One arm extended toward the sun, supplicating, as the tiny dustlike particles strained through the protracted fingers. When all the sand had drained away, the arm fell limp at his side, a futile gesture.

The two sylphlike females had stopped a little farther ahead, waiting for him in silence. He easily caught up with them and swept past without stopping. They seemed to understand, and followed him toward the broken-down ruins on the far horizon.

*   *   *   *   *   *

The dream shocked me out of my sleep with the force of a cannon.

For several moments, I feared a recurrence of the previous morning's agony. I suffered slight nausea, a creaking of the joints, and a dull headache: a minor recapitulation.

It was still too early to rise, and I was half tempted to force myself to sleep until breakfast. But apparitions from my dream were too poignant and alive. I was distracted by a faint, green glow in the room.

The computer monitor was switched off, the annunciator panel on night mode. On a shelf above the hatch, a bioluminescent emerald glimmered, fluctuated, strived for phasing.

I slipped out from under the covers and approached it, fascinated by the scintillations. The constriction in my chest eased, the feeling of dread subsided.

One only fears the unknown, but I understood it now. It was more than simple lichen, more than a leftover prehistoric plant — it was life itself. Its sterile charm did not lead to autism or death; areolichen pointed the way to another plane of existence.

I held the bowl in my hand, captivated by the brilliance of the thousand streaming points of light. I was able to study it in a detached way, scientifically. I reveled in its soft, curly spines, like slender petals, closely cropped. With one finger, I stroked the small, bunched mass: it was cool and furry, finer than velvet. Held closer to my face, its smell was fresh and rosy, like the blossoms of spring. I thought I might even have a taste . . .

I reacted galvanically. In one fluid motion, I turned and dashed the ugly mess into the sink. The plastic bowl bounced around the room, spitting out sand and shreds of lichen, and came to rest on the floor. I fought down the impulse to stomp on it like the foul, fetid substance that it was.

I grabbed my uniform off the hook, opened the hatch, jumped into the corridor, dogged the hatch behind me. I shivered with fear of what I had been about to do. My mind was turning against me. Nausea swept over me in waves as alien thoughts trampled through my mind, unblocked.

I needed to breathe.

But I could not force myself to go back inside for my exposure suit. I pulled the padded uniform on over my long-johns, and rushed for the Observation Deck. Despite the flurry of predawn activity, I reached the portal room with only minor delays and waves of the hand.

I irised open the windows, let the eerie bright starlight flood the room. The stars hung in the sky like miniature lanterns: without heat inversions, they remained steady and untwinkling. The pronounced blue shading was the result of early morning ice crystal fog. The ground was an amorphous gray. There was no wind.

The sun rose without warning, cold and colorless, and was hazy and indistinct because of scattering. Suspended ice now refracted kaleidoscopically. The gray ground became yellow brown and, as the angular direction of the sun changed during the day, it would grow to a bright ocher at noon, then fade to a dull red near sunset. Throughout the day, a few of the brightest stars would remain visible.

Color is an atmospheric manifestation. That very same sand transported to Earth would appear lighter and more yellow, despite the tingeing from iron oxides. It is merely the placement of the eye and the interpretation of the brain that determines color. And the eye can easily be fooled.

In this uncertain light, I saw several fleeting shadows dash across my field of view. In the coruscating fog and high contrast, the figures appeared evanescent, but I captured the impression of tallness, of leanness. Visions leftover from my nocturnal fantasy confused my sense of proportion, for what I saw appeared to be a group of naked bodies shuffling over the sand, not red and blue, but pale white.

I rubbed my eyes, and the rushing eidolons were

gone. I was left doubting my senses. What I saw could have been nothing more than sand spouts churning across the dunes.

My stomach grumbled, my body ached for food. Breakfast time or not, I had to eat. I remembered to close the ports before I departed.

In the mess hall, I picked up a tray of food, nuked it, and carried it steaming to the table where Major Tarkington and Doc Reynolds had saved a place for me.

"Good morning to you, Doug." The Major seemed to have forgotten our debates of the previous night. "Are you ready for the big day?"

I tempered my voice with affability. "As ready as I'll ever be."

Doc Reynolds held up a hypodermic syringe. "You're looking much more chipper today. How do you feel?"

I eased into the seat. "I felt fine until I saw that needle. Now I'm not so sure." Resignedly, I rolled up my sleeve. "You know, I'm having some pretty weird dreams, even when I'm awake."

The doctor dabbed my arm with alcohol, poked me with the needle. "You don't dream when you're awake. You either have expectations or flashbacks. No vest today?"

I rearranged the sleeve, charged into my food. "No, I'm not cold at all. And I'm famished."

"I told you that you'd acclimatize. Your body's producing more red blood cells, and you're metabolizing more nutrients."

The Major sipped his coffee. "The tower up on the Rim has been repaired. According to the latest weather report, there's a heavy sandstorm up north, but it doesn't appear to be moving this way. Looks like clear and sunny skies for the rest of the week."

"Great." I could hardly talk with my mouth full. "Are the crawlers ready?"

"All loaded and primed. One already left, towing a spare power plant. We need more electricity out there and this one has just been refueled."

I continued to stuff my face. "What are you using for power now — at the Caves?"

"We've already got one small nuclear reactor rigged for lighting and general power. Otherwise, we're relying mostly on crawler reactors and a lot of extension cords. But we're recalling two research stations — the one in Moeric Lacus, and one from Antigones Fons. We want them set up inside the Caves, hopefully by the end of the month. Once we do that, erect a few more emer-gency pods, and have them powered independently, we can release the crawlers from duty."

"Will the removal of the emergency reactors leave enough reserve power for the City?"

"Sure. We've cut back on a lot of our requirements here. Besides sectioning off and powering down wings no longer in use, we've dimmed the lights."

Between bites, I looked up at the fluorescents. "I didn't even notice. Is that part of your acclimatization project, too, so visiting Martians don't have to wear shades?"

For once the Major's smile faded. "I'm glad you brought that up, Doug — "

"Somebody had to, and you weren't making any effort."

"I was going to discuss it with you today, but could-n't figure out how to lead into the subject."

"Now that Linda has spilled the beans, you mean."

"Now, son, there's no reason to get riled — "

"Forget it, Major. I'm not interested." I got up from the table, hastened to the food dispenser. I poured a cup of hot coffee, gulped it down black. "You're just making a complicated situation worse."

"I'm just trying to handle it the right way — "

"I said forget it." I stuck another tray into the microwave oven, heated it, brought it back to the table. "I've heard all the analogies, and I'm not buying it. As mysterious as you make it sound, this isn't a detective story. It's a formal and possibly punitive court of inquiry. All of you here are suspect of breach of con-tract and can be handled accordingly. And unless I get

some decent explanations, I will radio my report immediately and take over command of this post."

"Doug — "

"I do have that authority."

"Doug, just listen, will you? We're going to be
packed in that crawler for two days, so there's plenty of
time to talk things over. It's just that, well, I would have
preferred to have you see the Martians for yourself
rather than to have them described to you." The Major
halted and rubbed his chin. "Doc, you've had more of a
personal view of the whole deal, and you can sum up
the medical aspects, so why don't you fill him in?"

"Thanks a lot," Doc Reynolds said flippantly.

I was not in the mood for humor. My face stayed
deadpan while I continued to shovel food into it.

"You won't think I'm beating around the bush if I
give this to you in a chronological sequence?"

Between bites, "I'll bear with it. Just don't pull any
punches."

"Sure, Doug, but that's a tall order." The doctor
stirred his coffee, but did not drink any of it. "Well, the
story begins with Sanders, and goes a lot deeper than
the geological details that Keppert highlighted yesterday. During his exploration of the Caves, Sanders was
radioing a minute-by-minute account to the two other
crawler crews, who patched it through to us. We were
all in shock, and practically all work ceased. A few preliminary transmissions were sent to Earth — prematurely, as it turned out. They would have been better off
knowing nothing. Anyway, they all found lichen samples, but Sanders and his crew delved deeper into the
Caves.

"First they found chipped rocks, then ruins, then
artifacts. Sanders became more and more excited. As a
doctor, I'm supposed to be used to this, but I still find
it astonishing when one of our deeply entrenched scientific boys shows signs of real emotion. It makes them
seem almost human. In this case, of course, it was
understandable. First his speech began to slur, then all
four of them started jabbering at the same time. No one

could make any sense out of what they were saying. We caught phrases here and there, like 'sarcophagus,' 'cache of mummies,' and 'machine.' But we couldn't calm them down. They got worse and worse. Eventually, they were quite mad.

"A second crawler team went in after them. They found two of the men already dead. They — " Doc gulped and stole a glance at the Major. "They were halfway out of their exposure suits — it wasn't a pretty sight. The third, a technician, succeeded in pulling out his oxygen hoses as the rest struggled with him. He suffocated before they could get him inside their crawler. Sanders was hysterical, but they managed to drag him back to the crawler. They sedated him, but he went into convulsions and died."

"I ordered the expedition to recover the bodies and return at once," interrupted the Major. "I didn't want to take any chances with what I believed was an alien infection. I also didn't want to alarm the Committee with our predicament, so I put a hold on further broadcasts to Earth until we could determine exactly what we were up against."

Doc Reynolds pushed aside his coffee. "When the expedition returned, I quarantined everyone on it, as well as their crawlers and equipment. I sealed off the infirmary and packed in all eight survivors. I gave each one a complete physical and ran them through the Medwife, but neither the computer nor I could find anything organically abnormal. I finally gave them a clean bill of health, but kept them in quarantine. Then I examined the bodies for signs of alien contamination."

I scooped up Doc's discarded coffee, and drained it. "You were taking a hell of a personal risk."

The doctor shrugged it off. "I wore an exposure suit that had been sprayed with every anti-infectant we had. I conducted the autopsy alone, but was monitored on video so any mistakes could be modified by my successor. Without going into the gory details, I found no signs of contagion or any physical cause of death.

"Meanwhile, Phyllis began observations of the

lichen. The men had done their job thoroughly by bringing back the samples in anti-contamination chambers. She ran through a whole gamut of chemical tests with some interesting results — you've gone through the disks, of course — but nothing deadly. The most shocking discovery, as you know, was the apparent hypnotizing effect. But even that wears off as you get used to it. And laboratory animals couldn't sense it at all. I would have given my left lung for a couple of chimpanzees, but the closest we could come was white mice. So, when the rodents showed no ill effects, Phyl took matters into her own hands — and exposed herself to the lichen."

"It was strictly against orders," boomed the Major. "Four good men had already died, and I sure as hell didn't want to add any more casualties to the list. I screamed bloody murder at her, but there was nothing to do but put her in separate quarantine."

"When I completed the autopsies, I joined her in *her* quarantine," continued Doc Reynolds. "I examined her and found her fit as a fiddle. Next, we did some chemical analyses on the lichen and came up with nothing. Eventually, we concluded that the lichen was not the cause of death."

Major Tarkington interrupted. "I was still keeping the Committee at bay. We had to know more about what we were up against, and the only way of finding out was to form another expedition. I didn't want to expose any more people than I had to, despite the medical reports, so I asked the quarantine crew members to go back. That gave me eight, plus the Doc and Phyl. Keppert raised a stink because I wouldn't let him go along. But with Sanders gone, he became our chief geologist and that made him too valuable to lose. Finally, though, I had to give in because I needed his expertise in the field."

Doc Reynolds took the ball again. "I needed an assistant with medical experience, but couldn't afford to lose any of my staff — in case I didn't make it back. We need doctors more than biologists, so I asked Dr.

Malle to join. We still had to consider the possibility of finding something that might fall under the category of mummies. We did. But not as we expected them. There was a whole cache of actual Martian bodies, preserved perfectly down to their toenails. But they were encased in a clear, crystalline material which, so far, we've been unable to penetrate — even with lasers. No, don't interrupt. There's more.

"Beyond the sepulcher is something even more profound. It's something we don't yet fully understand, something that may be beyond our understanding altogether. It's a kind of living machine which, after five million years, and through the agency of some unknown power source — " The doctor drew in his breath. " — is apparently still functioning."

Chapter 13

Linda entered the crawler through the open airlock and threw her exposure suit onto a lower bunk. "I guess the latecomers get the uppers."

"Come help me with the safety checks. I'm a little rusty yet." I leaned forward in the seat, reading the checklist and flipping switches.

Linda pirouetted to me, gave me a resounding smack on the lips, and sat in the adjacent control seat. "Looks as if you've got most of it done."

"I had to skip a couple that I didn't understand. Hey, what happened to you last night?"

She glanced at the manual, tried some of the gauges. "What do you mean what happened?"

"I mean, I woke up without you."

She looked shocked. "Doug, I woke you up when I left. I told you I had some things to do."

"What time was that?"

She pursed her lips. "About four. Don't you remember?"

"I must have still been asleep."

Linda leaned over and kissed me again. "Oh, Doug. I'm sorry."

I stored the thick manual under the dashboard. "No, that's all right. I was just a little confused."

I heard a clamor aft. Doc Reynolds stumbled through the airlock bearing a large box. "Come help us with the supplies."

The Major stomped in right behind him, crates under both arms. "Stash these equipment cases under the bunks. I'll go back and get the food."

"Careful, that one's got medical instruments."

Linda completed the crawler preparations while I helped stow the gear. The Major returned with an armful of frozen dinners. While I made space in the freezer for the provisions, he went out for the rest. When everything was aboard, and stowed, he dogged down both outer and inner hatches.

The Major stared at the exposure suits denoting possession of the lower bunks. "You'd think that being commander of this outpost, I would have first choice of a place to sleep."

"Rank has no privileges," Doc Reynolds said.

"Airtight integrity checks. We're ready to go." Linda pulled out the dampers, the engine whined. "Who wants first turn at the wheel?"

"I'll take it," drawled the Major. "Since I've lost the good bunks, I at least want to start out with a good seat. Who wants shotgun?"

Linda cinched her safety harness. "I'm already here, so I'll stay."

The Major keyed the microphone. "All clear in garage three. Cycling air." Suction pumps went into action, the garage airlock door opened, and the Major moved the crawler ponderously out through the cloud of dust and onto the cold sands of Mars. The other five crawlers in the caravan were already outside, hitched to trailers.

"Hey, is anybody else on the air?"

One by one, the other crawlers checked in, with only one snag.

"Just like Keppert to forget something." The Major pointed to the starboard monitor.

The tall, lanky figure carried a box, while a shorter one checked the trailer hitch and safety cables. They entered the crawler airlock and sealed it shut.

"He's towing some electronic monitoring equipment, x-ray gear, stuff like that. I hope he remembered to tighten his neck bolts."

Leading the wagon train, we swung in a wide arc around the City, heading west toward the open plain. The sand was soft and gentle as we weaved around the larger dunes before turning south. Linda turned on the grid map. The red blip in the middle showed our vehicle as it left the outskirts of town. The contour lines were vague and the elevations approximate because the dunes were in a constant state of change. The map followed automatically in the direction of motion, keeping the blip constantly in the center. The blob of other blips behind us slowly straightened out to form a jagged line.

"Isn't our first gravimeter check just up ahead?"

"Right you are, my boy. I see you haven't forgotten much since they put your behind behind a one-gee desk. Turn on the scope, Linda."

I watched the display grid between them. The device sensed the minute difference in gravity resulting from hollows or less dense material beneath the sand. Without it, we could not avoid soil domes and quicksand, either of which could easily swallow a crawler and its crew. As we touched the edge of an amorphous yellow area overprinted on the map, the needle deflected sharply, but not into the danger zone.

"There she is, right on schedule," the Major boomed.

Doc laughed. "Whoever designed this thing had a good sense of humor. The really dangerous zones have red overlays, and the crawler blip disappears when they coincide."

The Major keyed the mike. "All right, people. Listen up. Proceed with gravimeter check over SD-31 and report malfunctions." Aside, "Gotta keep up *some* formalities."

Linda switched the map grid to a larger scale, showing not only Syrtis City but the spaceport as well. To the west, the thickening contour lines bunched up in two-dimensional relief. A green blip flickered continuously atop the Western Rim — a remote weather station and marker beacon. All vehicles, weather stations, emergency pods, and way stations emitted a coded signal at all times. One could never become lost on Mars because satellite relay stations kept all signals monitored.

"Look at the thermometer," Linda muttered. The instrument read seventy-four below zero Centigrade. "I didn't realize it was that cold out today."

"One of the advantages of keeping the crawler in the garage overnight," said the Major.

"Aw, that's nothing." Doc glanced at the digital readout. "Last winter we had a cold spell that didn't go above seventy below for ten days straight. And it went as low as ninety. Of course, in a few more months, we'll all be walking around in our shirt sleeves."

The temperature could go well into the twenties — above — on a still day at high noon in the middle of summer, but could drop to fifty below in the first hour after sunset. Without a substantial atmosphere, heat poured down from the sun with an intensity equaled only by that of ultraviolet radiation.

"Yeah," I said. "And maybe you can get a tan before you die."

The crawler crunched slowly over a desert of small, reddish rocks. Two hours later, Linda took the wheel and I copiloted. The Major climbed into a bunk and propped himself up with a book, but within minutes I heard his stentorian snore.

Doc Reynolds whispered, "The old man's had a lot on his mind lately."

I merely nodded, deciding to guide the future instead of condemning the past. All the red blips were strung out faithfully behind us. In the rear-scanning camera, I saw the churning sand, but could barely make out the next crawler through the settling dust. The left and right screens showed nothing but track-less, hilly terrain. The upward facing screen had been turned off because it showed nothing but a bright glaring sky: but it would come in handy in the bottom of a deep ravine, or when making steeply angled climbs.

"Some boulders up ahead." Linda pointed through the viewport. "You want to check the Major and make sure he's tucked in?"

Doc swiveled in his chair, unstrapped himself, and rose to look over the slumbering leader. "Seat belt's all nice and snug. Never knew him to hedge on a safety procedure, even in his sleep."

Linda alerted the other crawlers. "Rough terrain ahead, people."

The boulder field did not last long, and soon we

were picking up speed on flat, granular sand.

An hour later, Linda said, "Don't everyone talk at once."

I smiled. I felt unusually good: no muscle aches, no temple pain, no nausea, and chronic hunger. I munched on my third cold biscuit. "Why don't we talk more about the Martians?"

"I can start out by telling one important fact," offered Doc. "Visual analysis of their dentition proves that they were vegetarian."

"Not so odd, considering that every other animal found on Mars has been herbivorous. Rounded teeth and slanted jaws are a pretty common sight on Martian fossils."

"Yes, I'm not saying it's odd from the biological point of view. But it does affect the evolution of civilization."

"How so?"

"Take a picture of Earth — in its prehistoric state. It's a hostile place, with predators lurking around every corner and plant eaters building intricate defense mechanisms. Everybody is on edge and lives in fear. Strangers are to be avoided at all times, at all costs. Every person has this deep-seated psychosis. He fears any stranger, including others of his own species. This edginess has pervaded his world and has shaped his growth pattern. Suspicion, you must agree, is one of our most pronounced features."

"Mine started only two days ago."

"Doug, I'm being serious."

Linda hunched over the wheel. "That's a switch."

"You want to hear this, or don't you?"

I spun the chair around to face him. "Go ahead, Doc. I'm all ears."

"All right, in one respect this helped the Martians, in another it held them back. With no personal conflicts, no hostilities or special dangers, they were able to develop a higher degree of social civilization before turning down the road to industry. According to our standards, this means their technology lagged their civilization and that, having peace to spare, they were not forced into developing machinery as a way of survival, but at a slower and more natural evolution. Conversely, we can say that man on Earth, by nature of his bestial domicile, has reached a destructive state of industrialization long before he is socially mature enough to know how to cope with it."

"I don't know, Doc. The Martians had a pretty tough enemy just in their environment. They must have had to build defenses: against cold, against evaporation from a less dense atmosphere, against stray solar radiation and cosmic contamination due to the lack of a protective ozone layer — "

"So their skin was thicker and lacked pores. No, their environment was no more an enemy to them than ice is to a polar bear, or heat to a desert rat, or pressure to a tube worm living at the bottom of the sea. That's a natural adaptation no more difficult to attain on Mars than on Earth. The Martians were just at home in their desert as you are in your apartment. This world wasn't hostile to them; it was their home. And as it changed to the almost airless world it is today — that it's been for millions of years — they evolved with it. They were as comfortable in the open as fish in the sea."

"Is all that evidenced by your visual autopsy?"

"Some is, and some is conjecture. But it must be true because they lived. If I could break through those plastic coffins, I'm sure I'd find under the skin, layers of subcutaneous fat that acts as an insulator against cold, light, and probably radiation. Their larynx must be constructed differently so they can talk in a thinner medium. Their large ears are obviously able to collect more vibrating molecules."

"But how about intelligence? If they had no natural enemies and lived in a Garden of Eden, where did they get the ambition to progress? How does a stupid plant eater decide to raise his sights in a world of other stupid plant eaters?"

"Curiosity? Boredom? Instinct? These may be inherent factors of intelligence, drawbacks that must have their outlets. Incentive is a byproduct of intellectual growth. And then there is procreation and specific extension. In any species of plant or animal, microscopic or mammoth, the prime survival factor is expansion: the insurance that there is a large enough gene pool to cover random environmental changes, and that should a species be overtaken by sudden catastrophe, there are sufficient members of that species spread over a broad enough geological area to ensure survival."

I heard scuffling from the back of the crawler. Looking over Doc Reynolds' head, I saw the Major descend from his bunk. Rubbing his face and eyes vigorously with his hands, he plopped into the remaining seat and strapped himself in.

"Allow me to interrupt the good doctor's argument. Human migration in the past has permitted great increases in the population by extending the range of mankind. He has expanded until he covered the entire globe: every niche and every environment. And not because he wanted to, but because he had to. The need for expansion is part of his genetic makeup. And now, in space, he must continue to expand like he has in the past because he doesn't know how to stop. It's this single fact on which the future of the space program is guaranteed. It might meet with temporary setbacks, but in the long run, it'll survive, just as man has survived — just as man *must* survive."

"Then why didn't the Martians survive?"

"Wait a minute," Linda interrupted. "Before we start round two, I want a relief. Despite the fascinating conversation, I'm falling asleep at the wheel."

"I'll take over." I spun around, dropped my steering wheel into place, took over the controls.

"Great. And I'll rustle up some lunch."

Doc jumped out of his seat. "I'll help."

I shouted whenever I saw trenches or moguls, to give them fair warning. After a little confusion, Doc claimed the other front seat and passed me a sandwich and a cup of steaming hot coffee. The crawler's hydraulic steering system was easily manipulated with one hand. The cup fitted snugly into an indentation in the console.

"Either my taste is changing or the coffee is getting better."

"I made it, so I'll take the credit," said Linda.

Doc held up his cup, as if he were toasting. "Thank Phyl for the additives."

"Hey, let me get a few brownie points for something, will you?" Linda objected. "Let him think I'm a good cook — at least until after we're married. Then he can find out for himself — when it's too late."

"What's all this about marriage?" boomed the Major.

I could feel my face reddening, feel waves of heat crawl up my back. "Linda!"

Linda was demure. "As of last night, we were informally, on a contingency basis, conditionally engaged."

"I've been hoodwinked."

"Congratulations, son. You, too, Linda. You know, it's been quite a while since I performed a marriage ceremony. Six months at least. Most folks get hitched the first year of their tour."

"And spend the next four regretting it." Doc Reynolds went into a mimicking voice. "Come to Mars, the honeymoon haven of the solar system. Two moons to make love under. And welcome to Syrtis City Spa. Luxurious accommodations big enough to turn around in, each room equipped with its own introspective view and cold dripping water."

"Doc, you're just jealous," Linda chided. "If you weren't so busy chasing nurses . . . "

"I never mix business with pleasure."

"Your business *is* pleasure," I added.

The Major said, "His studies of incontinence have not all been medical."

"Whoa. Wait a minute. Why's everybody picking on me?"

Linda tilted her head. "Because you're the best man, silly."

"I'm honored. Oh, and by the way, congratulations."

"Thanks, I think." I swallowed the last bite. "Linda, what else have you got to eat?"

"Where are you putting all that food? Have you got a hollow leg?"

Doc said, "He's a growing boy." To me, "Just practicing giving orders, right? Shape her up now, Doug, while she's still moldable."

Linda handed me another sandwich. "Don't listen to him. I've already decided to be just the woman you want."

"And I've heard that before."

Linda slapped the doctor playfully. "That's enough out of you."

"No, it's not." I finished my coffee, handed it back for a refill. "I want to get back to the Martians."

Doc cleaned his teeth with his tongue. "Where was I? Oh, yes. Well, Keppert has postulated that about five million years ago, there was a surge of meteor activity in the solar system. Every planet was deluged with millions of tons of flying debris, but with different results. The gas giants simply absorbed the rocks without a trace. The smaller planets with comparatively dense atmospheres, like Earth and Venus, suffered some damage but managed to thwart disaster by burning up a lot of them. Mars, the Moon, Mercury, and the moons, were devastated. Craters pockmark all their surfaces today, except the volcanically active ones that have wiped out all traces. Mars, although nearly stable tectonically, was pummeled so hard that plates slipped, gases erupted, and the atmosphere was slowly being poisoned.

"Not that this happened overnight, you understand, and not that all the Martians were killed right away, but it decimated the population to the point where recovery was impossible. First their technology fell apart because of the loss in the flow of raw materials and the lack of manufactured goods that kept it in motion. Civilization is like a ball swinging around a central point at the end of a string: if you cut the string, the ball flies off at a tangent.

"After that, it's all downhill. They broke up into little pockets, or tribes: parts of a circle but not a whole. Their air was slowly becoming unbreathable, so they began dying off. They fell below what is known as the minimum population limit: when there is not a large enough genetic pool to ensure racial survival. Although individuals may be healthy, procreation drops off, as if the personification of species or race has lost the will to survive. The wasting away becomes racial suicide."

"In other words, an endangered species can become extinct because of an inability to cope with new environmental conditions."

"A fair way of putting it. Many animals on Earth died out during the twentieth century for the same reason. Biologists could save individual members of a species by placing them in a controlled preserve. Those individuals would survive and carry on as always. Copulation continued, but fertility dropped off, for no known reason other than that the specific vital force simply gave up. In captivity, many animals languished; eventually, the species became extinct through attrition."

"And where's Keppert's evidence for this theory? How did he come upon it?"

"He didn't just come upon it," said the Major. "He learned it, or deduced it, from the Machine."

"How?"

Major Tarkington paused before answering. "It's hard to explain about the Machine until you've experienced it directly. That was the reason we didn't tell you about it before — and why we couldn't . . . even begin . . to explain it to Rogers. Not over the radio. We're not sure ourselves what it is, or what it does, or how it operates."

"Yet you think it's some kind of memory bank, some storage center for all Martian knowledge, left like an epitaph to explain to all those who found it what befell the Martian race, and what pitfalls others should avoid?"

"That was our first impression. But it's more than

just that — it's something on a scale much vaster than a simple racial diary. It's a kind of educator, or mind expander, that induces an awareness of knowledge through some unknown means by direct stimulation of the brain. After a session with the Machine you seem to . . . to know things that you did not consciously know before. Or, perhaps things suddenly make sense. Whereas before your mind was clouded by uncertain knowledge, now various unrelated data are connected in a recognizable form. It's as if you were already acquainted with the parts of a puzzle, and the Machine has arranged the pieces so you can see how the whole will look. You merely pull them together."

"What makes you think you're not being misled?"

"Oooh, the mind knows. After the session, you're positive that what has transpired in your brain is actually true, that you know more than you knew before. But you can't pin down any single fact that has been learned. It's as if you learn concepts, or were given insight."

"Mind expansion drugs do the same thing, Major, by inducing feelings of well-being and increasing awareness of self and symbolism. But these changes occur only in the mind, solipsistically, not in the greater consciousness of reality."

Doc Reynolds gesticulated with his hands. "But this is different. This sensation of greater knowledge doesn't fade. You don't 'come down' later."

"So you get high and stay that way?"

"Well, if you want to put it like that."

"And without knowing exactly *what* you've learned, you seem to think that you *have* learned?"

"I can't explain it any better."

"In other words, it's brainwashing: a drug related experience from which you never recover."

"No, it's real."

"Subjective reality, not objective."

"Wrong, because everyone who goes through it becomes aware of the same concepts. Hallucinogenic drugs act on an individual's subconscious desires, wants, weaknesses. But this is the same for everyone. I'm sorry, but you can't possibly understand until you've experienced it yourself."

A one-way street from which there is no return to sanity. I kept one eye on the viewport, one eye on the doctor. "And tell me, Doc. Once you experience this sensation of learning, as you call it, from the Machine, does it affect your mind at all? Does it affect your sense of judgment, or your rationale? And does it leave you with an overwhelming compulsion to return for . . . further sessions? Do you become addicted to it?"

"No more than the thirst for knowledge can be called addicting. No, there's no compulsion. But your curiosity causes you to want to learn more — to learn whatever the Machine has to offer."

"I see." I sat straight-backed in the seat, watching the sand disappear under the viewport. For a moment, I felt disembodied, as if the planet were not real, but an old time movie with the background filled in and poorly matted.

If every person on Mars had been subjected to this alien Machine's power, if everyone suffered the same delusions, how could anyone from inside the community detect the difference? Sanity is nothing more than a point of view, a majority rule. Insanity is a radical departure from an established norm. But should the norm change, the rules would be reversed, and sanity would be outcast. In an irrational world, logic does not make sense.

"And Dr. Keppert, in his wisdom, has learned of this worldwide catastrophe from the Machine?"

"Yes, he's spent more time under its sphere of influence than anyone else," admitted the Major. "And he's attuned his mind to a higher retrieval level than the rest of us."

"Do you mean he's had his mind expanded more than anyone else?" It was difficult to keep the sarcasm out of my voice. "Or has he suffered more delusions than the rest of you?"

"He's been educated more," said the Major calmly,

but firmly. "And he's communicated his advanced learning to those of us who have not yet experienced it ourselves due to our level of tolerance."

"And what does that mean?"

"Doc, you explain it to him."

"Yes, well, the best I can do is compare it to a function of intellectual aptitude. Each individual has a certain rate of data assimilation: what we call learning capacity. A genius soaks up knowledge like a sponge, while a moron soon tires and his mind wanders. The Machine's output is almost infinite, but the brain's willingness to accept input is limited. If input exceeds limitations, the synapses of the brain burn out like an overloaded circuit. In mild cases, this can lead to unconsciousness with no permanent damage. In the most serious cases, it can lead to death."

The thought struck me like a bolt. "Dr. Sanders?"

"I'm afraid so. When he and his crew first found the Machine they all entered its activity field. Without knowing the danger, they took no precautions. The Machine hammered them with knowledge, more than they could absorb. But the Machine didn't know what it was doing. It's been waiting for five million years for someone to use it, and when the opportunity finally arose, it couldn't hold itself back. The men weren't mentally prepared to receive it, and they died."

"In simple medical terminology, they overdosed."

"A crude way of putting it, but roughly the case."

"And this is what you call 'immense cultural shock'?"

"For lack of a better term. It isn't just brain shock that causes the loss of mental equilibrium. It's because the knowledge absorbed is Martian knowledge, and meant for a Martian brain. It's not easily accepted by a brain that has been conditioned on Earth, from an alien point of view. But with proper conditioning — warning, that is, not brainwashing — we can build up resistance to the Machine's overloading influence. We can extend our time within its aura, and learn secrets that have taunted mankind since his meager beginnings on Earth."

Knowledge is always a double-edged sword: it can kill or cure, depending on the wielder. "You've got a real Pandora's box here."

"And if it's handled wrongly, it can be deleterious to the entire human race," said the Major. "We've got to proceed with our hearts and our minds open. We've got to know what we're about before we tip our hand to the world. That's the caution you've got to carry back to Rogers and the Committee. We can't go ahead too fast, or we'll do more harm than good."

"For the first time, Major, you and I agree."

Chapter 14

The great, gray walls of the cave arched high overhead, alive with a green twinkling light that sent soft waves of sibilant illumination across its wide expanse. A wonderful city rose up from the sandy floor, squat buildings spun like swirling spumes of dust, tall spires like dried out flames licking the roof of the vaulting cavern in which it was housed. Each structure possessed its own color scheme, seemingly splashed together in absurd disarray that was arresting to the eye.

Outside the cave entrance, a bright yellow sun spun golden webs of haze as it refracted through suspended dust and wind-borne sand. Rainbows, glittering prismatically, danced along the ground as winter ice sublimed into the rarefied atmosphere.

Seeking protection from the abrading wind, the cave was home to a luxurious growth of plant life, to the feeding animals which thrived off the wild vegetation, and to the myriad inhabitants of this thriving city. Laughing children launched themselves into the air with glee, leaping impossibly high. Parents and the elderly performed their tasks, ate meals, made love, worked and played, studied and taught, bathed in dust, washed in sand, manufactured products, gathered food, carried away trash, built and rebuilt.

They grew. They were a happy people who expanded slowly, as if to spread throughout all eternity their happiness and their progress. They did not dally, they did not procrastinate, but they enjoyed. They lived by their own formula: a touch of work, a pinch of play. There was no pressure, no intensity. No one was going to take anything away from them. So when they built, they built strong, and to last. When they learned, it was forever. And so it might have been — forever.

Then came the things from the sky, searing the atmosphere, crushing the land, draining the water, releasing from within the bowels of the planet the poi-

sonous gases. The steady life passed on, limbo evolved, death became the future.

And for those who lingered on, the gust of life was gone. The will to survive withered like the blossom in winter. An age had come to an end.

      *   *   *   *   *   *

When I awoke from the dream, I was simmering in sweat and clothed in unbearable heat. I longed to rip off my thermal uniform, to run naked in the open coolness of the desert, to feel the sun beating upon my bare back. I wanted to bathe in the raw, Martian atmosphere, to inhale its vacuous, carbon-dioxide-laden air. I even entertained quaint feelings of — nostalgia.

I wanted to scream. Instead, I lay perfectly still, so as not to alarm my sleeping companions. I must work this out for myself: with no outside help, with no inside conspiracy.

The covers lay a sodden mess at my feet. When I regained my composure, I wiped my soaking forehead with a sleeve. I was attacked by an unnatural thirst.

I eased out of the bunk, unlatched the food locker door, pulled out a plastic jug, and gulped down great quantities of cold water as if it were the last drink I would ever have. When the quart bottle was empty, I pulled out another and drank half of it before I forced myself to stop.

My uniform was drenched, and the heat was still generating from within my body — like a fever without pain. I unbuttoned the thermal shirt down to the navel and let the cool air of the crawler evaporate the perspiration. The reactor had been partially damped so, away from the bunks and the heating ducts mounted above them, it was moderately cool.

The crawler was abysmally dark, the diaphragm having been closed over the front port as standard operating procedure against a night wind kicking up sand and scratching unnecessarily the protecting lens. The cameras were all withdrawn. A few indicator lights were illuminated, denoting that all life systems were functioning. The radio beacon and receiver were always operational.

In this darkness, I noticed the green glow emanating from the food locker while I replaced the half-filled water bottle. I pulled the little box from the back of the cabinet where it had been tucked away, and stared at it for a moment, interested in the weird, hypnotic effect of the areolichen, but no longer captivated by its charm.

Although it held my attention overlong, I was able to look at it with objectivity. I remembered the green walls of my dream with distinct dé·jà vu — the two elements were connected by their common color. The lichen, I finally decided, was oddly likeable.

My hand drew closer to my face, as if it had a will of its own. I was repulsed by the reeking fetor, but kept my self-possession. I shoved the lichen back into the icebox.

I went to the front port and activated the outer diaphragm. The stars in the sky shone down in silent serenity upon the wild, eolion dunes. A light wind rippled across the desert like the golden, textured fur on a stalking tiger's muscular back. The bleakness overwhelmed me with longing. Some mysterious force, out there in the void, seemed to be calling me . . .

I heard a soft step and found Linda standing next to me. She wrapped her arm around my waist and held me tight. She leaned her head against my shoulder, and I could feel her humming a tuneless chantey. She did not look up, she did not speak, yet she comforted. I raised my arm over her head and squeezed her shoulder, feeling the coolness of her body, the warmth of her soul.

Neither of us spoke — words were unnecessary, for we talked in silent communication. We clung together for many minutes. Her humming became a dirge to the world beyond the port, an unreal world, a familiar world. My heart pulsed with poetic platitudes.

As if on cue, we let our arms fall together. Linda leaned up and kissed me softly on the lips, a kiss that seemed to linger long after she had stopped. I could still feel her breath on my face, caressing me. Without a word, but with silence betokening understanding and deep emotion, I closed the port as we turned and fell into our bunks. I lay down in blissful tranquility.

    *   *   *   *   *   *

I awoke again when the Major jumped down from his bunk with the ease of a trained acrobat — and aided by the partial gravity. A second later, the silence was torn asunder by his booming voice.

"I'll rustle up some breakfast while the rest of you sleepy heads take turns in the head. Doc, make a general call and wake up the rest of the wagon train."

Doc Reynolds floated down to the floor wearing nothing but shorts. "Righto, kimosabi."

Linda ducked into the reclamation chamber, so I rolled over and planted my feet on the floor and rubbed my eyes with my palms. I felt better now than I had during the night, and was glad that I had not had any more dreams.

Doc completed his wake up calls, then prepared another injection. "Three down and two to go."

Wearily, I rolled up my sleeve. "Doc, how come you didn't inoculate the shuttle crew?"

"Well, since they're taking the shuttle back in a couple days, I figured why bother."

"But what about the side effects from the depressurization?"

The doctor inserted the needle, pumped in the clear fluid. "They spend most of their time in the ship, what with moving it out to the Caves. Besides, you know these hardcore spacers — they'd keep breathing in a vacuum and hardly notice the difference."

"Well, something must be working, because I feel better every day."

"You feel good enough to take first turn at the wheel?" The Major pushed some trays into the microwave. "Later on, I'd like you to just sit back and watch the approach to the Caves."

"Sure, I can handle that. How much farther is it?"

"Mileage wise, we're two thirds of the way; time

wise, about half. We'll pull into town this afternoon."

I devoured two trays of food and numerous cups of coffee. Daylight appeared suddenly, as if someone had flipped a switch. I switched on all the viewscreens, went through the safety checks solo, pulled the dampers out of the reactor pile, and gave the all clear. Like a lurching train, the other crawlers started spasmodically. Sand moved onerously but graciously under the wide flotation treads. The desert seemed to stretch to infinity in all directions of the compass, with no hint of life, no relief, no oases. Sameness was all around, and there was no escaping it.

I felt like a sailor in a North Atlantic storm. One moment I was surrounded by huge dunes hundreds — even thousands — of feet high, my view cut off completely. Minutes later, after climbing the steep, sliding banks, the crawler mounted the crest of the next dune, and I could see for miles around. There was nothing on the horizon but more, reddish-colored dunes.

As the morning wore on, the ground became less hilly and more rocky. Doc took the wheel and I retired to a back seat. The Major sat up front and played with the grid map, changing quadrangles and scales to give me an idea of our relative position.

"I know you've never been this far south, so you probably haven't noticed that we've gradually been gaining altitude." The Major pointed to the altimeter, still showing a negative value since we were below the artificial sea level. "If the Western Rim hadn't curved out of our line of sight, you'd see it's not as tall here as back at the City.

"Now, we're going to pass through here: west of the Sasquatch Mountains and east of the Western Rim, but you won't be able to see either one because we'll be traveling valleys and rills. Right now we're only thirty miles from the Caves, as the crow flies, but our route'll be three times as long. Besides skirting several mountains with unclimbable walls, we have to do a lot of detouring because the area is heavily faulted. Then we have to cross Ryans Rill, and there are only two places we can do that with the trailers."

Major Tarkington punched directions into the navigational computer and an electronic overlay appeared on the grid screen. It showed the different paths that were considered safe by sonar surveys. Wide, flat plateaus were unapproachable, and many fault zones were unstable and had to be avoided at all costs.

"We're actually climbing out of the seabed and onto what we can call land mass — that is, terrain that hasn't been underwater for at least a hundred million years. Later, we'll be coming back 'underwater' when we descend into the rills."

The ride got bumpy as we ran over a mixture of hard-packed sand and rock. The rolling dunes were still visible in the rear viewscreen, as well as the rooster tails churned up by our entourage. The giant treads crushed the loose shale, but up ahead loomed a boulder field strewn with house-sized debris.

Doc reduced speed, and threaded a course like an intoxicated snake: one that could be taken by the crawlers towing trailers. The crawler rocked from side to side like a subway train on a bad section of track. I gripped the armrests for additional support.

"There's a trail marker over there," the Major pointed out.

"Practically buried. Looks like there's been some frost heave action out here. What say we get a little ahead and scout out the bad spots?"

"I don't remember that hollow, either. Looks like there's been some breakdown."

For an hour, we beat a path through the rock garden, over mounds and into potholes, sometimes creeping along at a mere mile or two per hour. Our squiggles were stored electronically and printed as an overlay on the grid map, so the others could follow even though we were out of sight.

"Scouting hasn't gotten any easier since covered-wagon days," drawled the Major over his shoulder. "Doc, you'd better backtrack to that pass. Even with double-directional universal joints, those trailers'll never make it through here."

"I thought flags had been laid along this route," I said.

"Prob'ly blew away."

Doc found the main course just as the crawler train caught up with us. We climbed a rocky ledge so steep that I could see two of the following crawlers in the overhead camera screen. Then, the bottom seemed to drop out from under us. When the line of sight should have shown us the ground, there was nothing there but a hole. We plunged into it at an angle and the crawler slewed sideways as it careened down the near vertical incline. Doc fought to steer the crawler straight: skidding could be disastrous if we broached into a large rock formation.

"Hold your positions, people. We're in trouble."

The Major put the mike down just as one tread left the ground, then bounced hard. Linda let out a short, ear-piercing scream as we jarred to a stop with a loud crash and a screech of metal — steel tread on bare rock. Only the rarified atmosphere prevented sparks and possible fire: there was not enough free oxygen to support combustion.

Cabinet doors crashed open, storage lockers spewed their contents. Loose paraphernalia swept across the floor. The crawler lurched to a halt with a loud boom accompanied by the expulsion of lights.

With the darkness came silence.

"Nothing to worry about, folks." The Major released his harness and climbed out of his seat. "Shock just kicked some of the main breakers. We'll have it fixed in a jiffy."

Doc wiped sweat off his brow. "For a minute, I thought that hole was going to swallow us up."

Linda shrugged. "Just an everyday occurrence."

"Doc, you've been married to that Medwife too long," I laughed. "It's time for you to come out of the cocoon."

"I will when I'm ready. I'm not much of traveler. I never even left California till I came to Mars."

The Major got on hands and knees, pulled the panel

off the dashboard breaker box. Deftly, he threw the switches: first off, then on. One by one, systems functions flashed, and finally the interior lights came on.

"There doesn't appear to be any damage, but we'll go through the safety checks just to make sure."

I slipped out of my harness. "I'll clean up the back."

Linda disengaged her straps and slid out to help. "Anyone for a snack?"

"I'm famished."

"Honestly, Doug, I don't know if I can keep up with your appetite."

I repacked the loose gear, stowed it where it belonged. "I thought these catches weren't supposed to come loose."

The Major closed the panel. "They're not. But we're not supposed to do acrobatics, either. Doc, leave the flying to the shuttle crew."

"I should have flown over with them and the supplies. I hate ground travel."

"Don't apologize, just get us back on course." The Major scooped up the transmitter. "Okay, people, we're alive and back on line. Hold your position till we get back to you. Doc, swing this buggy around and head on back. And don't do any exploring on the way."

Treads spinning, the heavy machine crept up the hill we had just slid down. As we neared the top, the ground again disappeared until half the crawler was over the ridge; then we overbalanced and slammed onto the other side. In a few minutes we joined the rest of the train.

Doc Reynolds pursed his lips. "I see it now. We should have gone between those two big boulders and down that ravine. But it sure doesn't look like the route."

Linda squinted. "It hardly looks like a crawler can get through there." The Major lowered his steering wheel. "Let me take it from here on out. I know the way pretty well, and you've been driving long enough."

"It's all yours." Doc folded the port wheel against the bulkhead.

Major Tarkington keyed the mike. "If anyone's listening, we're going right through that mountain up ahead. Follow me."

For another hour, we caromed along uneven terrain until we came suddenly and dramatically to a halt at the very edge of a drop so sheer and deep that my stomach erupted with butterflies.

"Ryans Rill," announced the Major.

The precipitous walls fell away for half a mile to a floor that was, if my recollection of Keppert's monologue was correct, five miles across. The sight through the viewport was severely tunneled, but the lateral viewscreens showed the enormous gash extending out of sight to either side, the walls seeming to converge in perspective like railroad tracks in the distance.

"See that tongue of breakdown about two miles to the west?" The Major traced a finger across the screen, where a wild collection of rock extended about a quarter of the way across the floor of the rill. "That's where we climb down. The gradient is about one in three most of the way, easy for a crawler. The trailers will have to be backed down so they don't override their tow."

"And about ten miles west is another breakdown leading up the other side," Doc added. "You can't see it from here."

Major Tarkington backed up the crawler, threw one tread forward and the other in reverse, and spun the vehicle within its length. The radio chattered constantly as the crawler train inched through the rock field. Doc issued instructions on route changes while the Major brought us to the top of the talus slope. In the rear viewscreen, I saw the rest of the train approach the brink, then veer in our direction.

Doc squirmed in his seat. "Hey, do we need to be so close to the drop off?"

"You keep your nurses on edge, you should try it for a change," Linda chided.

"She's got you there, son."

The midday sun reached into the rill, painted the colorful sandstone with soft pastels. A huge geological upthrust forced an anticline on the other side. The crawler dipped down the top of the talus, moved at a snail's pace in low gear to counteract the force of momentum.

"I hate this." Doc gripped the armrests like a ten year old at his first horror film. "I can't stand heights."

"Come on, son. Didn't you go out to Meridian Sinus last winter, when Burkett broke his back?"

"Fractured three transverse processes, but I didn't want him moved till I could make an examination. He was replacing the battery pack for the prime meridian beacon in Airy, and decided to practice low gravity cartwheels. But they flew me out in the shuttle; I didn't have to drive. Look, I'm a doctor, not a daredevil."

"Just keep talking, son, and before you know, it we'll be on the bottom."

"How about you let me out here and I'll walk the rest of the way."

We reached the floor of the rill in a few minutes. Major Tarkington turned the crawler around, then headed back up. "Why don't you go lie down and let Linda take over? I need someone with a strong stomach to help out.

"Good idea." The doctor let himself out of the seat, climbed past, and launched himself into a bunk.

Linda sat in the other control chair. "Want me to give the orders while you drive?"

"That's what I had in mind."

We climbed up to the top, and waited for the first crawler to back its trailer over the edge and down the embankment.

"The coast is clear to the bottom," Linda transmitted.

The driver of the crawler was using his rear viewscreen, of course, but the position of the bulky trailer hampered his line of sight. We backed down first, issuing orders on the route and telling him to steer right or left, while his copilot performed the same task for the next trailer in line. Each crawler was actually being directed from the one down slope. In this laborious manner, we spent two hours getting all the crawlers down onto the level plane at the bottom of the rill.

"These Conestogas are easier to handle going up than down," the Major drawled. "Pioneering hasn't changed much in two hundred years."

What from above had seemed like a smooth, sand covered ground layer was in reality a rough landscape of small, twisting ravines. The rocky convolutions were the result of water receding from Mars' surface.

We bounced along the tortuous terrain for an hour before reaching the exit tongue of breakdown. The crawlers had no trouble hauling their trailers up the steep slope, and in a few minutes, we regrouped on the other side of Ryans Rill.

"Take a look at the grid map, Doug," said the Major.

I leaned forward as he changed to a smaller scale quadrangle. The contour lines clearly showed two major rills, Ryans and Sanders. The surrounding country was broken and uneven, fraught with soil domes. Half a dozen places were marked with red danger beacons, with many more in yellow. By connecting the dots, I could picture long fracture zones still covered by unstable ground.

The Major dragged a thick finger across the screen. "The place is crisscrossed with underground tunnels, part of the Martian highway system. We haven't even begun to explore them all, but it's a cinch these interconnecting passages are how they carried out their commerce. There's no telling what we might find there, once we can spare the personnel to go looking.

"This beacon here is the main opening leading to the inner city. This one here is the space shuttle — they hopped into orbit last night and settled down this morning. It's as close as they can get because the bottom of Sanders Rill is so rough. It'll have to do until a landing zone is bulldozed flat. It's five miles down this escarpment to the LZ, but dangerous because of the soil domes. A trail has been blazed along this ridge. It's a long way around, but the only safe way."

"How much longer till we get to the ruins?"

The Major bushed his shaggy brows. "We should be there in another hour. And the ride from here is smooth, even the downhill portion. Steep, but smooth."

"I'll just stay in the bunk," came the doctor's plaintive voice.

"Come on, son. This is nothing. You should see the Great Rift over by Nix Olympica. It's ten times deeper than this, and so wide the opposite side's out of sight over the horizon."

"That's one I'm not going to see. I just gave up house calls."

Linda pulled down her steering wheel and took over the controls. "Let's cut the gab and get this show on the road." She gunned the engine and pulled ahead of the slowly moving crawler train. "If we hurry, we can have dinner on a Martian table."

I rubbed my stomach, feeling hungry again. "As long as it's not Martian food, I won't object."

Chapter 15

The reddish, loamy ground supported a patchwork quilt of soft and resilient grass, cropped close so that it had the feel of crushed velvet. Placed contiguously were low bushes, leaves stained with chlorophyll, stems ripe with brightly colored vegetables. Spaced remotely were impossibly tall trees, their limbs effulgent with large, succulent fruits, reaching a thousand feet into the air, their tops lost in the early morning haze. Lying in the shadows of dead recumbent timbers grew stubby brown lichen, clumped together like miniature shrubs. Now, in the light, the lichen was quiescent; but come the dark, its collective glow would illumine the forest like a pageant of fallen stars. Beauty there was by day, glamour by night.

The many vegetables and fruits were of different sizes and shapes, different textures and tastes. Vegetables were always abundant on the bushes, fruit from the trees fell to the ground with year-round regularity. Those that landed on the bare soil were nurtured into sprouting roots, while those hitting the plush grass were cushioned in their fall and remained fresh and edible for foraging animals. Gladly did the trees offer their fruit to itinerant creatures that, while eating delightfully of the pulp, would carry the germ far and away and spread the seed over the land.

The plants fed the animals. And in return the animals helped the plants to reproduce. All were satisfied, for each had what it needed.

And through this planet-wide garden rummaged not only the lowly four-footed animals, but upright creatures that walked on hind legs and used the two forward limbs for manipulative purposes. And these creatures possessed something which none of the other animals had: intelligence.

The naked bipeds carried baskets woven from green vine, in which to collect fruit and vegetables. Some carried tools: long poles cut from downed tree limbs, with which they could reach into the higher branches to pluck fruit that was otherwise out of reach to all but the tallest and longest-necked animals. Others, those with pendulous breasts, slung woven sacks from their shoulders in which to carry the newborn.

And the land and the lakes and the forest were theirs. And their intelligence gave them rule of the environment so they could protect themselves from the savage storms and times of drought. They lived in delicate balance with nature, neither taking away nor adding to. Symbiosis was worldwide.

And the young in their sacks were more than the joy of the present and the hope of the future: they were the descendants of a heritage of peace. Peace that had always been, peace that would always be. And this love of peace was passed on from father to son, from mother to daughter.

And the happy people danced and sang, for their world and their loved ones.

*   *   *   *   *   *

The night vision, as I called it, instead of a dream or nightmare, was still vivid in my mind when I awoke, although its undertones were nebulous. As before, I experienced a driving thirst, an extreme rise in body temperature, but I was getting used to these symptoms — and they were diminishing. I lay quietly in my bunk until I got control of myself. Slowly, I moved about, unbuttoning my thermal top and descending softly to the floor.

After drinking a gallon of water and wolfing down some pre-packed food that required no heating, I sat in one of the driver's seats and gazed out at the Martian city. Parked in the great cavern, and free from sudden windstorms, the protective diaphragm had been left off the viewport. The sun had not yet illuminated the deep gorge that was Sanders Rill, but the luminescent glow from the thick lichen covering the cave walls was sufficient to outline the buildings in harrowing detail.

My cursory examination the previous night had been made by that ominous green glow. But I was no longer affected by the strange, hypnotizing characteristic which I had first experienced in Phyllis Trimble's greenhouse. I now felt at home in the eerie iridescence, free of all fantastic and unnatural urges.

"What do you think, Doug?" Doc Reynolds lowered himself into the other front seat, gazed out over the ruins. "It's enough to stir your soul. Sometimes, I think we don't have the right to be here, to disturb their greatness. As if we were walking in a sacred graveyard of saints."

"What? No witticisms this morning?"

The doctor slowly shook his head. "I feel so humble. It's a shame their civilization had to end. They were a marvelous race, a people of peace, a fountain of youth and exuberance and initiative. They were strong; it was their planet that was weak. Just imagine, if they had been allowed to continue, they would have had five million years more progress. Progress without war and suffering. And to think they've evolved from the same simple beginnings."

My seat crinkled as I changed position. "How do you mean that?"

"Well, we know that life on Mars developed from the same chemical constituents, according to the same genetic coding system, and developed similar form and function, as life on Earth. There were local adaptations, of course, but the morphology is the same. Martian animals are no stranger than the diversity between kangaroos and mastodons, mountain goats and giraffes. But man has more in common with the Martians than he has with other earthly creatures."

"In what way?"

Doc Reynolds rubbed his chin, pinched his eyes, stared blankly. "We share the common bond of intellect. Think how incongruous man is from all the other animals. We're born naked, unprotected, unarmed: an essentially peaceful being in an otherwise hostile world. In the wild, we are too slow to run away from danger, too small to fight, have no defensive armor and no offensive armament. Our aggressive violence is not inherited, but a learned response that's necessary to keep us alive.

"We're radically different even from our closest living peers: the porpoises and great apes. The internal organization of their brains has a distinguishable pattern: it's oriented toward controlling the lower functions. Porpoises can never achieve true intelligence because they lack the proper physical attributes: binary vision, useful appendages, and an opposable thumb.

"The chimpanzee, while meeting the physical requirements, fails at the message level. Even though it has a fully equipped larynx for making sound, the function overreaches the faculties of its brain. The chimp lacks the speech center, a region of the brain known as Broca's area, and can no more think how to talk than it can think how to fly. Without the advantage of communication, it can never progress to reason and abstract thought. It's doomed to a purely instinctive level of behavior.

"And our closest rivals of the past, the Neanderthals, represented an evolutionary dead end. By volume, they had larger brain capacities, but its growth was mostly parietal and occipital — again, lower function centers. They didn't have the building blocks for conceptual thought.

"But take the brain of homo sapiens. It's far more advanced because of the more efficient neural connections. It's composed of ten billion *billion* working parts, and has enough storage capacity to accept ten new facts every second. It's been conservatively estimated that it can store an amount of information equivalent to one hundred *trillion* words   and at that, we use only a fraction of our gray matter.

"But our brain can do more than simply store data. We have highly developed frontal and temporal lobes, which give us superior linguistic and anticipatory skills, foresight and analytical abilities, associative ideas, and creativity.

"Animals experience both sensations and perceptions, but only man has conceptions. And this basic difference isn't just another phase of evolution — it's a quantum leap. Our thinking processes are as far advanced beyond that of the porpoises, apes, and Neanderthals as theirs is beyond the stimulus response of the amoeba. And in all the billions of years of animal development, only we — and they — have that noble quality."

Doc Reynolds motioned with his head at the mysterious city which had kept its secrets so well hidden — and preserved — for so many long and lonely years.

Far, far away, I saw a flickering light, like a moving candle at the end of a long tube. It grew brighter, drew nearer, and finally split into three tiny pinpoints. My perspective was out of balance, so it was not until each of the three points of light further split in two and resolved themselves into twin headlight beams, that I recognized the crawlers. They were dwarfed by the gargantuan buildings, their feeble lights almost lost in the immensity of the cave: the height of the ceiling, the breadth of the walls.

As a city it was small, but as a cave it was tremendous. The thousand foot high roof was supported erratically by huge masses of natural stonework: lichen covered columns that shone like beacons on a distant shore, or streetlights on a lonely country road. It was the light that made the city so impressive.

The lead crawler turned directly toward us, and for a moment we were bathed by two intense shafts of light until the driver, seeing us, lowered his beams. On they came, moving slowly through the gloom like snails wading through water. The tanklike vehicles were lost in the colossal architecture. Carlsbad Caverns was a child's playground by comparison.

The crawlers ground to a halt in the middle distance and doused their lights. I could actually see better from the unobstructed green glow emanating from the walls and columns. Red and blue exposure-suited figures clambered out of the vehicles and dived into a pile of debris.

"Looks like an early morning work crew. Probably

got thrown out of bed by the night shift."

"Are they working round the clock?" I asked.

"Sure, why not? There's no 'day' in the Caves, and lots of hotbunking. Things'll get worse for a while once we start cramming in raw recruits."

"And where are you going to put them all?"

"Why not ask the Major? That's his department."

"If that's a hint for me to get up, it's well taken," Major Tarkington grumbled. He rolled out of his bunk and jumped to the floor in one clean motion. "Hey. You." He shook Linda by the shoulder. "If I have to get up, everybody gets up."

Linda groaned and rolled over sleepily. She cocked an eye first at the Major, then at Doc and me. "Who can sleep with these blabber mouths having philosophical discussions?"

The Major stepped between us and grabbed the radio transmitter. He flipped the switch to the emergency channel. "All right, listen up. We're having a general assembly of all project heads at 0630, so those of you who want breakfast better hop to it."

Swinging back to the kitchenette, he pulled out four cups, tossed a dollop of coffee mix in each one, filled them with water kept steaming by waste heat from the reactor.

"Need some help?" offered Linda.

"Sure, you can rustle us some breakfast while I talk with our early birds." The Major handed us each a cup, took a back seat. "Now, what was it you wanted to know?"

I gulped the scalding brew, hardly aware of the temperature. The taste was superb.

"Doug was wondering how we're going to live once we move our base of operations to the Caves. Especially if we're flooded with newcomers."

"Hell, I've got so many things on my mind, I plumb forgot about the minor details." He leaned forward and rested his elbows on his knees, with his coffee cup held permanently against his lower lip.

"Once you get away from the city and the main cavern, you'll find a regular warren of interconnected tunnels. Some of them are roads to other caverns, other cities. But a lot end in fair-sized chambers. What we've done is sealed off some of the smaller tunnel entrances with concrete and plastic, scavenged some airlock doors from spare emergency pods, and pumped them full of air. The rock walls are nonporous enough so we can maintain adequate pressure with very little leakage. We can get ten times as much living space as we can from using the pod itself. And if we can get some more hardware shipments, we can install as many of them as we want. We'll have all the room we need, for as many colonists as we can get."

"Providing you can supply them all with oxygen and food."

"That's no problem. With more people, we can increase our limonite mining. And the only thing limiting the expansion of our hydroponics production is the maintenance staff. Nutrient solution can be synthesized right here, and the plants will reproduce themselves."

"There's another plan I like even better." Linda handed each of us a breakfast tray.

"Why don't you tell him about it?" the Major suggested.

She perched on the arm of the other chair, tray in hand. "You see, the city is built out of the same dense rock that makes the cave walls. And the stones are fitted together so precisely that the rooms are almost airtight — a little plastic caulk will seal any small leaks. We can install clear sheathing over the window openings, an airlock door at the entrance, and presto: we have an instant house. We can convert the buildings into offices, laboratories, or domiciles."

"I've even been promised my own hospital," Doc said. "With enough space so me and my patient can be in the same room together."

The Major stuck a fork into reconstituted eggs. "What better way to study the Martian culture than from the inside?"

Chapter 16

"Mars is an old planet. That is to say, it is not older than the Earth, since both had their planetary beginnings along with the rest of the solar system. Rather, it is a more mature planet. Because of its smaller size, its core of molten iron, of superheated gases, and of inner warmth, it cooled much more rapidly than Earth's. This meant that the accidental appearance of self-propagating organisms occurred on Mars while Earth's atmosphere was still a seething, searing, steam-filled, slowly reacting alembic."

Dr. Keppert led me through the alleys of the Martian city, describing structures with poetic description, maintaining an attitude of warmth and affability, and without nervous gestures.

"Organisms were growing and evolving on the Red Planet while Earth, still in her infancy, was too hot for stable organic molecules to exist. Mars originally possessed a dense atmosphere resulting from the byproduct of second-generation stellar formation. It could not compare with Earth's thick blanket, to be sure, but it was sufficient to hold water in the liquid state. Also as important was the fact that it offered the basis for planetary heating — the so-called Greenhouse Effect, whereby light and energy from the sun are trapped in a gaseous envelope and reach a temperature sufficient for life to begin.

"Once entrenched, life is hard to stop. The cooling of the planet and the absorption and leakage into space of the lighter elements of its atmosphere took place on such an elongated time scale that already established life forms had countless millennia in which to adapt to slowly changing conditions. It's possible that the high level of radiation caused an increased rate of genetic mutation so that more viable species were available during climatic decline."

"Does that conflict with the theory of parallel evolution?"

"No. Life and its evolution is a science as predictable as physics. We can say this now with assurance because of all the fossil evidence that bears it out. Barring drastic possibilities such as silicon based life, or antagonistic environments such as the heat of Mercury or the gravity of Jupiter or the cold of Uranus, our kind of life - based on carbon - can occupy a wide range of conditions and still evolve approximately the same. Our particular niche, I venture to say, will be found on many solar systems throughout the universe.

"What we know as life, that which stemmed from the soup of amino compounds in the Earth's sea, must, because of its design features, follow a prescribed set of rules. Just as gravity on Mars works exactly as it does on Earth, so life from the same compounds must evolve according to the same laws. The variations caused by local environmental differences are to be expected — but in general, life is life."

We strolled through the ruins of the Martian city with our radios on low power, so our conversation would not be interrupted by the constant chatter of working personnel.

"However, Mr. Martin, there are points of divergence in the evolution of life as we know it. One is the splitting of life into two kingdoms: the plants, which are stationary and rely on sunlight and nutrients in the soil for nourishment, and the animals, which are mobile and independent but in a manner parasitic. The second is the growth and development of a central nervous system. And the third is the implementation of intelligence.

"We must allow for other divergences which may be discovered in the future. These could be as wild as the imagination will take us. For instance, there may be a fork in the plant kingdom of which we are unaware, either because it was tried and found nonviable, or because it hasn't developed yet. I can conjure mobile plants and intelligent plants and carnivorous plants — that is, plants with a greater degree of sophistication than those we already know about. Then again, there may be further developments in the evolution of the brain. I liken mankind leaving his planet to explore the universe to the first fish leaving the sanctity of the sea to explore the land. On a larger scale, we are just now emerging from the cradle of our own meager beginnings. What will happen to us in the future only time will tell.

"In any case, I digress. While life on Earth was evolving parallel to life on Mars, it was always one step behind. When Earth was in her adolescence, Mars was an old woman: as if the planet, in attaining maturity sooner, reached senility quicker. And while Earth supported nothing but wild animals and clever apes, the Martians had attained a high level of civilization, both cultural and technological."

We entered an area well lighted and bubbling with workers. Six crawlers had formed a circle like a wagon train warding off an Indian attack. Their aim was to throw light on a spot that was under investigation. Workers were setting up other lights, dragging into position long rubber extension cords.

On the ground, and on the walls of the buildings, patches of brown lichen grew in profusion, its eerie green glow flooded out by the brighter, white light of the crawlers. Men and women were dusting frescoes that adorned the upper part of a wall, while rubble was being cleared from its base to expose a stunning and colorful monolith in high relief.

"Then came disaster to the solar system and the Martian people. Until five million years ago, there existed between Mars and Jupiter, in the orbit now occupied by the Asteroid Belt, a double planet system, each body of which was larger than the Moon but smaller than Mercury. A gravitational imbalance caused the two worlds to break apart, littering the solar system with deadly missiles like shrapnel from a grenade. The effect was to spread devastation among the planets.

"For a million years the Red Planet was pummeled from space until not only the Martian civilization but all indigenous life succumbed to the violent and shattering onslaught. The only remnant of this great race and worldwide ecology is the ruins of these once thriving cities, and their crops."

"Crops?"

"Yes, Mr. Martin. The areolichen that you see so much of was, at one time, grown in huge quantities — not just for lighting their homes and highways. It was their major staple, like rice to the Chinese."

"But — how has it survived unattended all these years?"

"It needs no attention, only harvesting. It's an extremely stable and hardy organism."

"Then that explains . . . "

"Mr. Martin?"

"No. Nothing. I was just — I never thought of lichen as — food."

Stepped back from the ground were layers of cliff dwellings sculpted from the rock, flaunting majesty with its green blanket of lichen. The intricate and interwoven warren rose several hundred feet, to a point at which the wall curved out to form the arch of the ceiling.

"Lichen was the Martian's water source as well. Just as desert mice live without ever taking a drink, so the Martians lived. Like cactus, areolichen stores moisture recovered from the rocks. Mars is not at all a dry planet; it's just that its water is chemically combined in a state of hydration. If you will excuse a curious paraphrasing, deep waters run still. Areolichen is nature's extractor, breaking chemical bonds which hold water much more efficiently and economically than any man-made method."

I shook my head. "Then you mean that this — lichen — is a reservoir that can be tapped at will?"

"Once we learn how to use it, yes. Don't you see what this means for the Project, Mr. Martin? An unlimited supply of water can free us forever from the shackles of dependency. With an overabundance of water, we can crack it electrolytically for its oxygen as well. I'm talking about freedom, do you understand?"

"Freedom from, or freedom for?"

Dr. Keppert stopped in his tracks. His hand went to his chin, bounced off the oxygen diaphragm. "I don't follow you."

"Don't you? I keep getting the feeling that you people want to withdraw from Earth control, to be the master — of all this." I kept walking, sweeping my hand at the slabs of faded marble.

Keppert struggled to keep up. "No, you misunderstand. We don't want to be the masters, but the guides. We don't want to separate from Earth, we want Earth to see the significance of what we've found. We want to build another civilization, based on Martian ways, Martian ethics. Why do you think I'm taking such pains with you? I'd rather get back to my work, to uncover more of the mystery. But I want you on our side. Major Tarkington handled this whole thing wrong right from the beginning, and I told him so. I want you to understand exactly what we've got here, so you can spread the word. Come up here and look upon the faces of the past."

He dragged me up those marble slabs, to a long line of coruscating blocks of glass that reminded me of museum cases. They stood perpendicular to the length of the narrow tunnel that we had entered, and continued on like lonely sentinels as far as I could see.

The floor was polished obsidian. I held back, but Keppert pulled me with uncommon strength toward the ancient, crystal coffins. The surface of the blocks was fogged, as if blasted by sand. The figure inside the first was shrouded in mystery. I could see a body that was unnaturally long and thin, clothed in a diaphanous gown that covered the torso and upper legs.

"She's not really green." Keppert pulled out a handlight and directed its beam onto the case. In the white light, all the surrounding lichen blinked out, becoming brown and ugly. The sharp light reflected annoyingly from millions of tiny scratches, scattering so that I saw less than without it. The dress was pastel blue, the skin pale and sickly. She was a creature of dull sun and light gravity.

Reverently, I rubbed a gloved hand over the coarse surface. "Are — are they all like this?"

"Some are better, some are worse. I suspect that time has had its toll. But at least we know that the material is not invulnerable."

I walked around the crystal coffin, inspecting it in awe from every angle. "She seems so — lifelike. So — alive. Like Sleeping Beauty waiting to be kissed."

Dr. Keppert whispered, as if not to interrupt the sepulchral sanctity. "There's no decay, no cellular collapse. They appear to be held in stasis: frozen in time as it were."

"Waiting to be awakened?" My voice was clacked.

"I thought so at first, Mr. Martin, but have since learned otherwise. An organism as complex as the human body is beyond recall. What you see here are mere physical remains: without a soul, without personality, without knowledge and memory. All of that is housed at the end of the corridor."

"The Machine." It was a simple statement.

Keppert moved on, past alabaster caskets. They were all fogged to different degrees, and I was able, after a while, to conjure a composite picture: here an arm, long and graceful, there a leg or a foot, an oversized ear. The charnel house went on and on.

"Science and technology on Mars have pursued an alternate path than that which we have taken. The near vacuum does not support combustion, so the ancient Martians never discovered fire, nor felt its warmth, nor watched by its light on a cool summer's evening. The steam engine or the internal combustion engine would have been complicated and cumbersome devices without an understanding of the principles of oxidation or pressure. Consequently, they bypassed that stage of mechanical development.

"Electricity, on the other hand, would have come quite naturally. Without the hazard of fire, their biggest problem was conductor insulation: circuits would readily go to ground in the airless void. But then vacuum electronics would have been a short step away. We've actually found the remnants of wind generator stations."

I came to the last crystal sarcophagus. The figure, a male, was dressed in bright red cerement, but the form and features were obscured. When I backed away from it and looked toward Dr. Keppert, I saw over his shoulder a tenuous auroral shimmering, a curtain of changing colors.

"And here is the consummation of that search for power: a self-perpetuating energy source that knows no end. It has kept the machinery going for five million years, and has powered a protective force field that has kept it from harm."

Dr. Keppert melded into the coruscating field of energy, and as he crossed that wispy boundary, I saw him as one sees through heat waves over a tropical beach, or over a hot macadam road. The last of his words came through as multiple voice tracks slightly out of phase.

"Behold the Machine, Mr. Martin."

As I neared the unsubstantial wall, I felt a kind of — presence: some ineffable force impinging on my mind like a mental probe. For a wild moment I could see my brain, see the thousands of convolutions, see the synapses open and close like electric sparks between two electrodes. My mind was flooded with esoteric — thoughts? Knowledge? Memory?

"Do not be afraid," Dr. Keppert breathed. "I want you to learn. Forget what those fools have been telling you."

Standing at the very edge of the barrier, the pulsating force field sometimes enveloped me, sometimes receded. I felt the induction of energy whenever it caressed my skin, raising tiny goose bumps all over my body. Kaleidoscopic configurations reflected off my faceplate — or perhaps were burned directly onto my cornea.

"I sense strange mental images."

"It is a natural effect. It will not harm you."

I thought of Dr. Sanders and his crew. "Suppose I can't absorb what the Machine is projecting?"

"It will be all right. You have been conditioned — you are prepared for the experience. Come, Mr. Martin. You must find out for yourself."

I took another step forward. Pushing against the invisible force was like wading through a sea of thick oil. I forced myself onward, straining against the threads of force.

I was horrified by what I saw and felt. My mind expanded into nothingness. A fantastic knowledge was attaching itself like a leech to my brain, blending memory with reality. I was struck by exotic and deep-seated feelings. I harbored primal urges that had been suppressed — not just in my lifetime, but for the lifetime of humanity. I wanted to scream, to run, to retch, to breathe the air, to feel the sun, to sing.

The Machine was all around, millions of points of light which all seemed to focus on me. There was no physical movement: it was solid and static. Yet it beckoned to me with open arms, soothing like a Madonna, protecting like a womb. I was overcome with emotion, with nostalgia, with sadness. I sensed a flowing motion: not mechanical, but electrical, as if the Machine were a giant brain, thinking. I felt relays clicking like synaptic discharge. I felt my loins tingle with the thrill of homecoming. I felt warm and safe. I felt great rumblings deep under the structure of the Machine: the rumblings of a hungry beast. But I knew I was snug in its influence.

I felt that the Machine was alive.

The Machine was a magnet and I was an insignificant iron filing. My body twitched and skittered toward the center of its being. My limbs were paralyzed. They reacted to no conscious control, yet some stimulus, some command, carried me unhesitatingly toward the maw that fed into the alien, inner workings.

The Machine.

It was a gigantic recorder and my brain a sensitive playback scanner. The things I learned. The things I knew to be true — about the world, about the universe, about myself. A mercurial montage, like a newsreel film, paraded through my mind, thrusting so many facts at me that I could not absorb them all, but could only catch glimpses of each item. It was like watching a motion picture running at ten thousand frames per second: every frame flashed on my brain, but I was unable to grasp the rapid content.

I felt myself spinning in a silent maelstrom. I floated in an outpouring of knowledge. I no longer existed as a corporeal being, but lived only as a disembodied consciousness.

I approached the bottom of the infinite vortex that was my inner soul.

Chapter 17

What seemed like an eternity had been but an hour. The Valkyries who had been my friends had left me behind. Yet, the influence of the Machine lingered on, not like a bad aftertaste, but like the sweet scent of honeysuckle, nurturing my mind with pleasantries. Slowly, so slowly, the feeling of euphoria left me, and I crawled into the gutter that was reality.

"Somebody call Linda."

"I already did. She's on her way."

"Is he going to be all right?"

"I think so, but he's had a pretty heavy dose."

"I was going to bring him out in another minute. You didn't have to spoil it."

"*Shut up!*"

"I think he moved."

"I'm going to give him another shot."

The stabbing pain in my arm captured my attention. I tried to get away, but was held in place.

"You'll be all right, son."

I opened my eyes. Doc Reynolds withdrew the needle. Major Tarkington swam into view. My head lolled; I took in my surroundings. I saw four exposure hoods on the table, names and faceplates up, packing cases, aluminum bunks, sleeping bags, a long row of hastily stacked oxygen bottles, survival gear, deflation annunciator speakers, plastic walls billowed outward, an airtight zipper. We were in an emergency pod.

The Major stabbed a finger at Dr. Keppert, huddling in the corner. "You should have known better than to leave him in there so long. What the hell were you trying to accomplish?"

The geologist looked away. "I thought he was prepared for it."

"Not for that kind of exposure." The doctor sterilized the hypodermic, stored it in its case. "You might have done him irreparable harm."

"So now he can appreciate what we have gone through. I still say let's face up to it without the childish intrigues."

"We've been through all this before." The Major's face was contorted in anger. "We'll go about this in a prescribed, methodical manner. There's more at stake here than the salvation of one soul. We have the whole of humanity to worry about."

Dr. Keppert scowled. "I understand what you are saying, but I still submit justification for disagreeing."

"You can think what you like, as long as you do as you're told."

"Why beat around the bush?"

"What's your goddamned hurry?" Doc Reynolds shouted. He checked my pulse and placed a professional palm on my forehead. "It's waited five million years, another day won't matter. Not even a century."

Keppert pouted, his tall frame bent forward and his lanky legs spread wide. He stared out through the clear plastic walls.

Doc Reynolds let my wrist drop, helped me to a sitting position, put a cup to my lips. "Here, have some of this."

I gulped the sweet tasting coffee greedily.

The Major gripped my forearm firmly. "Doug, please accept my apologies for Keppert's action. Not that I didn't want you to see and experience for yourself the power of the Machine. But as you are well aware, it can deliver more stimulation to the neural passages than the brain can endure. You're very lucky that the good doctor here knows as much about medicine as all those fancy letters after his name indicate."

"Well, I don't want to take all the credit . . . "

"But you'll take the lion's share."

Finally, I found my voice, although, despite the coffee, my throat was still dry. "What — what happened? The Machine — "

"Doesn't know when to stop. You almost overdosed, almost had your brain burned out like Sanders and his crew. Because of the good doctor's experiments with lichen extract we've been able to accelerate your meta-morphosis. You've changed more in a week than we have in months. Instead of minutes in the Machine, you withstood an hour. You — "

"Doug, do you know what the Machine does? Did you get that far?" The doctor's words made no sense. "It's a tremendously complex educator, more sophisticated than any computer you've ever seen. It has no input terminals, no output terminals, and no push button for hard copy. It's designed to register directly on the brain — but on a Martian brain: with Martian thoughts, with Martian experiences, with Martian outlooks. A Martian could glean information by having it implanted right into his memory.

"But we were born and bred under different circumstances. Our thought processes are not the same. When we listen to the Machine, we hear babble. We can — and do — train ourselves to interpret these mental signals. But in the process, as our minds are imprinted with Martian knowledge, our psyches are imbued with Martian attitudes and feelings. With enough practice, you not only learn to think like a Martian, but to feel like one as well."

"Wait a minute!" I did not mean to scream. I pushed the cup away. I was beginning to wake up, to think clearly. "Are you saying that this Machine distorts your psychology with alien patterns?"

"No. I'm saying that it's a psychometric device which prepares our mental attitudes so we can accept and believe in the Martians as real, living beings. Understanding them is the key to understanding Mars, to understanding ourselves, and coming to grips with our existence. It represents the psychological adaptation factor which is necessary for a successful colony, and in conjunction with physical adaptations, prepares us for our future life."

My whole body shivered. "What physical adaptations?"

"Well, let's go about it another way. The biochemistry of areolichen has the same amino protein base as

Earth forms. But because of its alien phylogeny, it has a chemical constituency which enables it to survive on Mars: it's a product of its own evolution. I've been able to extract those specific chemicals and infuse them into Earthly biota, thus endowing a physical change more resistant to ambient Martian conditions."

Phyllis Trimble's plant treatments immediately came to mind. "You mean you can inject a plant with chemical derivatives which will induce genetic mutations that adapt the progeny to Martian habitudes?"

Doc Reynolds took in a great breath. "Not exactly. Although it's true that survival traits are transmitted to offspring, it's only half the story. What I'm saying is that physiological changes can be induced in the parent plant. Just as hormone injections can stimulate growth, or alter the sexual balance, so this serum can affect the body's adaptability.

"Dr. Malle went further and experimented with animals: not just with worms and ants, but with mice. He found that by keeping the mice on an increasingly stronger diet of areolichen extract, amazing modifications began to take place in their bodies, right to the core of cellular structure. They became able to withstand less atmospheric pressure; the skin shrugged off ultraviolet radiation; the pores sealed themselves against unnecessary evaporation; the whole metabolic process acquired optimum efficiency so that less oxygen was required, and less internal heat needed to be generated. The eyes saw into the infrared. The entire body was in a state of anabolism: like a tadpole becoming a frog, developing from one stage of life to another and greater stage."

I covered my hand with my mouth, suddenly sick.

"Of course, we now know that the process can be accelerated by injecting the serum directly into the bloodstream."

I swung myself off the table, backed away. I kept the three of them in sight. "You've been poisoning me, haven't you?"

"Now, son, don't take it like that. Listen to what the

good doctor has to say before you jump to conclusions."

"The only obvious conclusion is that you're all mad: totally and utterly insane. This Machine has — affected your brains."

"Oh, much more than that," Doc Reynolds admitted calmly. "It's affected our bodies. We have in our grasp the perfect colonist. Since terraforming the planet to meet human physical requirements is beyond our present state of technology, what better solution than marsforming the body?"

I stared at them one by one; they held their ground. "You can't do it. You don't have the right. Even if it works, if it isn't some induced delusion, you're condemning people to permanent exile."

"It only becomes exile if it's against one's will," said the Major. "Otherwise, it's immigration."

My foot came up sharply against a crate. I felt behind me, touched the sleek, plastic walls, felt around for the table and my hood. "So how do I fit into your scheme? Am I supposed to go along with this preposterous plan and persuade people to come here from Earth, so they can be turned into monsters?"

"Son, all you have to do is the job you were sent here to do. Write your report, make any recommendations you feel warranted, but first take the time to examine the situation fully. Trust in our allegiance to the Project, and to humanity. Tell Rogers what we've found — and how we intend to use it. I have faith in his vision to understand our needs."

"Do you honestly believe he'll send guinea pigs for this madcap plot?"

"We need industrious people to help this Project grow. Offer them a parcel of land, and you'll have as many pioneers crossing through space as you had crossing the American continent. But give us some more time before you make any decisions. You need a bit more information."

"You mean indoctrination, don't you? Brainwashing?"

"No, merely understanding. It will come in time.

We've sought only to cut that time short."

I sidled sideways, reaching behind me. My hand fell on the hoods. I clutched one, and drew it close. It knocked another over the edge, against the packing crates. Like toppling dominoes, the uppermost crate crashed into the next pile of crates and knocked it into the hastily unpacked oxygen bottles standing along the wall.

Two of them bobbled back and forth, rocking precariously for a long moment, then continued beyond the balance point. With the slowness induced by Mars' gravity, they fell with a thud to the canvassed floor lining. In a sudden and never-ending explosion, the valve sheered off and, like a missile, soared across the pod between two bunks, and without ever slowing down tore through the inflatable fabric of the wall.

Some seven hundred cubic feet of air, suddenly freed, tried to escape through the narrow neck of the bottle, like the genie from Aladdin's lamp. The expanding oxygen converted the spun aluminum cylinder into an aborting rocket. With a great roar, the bottle whirled around in circles almost too fast for the eye to follow. Ricocheting off crates and gear, and describing a large arc through the air, it snapped two legs off the central table, sending coffee cups clattering, and crashed through the lower bunk and took half of it through the hole that it made in the pressure skin.

With it went the bellow of escaping gas, but almost instantly blazing klaxons sounded the warning of depressurization. And just as instantly, everyone burst into action.

The Major vaulted to where the oxygen bottle had gone through the wall, ripped the mattress from the upper bunk, laid it flat against the large tear. Dr. Keppert grabbed an emergency patch kit and, squirting glue from a tube on one side of a plastic patch, slapped it against the hole made by the flying valve. Doc Reynolds ran to the oxygen system bank and opened the valves to their fullest extent, compensating for the immediate loss. I dived into the jumble of exposure hoods and hurled each one at its owner.

I scrambled for a backpack, plugged in the intake hose and flipped the regulator selector switch from demand to force flow. Oxygen hissed out promptly and I jammed my face into the mask to take a couple of quick breaths. Then I pushed the rest across the floor to where the others could reach them.

"It's no use. This hole is big enough to walk through." The Major's voice sounded tinny and far away.

The klaxons continued to hammer at my ears, adding such a frightening squelch of sound that I found it difficult to concentrate. Waves of vertigo swept across my brain, and I fought unconsciousness. My head seemed to be expanding and, despite the oxygen from the mask, I was getting so dizzy that I could not stop from weaving. I fell to my knees with the thought that explosive decompression was not a pretty death — nor a painless one.

The pod's internal supports began to sag, the fabric hung loosely. I found myself on hands and knees, staring stupidly at the floor. In my weakness, I had dropped the exposure hood. It dangled from its hose, and oxygen still issued from the support pack.

My eyes were pulsing; my skin itched all over. I felt a fullness in my chest: I exhaled before my lung walls burst. My bones began to ache at the joints: elbows and shoulders, knees and ankles. When I picked up one hand to make a feeble scratching motion, I fell headlong onto the flooring. I rolled over and stared at the drooping ceiling, only vaguely aware of what was occurring around me.

The itchiness in my joints was replaced by a queer numbness. My body went slack; I could no longer feel my fingers or toes. I tried to wriggle them, but they did not move: it was as if they did not exist.

My arms weakened and flopped uselessly to the floor; my head lolled. My arms and legs were gone, as if they had been neatly amputated. There was no feeling anywhere in my body.

Somewhere in the distance, I heard voices convers-
ing dimly and at fantastic speed. My body was dead, for
none of it responded to my will. Then my stomach
retched and I felt the vomit belching up out of my
throat. Powerless to roll over, it streamed from the corners of my mouth, choking me with its bulk. I went into
convulsions, inhaled involuntarily: there was nothing
to breathe but my own vomit.

Naked faces appeared above me. They seemed
familiar, as if from a childhood dream.

Choking and coughing, darkness mercifully closed
in on me.

Chapter 18

Space.

Infinite space.

Swirling galaxies. Converging nebulas. Exploding supernovas. Stars coalescing from vast clouds of hydrogen, rotating madly, spitting thin streamers of gaseous matter that further coalesced into planetary masses.

Suns of many colors and hues painted a spiral galaxy with rainbow pastels that glinted and scintillated in kaleidoscopic variety. Long, tenuous, tapering arms, themselves consisting of millions of stars, manifested circular motion. Some suns strode their well-worn paths as solitary meanderers. Others traveled in twos or threes or fours, describing interstellar configurations that revolved in perfect symmetry.

Worlds, wondrous in their infinite variety, strove into view. Enormous cold, dead planets supporting atmospheres thick with methane gas and continents surrounded by liquid ammonia, shared solar systems with dainty globes dotted with water-vapor clouds, caressed with warm seas and gently rolling hills, and carpeted luxuriantly with vegetation that was both primitive and yet biologically advanced.

All this was visible from the port of the — starship? If it was a starship, it was immensely large: the size of a small city, and just as formless. Yet it moved as one coherent body, cruising through the cosmos on a never-ending journey of interstellar enlightenment and exploration.

Through a dimension that was both timeless and directionless, the starship moved: through a space that was neither here nor there and could have been anywhere or anywhen. From this nether place of unreality, it dropped into real space.

A typical star system swam into view: average, yellow sun; family of ten attendant planets; life on three of them: one primitive and close to its beginnings, one bar-

barously adolescent, one sere and dying.

And one held true intelligence: that scarce commodity but rarely encountered in the broad reaches of the universe. It was a civilization of quiet, beatific refinement, of simple, unassuming naïveté, of a people both bold and gentle, sanguinely struggling against the forces of nature.

But thrown into the midst of their struggles was an imbroglio from which there was no escape. This peaceful system was suddenly bombarded with millions of meteoric fragments as one of its orbiting children erupted from interdimensional stresses. It spelled disaster for that noble, striving race.

Those in the starship must stop and help. That was their destiny. That was their purpose in the scheme of the universe. That was the price of ultimate sentience. Not just to collect and catalogue, not simply to analyze and itemize, but to pluck each precious flower efflorescing with dim hope for the future.

Contact.

    *   *   *   *   *   *

I opened my eyes to a silver sky and a pale yellow sun, radiating comfort and dim warmth. An alien landscape was dotted with odd-looking trees and dull, grayish rocks. I felt a chill in the air, but it did not make me shiver — I accepted the cold stoically.

A group of strange creatures stood off to one side, mumbling unintelligibly to themselves. As I turned my head toward them, one detached itself from the group and flowed in my direction. My ears sensed a sibilant, chirping voice that spoke in a tongue that was foreign but somehow familiar.

A mist rose from my eyes like evaporating dew. The trees and rocks and creatures dissolved into more recognizable shapes: cabinets and chairs and people. The sun overhead became an incandescent lamp. Hallucination became reality.

"Doug? Doug, are you all right?"

Linda stared down at me, one hand held to her breast, the other clutching my shoulder tensely. Blonde curls hung loosely around her face, framing taut features. Her blue eyes blazed like a hundred fiery stars, sparkling with life.

"How do you feel?"

Her voice trembled. Her eyes cared. But her demeanor patronized. Just above the neck seal of her exposure suit, I watched the faint pulse of the carotid on her slender, white throat.

My natural inclination was to sit up. But as I pulled my elbows under me and pushed upward, I managed only a slight rise before waves of vertigo caused me to restrain my effort. Linda seized my head with both hands and eased me back onto the pillow.

I opened my eyes a minute later. "I guess I'll live."

Another face swam into view. My right hand was picked up and held clinically by the wrist for a quarter of a minute. "You'd be dead by now, either of pneumothorax or embolism or decompression injury, if you weren't such a tough son of a gun."

I squinted my eyes, and recited anathema. "And if I hadn't had the benefit of Dr. Reynolds' panacea made from rare Martian herbs."

"That, too, of course," he admitted cheerfully.

Major Tarkington's face appeared next to Linda's. He laid a heavy hand on my shoulder, then pounded me several times. I shrank from his grasp.

Why is everyone touching me?

"You can thank Dr. Keppert for some quick thinking," the Major boomed, nodding behind him. "He dragged you into the airlock and sealed it tight."

I rolled my head and saw Keppert skulking against a far wall. He seemed not to have heard. "Thanks."

He glanced at me, his bewhiskered face cold but sincere. "It was the only thing to do."

"I feel weird." The dizziness had gone, but my body felt different — somehow detached from my mind. The aches of the past few days were intensified. My lungs were hot, as if I had inhaled fire. My muscles responded in an unfamiliar way, jumping erratically as if my motor coordination was out of phase.

"Nothing that a good night's rest can't cure," the doctor prescribed.

"He's been sleeping all afternoon," Linda said, pleading.

Doc Reynolds shone a small light into my eyes and peered in after it. "You're a very lucky man. You have a few distended vessels, but no bubbles or clots. You'll be sore for a little while, but with no lasting effects. A little more rest wouldn't hurt."

As the doctor stepped back with his instruments, I made another attempt to rise. Moving as slowly as my sore muscles would allow, I pushed myself up. Without the sudden urge of blood away from my head, I managed an upright position. Linda reached out to help, but I shrank from her touch. Her fingers felt cold, inhospitable, *alien*. My skin crawled electrically.

I swung my feet out over the edge of the couch between Linda and the Major. "The Machine," I started. My head swam. I did not know exactly what I wanted to say. "The Machine. It's out of place. It doesn't fit. I've studied the slides and read the reports. I know what remains of their science and technology. I spent all morning visiting the ruins and — nothing I've seen intimates the degree of skill required to design and build a device as advanced as that — divine computer. It's an obvious and enormous singularity planted in the middle of a lesser civilization. I know this. I don't know how, but I know.

"You've led me to believe that everything here is a product of Martian genius. But no other relics precede such refinement. It's totally incongruous. So how is it that they were suddenly able to construct a mechanism on that order of magnitude?"

"They weren't."

In unison, all eyes turned toward Dr. Keppert. He came away from his perch, his arms dangling loose at his sides.

"They didn't build it. It was built for them."

In the dead silence of the pod, I was acutely aware of every minuscule sound not normally heard. Linda's manicured fingernails beat a steady, staccato rhythm on the plastic side of the couch. The circulator breathed a faint hiss of oxygen into the room. My heart beat furiously within my chest.

I tried to sound calm, professional. "By whom?"

Keppert shrugged his bony shoulders. "Shall we say — extragalactics?"

"And why did they do such a thing?"

"As a repository of vanishing Martian knowledge. As a monument to the prominence of their culture. As an everlasting beacon in the universe to their greatness. And for others to find — and emulate."

My spine raced with chills, my voice broke up. "And what makes you so sure?"

Keppert smiled. "The Machine."

I made an instantaneous decision. Without taking my eyes off Keppert, I said, "Major, the time has arrived. I want to collect my notes and disks, and put together a preliminary report."

"Well, don't you think it's a little early for that, son? After all, you have a lot more to see. And maybe we should discuss this in more detail when you — "

I faced the Major. "We will discuss it — in depth. But that won't affect my present report. I want to sketch out the particulars for Rogers, and let him know how the investigation is proceeding. He will be concerned about my progress, and I think it's within the bounds of protocol to deliver such information as I already have on hand."

"Well, of course, I wasn't trying to prevent you from fulfilling your obligations. It's just that — "

"Good. If you'll locate a recorder for me, I'll file a verbal report at once."

"I think you're making a mistake — "

"Any mistakes will be my responsibility."

"I didn't mean — "

Slowly, deliberately, I pronounced my words. "I'm taking over. Do you understand?"

Major Tarkington's massive chest heaved a great sigh. "We don't have the computer tied in for direct broadcast from here. Do you want me to patch it through the Syrtis City transmitter?"

"That won't be necessary. I've come to understand the sagacity of your original management of the situation. You're right: a radio broadcast is too risky. I want my report hand delivered — by space shuttle."

"You may not have enough time. The supplies have been unloaded, and they're putting aboard some — samples, relics, for the return flight. There's a window at sunrise that Hodges-Smith plans to take advantage of."

"I'll try to rush it. I'll prepare my report tonight and we'll deliver it first thing in the morning. Forward a restraining order that the shuttle is not to take off without me."

"I still wish you'd wait."

"I'm sure you do. But this is the way I want it."

Linda placed a hand on my shoulder, looked at me with warm, blue eyes. "Doug, are you sure you're up to it?"

"I'm fine," I said, more harshly than I intended. I turned to the geologist. "Dr. Keppert, do you have any photographs of the Machine? Do you have any idea what it looks like?"

He shook his head slowly. "You remember that the end of the tunnel is barricaded by a force field. Whatever energy it possesses has kept us out of it. We can so far penetrate only the outer extremities. What is inside, what it protects, I have no idea."

"You really should get some more sleep." Doc Reynolds fiddled with his stethoscope. "You'll be pretty sore after that experience. And," he glanced at Linda, "you might need some watching — in case there are aftereffects."

"No! I want to be alone." I switched my attention from the doctor to Linda. "You understand, don't you? It isn't over yet."

A watery pearl flowed from one eye. "Of course." She opened her mouth, but no sound emerged.

The Major headed for the airlock. "I've got your

notes and disks out in the crawler. I'll put them in the airlock."

"Thank you, Major. And you, too, Dr. Keppert."

The geologist nodded. The Major unzipped the inner door, and together they cycled themselves out.

"I left some pills for you on the table." Doc Reynolds pointed. "They're just muscle relaxers. If you start feeling twinges or spasms, I'd advise you to take a couple."

"I'll keep it in mind."

I tucked Linda's blonde hair into her exposure hood. I wanted to kiss her red lips, bury my face in her curly tresses. "Don't worry. Everything's going to be all right."

She nodded, smiling faintly. The ready light illuminated and Doc unzipped the inner door. He took out a briefcase and handed it to me. Then he and Linda stepped in. I closed the door behind them. Linda waved forlornly. I winked.

I took the briefcase back to the couch and went through its contents. All my notes were there, as well as the departmental reports that I had collected. I listened to several audiotapes in random places, put the hard disks in the computer and read the file menus. Nothing appeared to have been erased.

The pod was filled with medical supplies, x-ray equipment, surgical instruments, and a portable Medwife with diagnostic disks. I found the pills that the doctor had left for me, threw them into a corner. I checked my life-support backpack: the scrubbers were still operations, but the tanks were low. I refilled them from the medical oxygen system, waited until the tanks cooled down, then topped them off.

I switched off all the lights. Without the glare from the plastic panels, I could see outside through the clear inflatable walls. The Cave was dark. In the distance a few headlamps bobbed near the ruins. Green light glowed from patches of lichen.

By feel, I donned the backpack and exposure hood, plugged in the hoses. I cycled through the airlock. No one was close. The crawler viewport was open; it was dark inside. I slipped inside through the rear door. I checked the bunks with my handlight. They were empty.

Sitting in the dark, I hurried through the safety procedures. When everything checked out, I flipped on the external camera screens. There was no motion in any of the four horizontal directions; overhead, from the cavern roof, the green aura shone dimly, suffusing its shadowless light throughout the immensity of the Cave. The Martian city was cold and still. From the far edge, a faint glow of starlight peered in weakly from the ragged opening into Sanders Rill.

I threw my exposure hood on the other seat and strapped myself in the seat. I eased the dampers out of the atomic pile: it fed energy to the waiting engine. With no headlamps or signal lights to attract attention, I steered by the ambient emerald sheen until I was safely in the rill and clear of the entrance. The eerie silence of near vacuum aided my escape.

Once out of sight of the Caves, I pulled over behind a large boulder. The bottom of the rill was dark and foreboding: the stars had only a narrow slice from which to peer down, all else was blocked by the mile-high walls.

I unclipped the dashboard locks, pulled off the panel, laid it flat between the seats. Methodically, I traced color-coded cables from the signal beacon through a splice box to the control panel. The signal beacon was not connected to any of the distribution circuits, but came directly off the main breaker. It was not intended to be disconnected — ever.

From the tool kit I took a pair of pliers and snipped the wire in two. On the grid screen, the red blip representing the crawler blinked out. I taped the hot end of the lead. The crawler was now electronically invisible and, for all practical purposes, no longer existed.

I tucked in the wires, replaced the panel. I switched on the low beams, but left the running lights off. Gently, I maneuvered the crawler back onto the trail and started up the precipitous slope.

The treads kicked and gouged at the loose detritus, but moved upward steadily. The ground was torn up by heavy traffic. I saw the space shuttle on the screen, and a bunch of blips clustered around it: crawlers still on the launch pad. Free from surveillance, I was a phantom of the night.

When I veered around boulders, the crawler had a tendency to sideslip. Rocks acted like roller bearings on the steep talus. By the time I climbed out of the rill and onto the plateau I was drenched with sweat. The air was clear and windless, and ten thousand stars shone down like klieg lights on a movie set.

While I rested from my ordeal, I noticed movement on the grid screen. The blips previously surrounding the space shuttle had moved into a line. They were on their way to the Caves.

I studied the contour lines. It was a tortuous country ahead, fraught with mountains and ravines and dangerous soil domes. A more fractured, fissured and inhospitable terrain existed nowhere else on Mars. I keyed in the overlays of acceptable routes. The returning crawlers were taking the long, circuitous, but safer route. The only way to avoid them was to take the short cut.

I threw the transmission into gear, headed for the fork. As I slowed down at the wilderness intersection, I caught a glimmer of red and green navigational lights off to the right. I switched off my headlights and studied the viewscreen. Silhouetted against bright stars on the horizon, I made out a crawler and its tow. It was Henderson with the reactor, waiting for an escort down the trail to the Caves. Now I saw the blip on the screen.

Unless he called on the emergency frequency, I could not hear him. The radio was switched off. Concealed in the darkness of overhanging cliffs, I turned down the abandoned trail to the south.

The crawler bounced and crashed over cragged terrain: I did not spare the machine. I raced at full tilt through light sand and dust and over small rocks. I spun the wheel like a racecar driver. It handled with perfection at lower speeds, but its momentum was not easily checked by the scant friction afforded in low gravity. And at higher speeds it tended to slew sideways so that the rear was constantly trying to overtake the front. But I could not force myself to slow down.

The trail gained altitude and rose to a high ridge. There were no tracks to guide me and, since I had disconnected the beacon transmitter, there was no red blip on the screen to show me where I was located in relation to the grid map. I had to make my own interpolations.

I saw what I thought was the right pass: a deep gouge between two spiraling peaks. I felt my way up a steep talus slope, consisting mostly of pebbles and granulated sand. Even the wide flotation treads sank deep. I lowered gears and revved the engine to maximum rpm's, afraid that the crawler would bog down in the soft, arenaceous ground.

Grunting and groaning, the crawler pulled itself out of the talus and onto hard-packed rock, dusted lightly with orange sediment. I continued to climb more easily now. Kicked up by spinning treads, a dry fog followed me.

When I reached the height of the mountain pass, I beheld a marvelous view of the surrounding territory. The rills behind me were bathed in dark shadow: thin penciled lines knifing through a montage of cliffs and ravines. In front spread a vast level plain, broken in the distance by other mountains and rills, but with a caldera of sand in the near foreground.

Straight across this isolated desert, searchlights stabbing the sky, perched the space shuttle. My hand went to the transmitter, but held there. Breaking radio silence might also tip my hand to the wrong faction. I wanted to get on that shuttle with no one the wiser.

Below me lay a long, winding trail. According to the elevation reports, the field of sand was on a plateau much lower than the side from which I had just climbed. The red splotches on the screen told of possible subterranean dangers. The plane between the base of the mountain and the shuttle had to be navigated with the same care as a minefield.

Again in low gear, with little or no acceleration, I coasted down the rocky incline. The overall drop was several thousand feet, with the upper part of the mountain stepped in a series of ridges: near vertical drops were separated by long horizontal stretches. But as I neared the bottom, the whole mountain fell away with amazing sheerness.

Grinding treads scraped on naked rock; sparkless shards were ripped off and sent scattering. The transmission whined in agony. Forward momentum overrode the brakes.

In the lowest range of low gear, I plunged down the sixty-degree pitch. I had made the fundamental error of descent: gathering more momentum than I could dissipate. A trained driver might be able to shift into reverse and by carefully balancing the torque between treads keep the forward direction perpendicular. But that was beyond my skill level as a driver. I could only cling to low gear, pump the brakes, and pray.

The treads scraping on rock ended suddenly as I plowed into the scree near the bottom of the slope. I had descended several thousand feet in a matter of minutes. The gradient moderated, pebbles and thick sand retarded my speed. But I could not swerve without fear of losing control. I was jolted around as the crawler collided with boulders, bounced over divots with jarring impact. Despite the high ground clearance, the undercarriage raked over rocky projections.

Loose debris kicked up by the plummeting crawler launched a landslide which, because I was decelerating, began to pass me. Stones and rocks rolled past on both sides. In the narrow beam of the headlamps, it looked like a living, moving ocher sea.

The ground rumbled and roared beneath me. I did not hear a sound, but felt the vibration through the flotation treads. It seemed as if the whole mountain were in motion — an avalanche of sand and stone. The crawler sank deeper into the pulverized dirt, gears screeching like a wounded whale. A fountain of dust and slowly falling debris was visible in the rear viewscreen.

A flash of red caught my eye at the same time that an ear-splitting klaxon sounded raucously. The grid screen was flashing a warning — the gravimeter needle was pegged in the danger zone.

Before I could disengage the alarm, the crawler lurched and leaned forward. I was pressed against the safety harness. Sand piled up halfway over the viewport. The headlamps were darkened, buried. I held the steering wheel with a death grip as my sense of orientation went completely out of kilter.

The nose of the crawler seemed to be pointing downward, as if it had gone over a sharp brink, and continued to flip over. I was in free fall — only my seat belt kept me from floating free. The crawler swung right on around in an arc until I lost all sense of up and down. Helpless, I braced myself against the inevitable impact.

When the crash came it was surprisingly soft, but still hard enough to cause serious concussion. I was forced down into the seat. The belts stretched, and my body was twisted through the interlocking straps. Ever so lightly, my temple grazed the rim of the steering wheel.

In an explosion of sparks and a clatter of shooting bullets, circuit breakers banged. My eyes closed a split second after the crawler lights blinked off.

Silence reigned.

Chapter 19

I awoke in a blast furnace. Waves of unbearable heat drenched me like rocket exhaust.

The blackness was absolute. I might have been at the bottom of a deep well, or in a coal bin at midnight. For a moment, I thought that I might still be unconscious, dreaming. But the pain across my forehead, the sticky wound I felt with a probing finger, the fierce, intense heat, were all too-real reminders that my sensory nerves were functioning.

In the utter darkness, I disengaged myself from the safety straps, stood slowly and uncertainly, stripped off the heavy layers of thermal clothing. The coolness of the cabin was a blessing. I ran my hand over my naked body — my skin was smooth and dry and painful to the touch. Every muscle was sore, as if I had been stretched out and sprung together.

There was no power in the crawler. The nuclear reactor still operated, the atomic core puking its guts out until it became an inert lump of stable elements. Blindly I felt my way to the provisions locker, fumbled until I located a portable lamp. It would not be wise to stick my hand unknowingly into the main breaker cabinet.

By the light of the narrow beam I opened the dashboard clips and exposed the wiring. All the switches were in the on position, but the main disconnect had been tripped mechanically. I grasped the thick handle with my free hand, pushed it all the way off, then threw it into the on position. It closed with a bang that made me jump back as all three phases arced under full load.

The armored, fluorescent lights shimmered, sending quivering spirals up and down the length of the tubes as the internal gas warmed to the overvoltage sparked by the ballasts. They peaked to full brightness, bathing the cabin in their warm, caressing glow.

The instrument panel sparkled like a Christmas

tree. Most of the annunciator lights shone green, some flashed red, while a few flickered alternately from one to the other, as if they could not make up their minds. The crawler had suffered some damage.

After that cartwheeling plunge, it still stood approximately upright. According to the digital inclinometers, the crawler listed to starboard sixteen degrees, with a forward tilt of no more than twenty.

The internal temperature was less than freezing, but I was comfortable without clothes. I turned off the heating coils and blower motors. Many of the more important functions were out of commission. Indicator lights had broken or were missing lenses, bulbs had cracked glass or burned out filaments, secondary circuits had loose connections or pinched wires or melted insulation. The gravimeter needle was bent out of shape. The grid screen display tube was smashed beyond repair. The air mixture gauges showed no response: I had to use my body as one might use a canary to test oxygen quality.

Blackness stared back at me from the front port, its glazed lens reflecting my naked body. My chest appeared bulbously distorted. All the external screens were equally as dark. Either the circuitry had been interrupted by the fall, or the cameras had sheared off their mounts. The swivel controls did not respond. But when I switched to test mode all telemetering systems proved to be operable. A touch of fear gripped my heart.

I climbed into my exposure suit and donned the hood and backpack. I stepped into the airlock, closed the door carefully behind me, evacuated the oxygen into the storage canisters. I spun the dogs on the outer door, activated the hydraulics. Nothing happened. With my feet braced against the inner sill, I thrust my shoulder against the heavy metal. It held fast.

The crawler was completely surrounded by sand and rock that had tumbled down into the crevasse. I was buried alive.

With the outer door hinged so that it opened outward, there was no way of digging a tunnel up through the debris. The viewport, built to withstand howling sandstorms and collisions with windblown rocks, could not be shattered by any force that I could wield.

Back inside the cabin, I felt infinitely tired of the whole game. I sat in the driver's seat, resignedly thumbed the radio switch, and scooped up the microphone. "Come in Cave Camp. Come in Cave Camp. This is Doug Martin. Come in please."

When there was no immediate response, I pressed the test button. It flashed brightly, indicating that power was reaching the set. I tried different channels. I played with the gain and volume. I switched to emergency frequency.

There was no reply. The radio was dead.

I sighed, leaned back in the seat, staring at my own distorted reflection in the viewport. When I switched off the cabin lights, my alter ego vanished. I stared at the annunciator panel, a grim reminder of my plight. With the utter calm that precedes death, I relaxed, thinking, dreaming, wondering, figuring a way out of my predicament. Eventually, in the semi-darkness, I dozed off.

Some time later, I came out of my drowsiness. I had hunched over the dashboard, cradling my head in my arms. Now I pushed myself upright, vigorously rubbed the sleep out of my eyes. Something was different, something on the dashboard — some kind of faint glow.

The central viewscreen was lighter than the rest, showing traces of pale pink instead of flat black. Like dissipating mist, the vision grew brighter, more distinct. I detected motion across the overhead viewscreen, as if the upward facing camera were being wiped clean. The sand was blown completely off it, exposing the luminous, starlit sky.

The crawler had been buried right up to the upper turret.

I pushed the rotation switch; grudgingly the scanner moved. When I tried reversing it, the head moved all the way back to the limit of its cam travel. It was above the sand, and the jerky motion had thrown the remaining fine dust off the screen. I could now see up from the bottom of a deep ravine.

With renewed vigor, I checked other crawler functions. Most of the external sensors were out, but the vehicle seemed to be in generally operable condition.

The top of the ten-foot-high flotation treads was probably only inches below the surface of loose debris. With the high-powered engine and low-geared transmission, there was practically nothing that could effectively stop the machine.

I engaged the clutch that connected the drive train to the atomic engine. I pulled out the dampers and let the oil warm up, checking for linkage malfunctions. In forward gear, I gently fed power to the transmission. The engine raced, but the crawler did not budge. I shifted to reverse, fed power — still nothing. The crawler was stuck hard, but if there were no large rocks wedged in the external sprockets, I might rock it free.

I shifted into neutral, revved the engine, dropped the transmissions suddenly into forward. The transmission clanked into gear, and the whole vehicle shuddered with the strain. It did not move. I put it back into neutral, revved it again, popped it into reverse. Again the crawler quivered, but it did not move in its track.

I revved until the whine of the motor became a madly racing, high-pitched squeal. I braced myself in the seat, half fearing the machine might tear itself apart. Holding my breath, I banged it into forward.

The crawler jumped right out from under me, sank back, the engine racing wildly as I continued to feed power. When it rolled back perceptibly, I threw it right into reverse, at full power. Every tooth in the heavy-duty gearbox ground together at once. Metal rasped against metal, linkage groaned, the flywheels vibrated. The machine bounded backward with such violence that I was thrown forward hard on the steering wheel.

I ignored the pain in my gut. As soon as the momentum ceased, I jammed the transmission into forward - never slackening the power input. Again came the terrible grinding of metal teeth as the synchronized transmission caught up with the madly racing gearbox.

There was an awful rending sound, and for a moment I thought that the steel alloy gears had been shorn of their teeth.

Instead, the crawler lurched up slightly, fell back. I hit reverse as soon as it started to fall. The crawler crashed into a solid wall, slammed me against the seat. I threw it into forward, reverse, forward, reverse, forward. The crawler climbed almost vertically, toward the sky, as if it were about to take off, then crashed into the ground with a soundless crunch, and raced away at top speed.

I whipped it out of gear, released the screaming power feed, stood on the brake pedal for all I was worth. The crawler skewered to a halt, skidding on its treads.

Sand cascaded off the windshield. I stared breathlessly at a nearby black wall of rock. The stars shone down with crystal clarity. How I welcomed that pink sky.

The motor faded to its usual, barely audible whine, but my heart continued to gallop unrestrained. For many minutes I sat still, until I brought my respiration under control. Even then I felt a strange gasping in my lungs. My chest hurt with every expansion.

I surveyed my predicament through the viewscreens. Ahead and behind, the walls of the ravine rose over three hundred feet, sheer and sleek in some spots, sloping and sand covered in others. To the right lay the huge mound of rubble which had followed me down from the surface. I swung the crawler to the left. The powerful headlamps pierced the darkness, but showed no end. The ravine was still bridged with hard-packed sand, becoming a tunnel which slanted downward, ever farther away from the surface.

Rotating the machine, I played the beams on the near vertical mound of rubble. The crawler could never climb it; a man might. But he also might cause a landslide. Even the lesser gravity would not protect him from being buried or crushed under thousands of tons of rock.

I donned my hood, plugged in the hoses, cycled

through the airlock. In the lights of the crawler, I climbed the loose talus, scrambling carefully in the sand and small rocks for two hundred feet. When the slope petered out and ended bluntly at a vertical wall, I worked my way up cracks and crevices, squeezed my fist into longitudinal fissures.

Debris still crumbled from the broken ledge. An occasional boulder fell, either landing with a plop in the soft sand, or bounding down the incline to the bottom of the crevasse, far past the crawler. Loose sand showered down on my already dusty exposure suit. Near the top, the rock face was overhung with a slender ribbon of compacted sandstone, waiting only for a feathery breeze, or slight vibration, to dislodge it. To continue climbing, or even to stand where I was, invited death or inhumation.

There was only one way to go — ahead, into the tunnel, and the darkness beyond.

The flotation treads spun easily over the soft sand as I executed a standing u-turn. The downward angle was not precipitous, but continued at a steady gradient. The walls came as close together as a hundred feet, spread as far apart as three hundred. Like all uncovered rills of Mars, it pointed in a straight line like the rectilinear fault that it was.

The sand floor came to an abrupt end. The stars were blocked out. The collapsed roof ended, and in front of me was a long, dark, ominous looking passageway.

I drove under a glazed ceiling hundreds of feet high. The steel treads grated over the smooth, hard floor. Like the void of space seen through the wrong end of a telescope, the tunnel stretched out forever beyond the cone of the crawler's headlights. I felt like an ant in a gopher hole, cowering in a chitenous, metal shell.

I played the headlights from side to side, and occasionally aimed them upward. Except for the gradual changes in contour, there was nothing to see but the stony surface. There was no growing flowstone, no imaginatively shaped stalactites and stalagmites. There were no twisting side passages, corkscrews, or key-holes. The cave was as barren and uninteresting as a Hawaiian lava tube. Or it could have been a Brobding-nagian subway tunnel.

Yards turned into miles, and still the tunnel descended deeper beneath the Red Planet's crust. The texture of the floor went through a gradual transforma-tion. Now it was covered with a fine, pulverulent coat-ing, inches deep and black in color, like coal dust. The crawler floated silently on this veneer of powder: a ghostly, mechanical Charon ferrying my soul to — where?

Without warning, like coming out of a funnel in reverse, the tunnel opened into a vast, boundless chamber. The headlights were like candle sticks in a forest, but I could see that the cave was miles across, and extended upward to a vaulted roof impossibly high. Every bit of the floor of this magnificent cavern was car-peted with thick, green, iridescent lichen.

And filling the unimaginable dimensions of this underground amphitheater, brightly illuminated by a glowing, sunlike ball, was a city composed of carved obelisks and tall spires and the symmetrical elegance of exotic and antiquarian art — all perfectly intact and protected by a shimmering force field.

Chapter 20

It would be a travesty to drive such a monstrous machine through the delicately laid out metropolis. Who knew what irreplaceable archaeological artifacts would be crushed under those massive, unseeing treads?

I doused the headlights with a flick of a switch - and fell back in awe when the ground before me exploded in a brilliant, celadon effusion of light, as millions of square feet of lichen covering the floor lent an eerie, green glow to the already alien appearance of the city. The artificial sunshine must have been on a wavelength that did not impinge on the fantastic glowworm display: the verdant bioluminescence sparkled with life and warmth and hope.

The graceful contours of temples and palaces stood boldly limned in the emerald radiance. Mansions beckoned to be explored. Streets cried out to feel again the familiar passage of trampling feet. A voice, the life force from the past, called for new blood, for the ultimate essence of being, in agonizing whispers.

The city waited.

Waited.

For me.

Forgetting my aching muscles and pounding forehead, I found myself strolling over fields of soft, spongy lichen, its effluvium concealed, its furry touch hidden by the thin sole of the exposure suit. The queer, hypnotic quality was forcefully rejected by the fabric of my mind, made stronger by my intentness of purpose. My muted footsteps sunk deep into the resilient sward, but the alien plant growth promptly sprang back to its former shape as if nothing, or no one, had dared to tread upon its sanctioned fibers. Like a psychopomp, it conveyed me toward the city.

I was conscious of my own breathing — the constant, rasping inhale-exhale of flowing oxygen grating past the regulating diaphragm. No other sound greeted, none departed. The city was silent — long silent — five million years silent.

I knew then that I had stumbled into a new realm of reality, a greater order of magnitude, a hitherto unexplored domain of that vast underground complex. I quivered with anticipation, knowing that I was the first man to witness the bewildering sights that lay before me.

The lichen stopped at the end of a hundred-foot-wide boulevard, which ran straight as an arrow for nearly a mile to the city limits. It then continued right through the city, dividing it into two equal parts, and emerged on the other side miles — *miles* away.

When I reached the outlying buildings, I sank in proportion as the tall, spindly spires soared aloft. My perspective stretched into a new dimension. I felt as if *I* were shrinking down to insect size while the buildings remained static. The city was built on a truly mammoth scale.

I reached the twin thousand-foot-high towers which defended the entrance with castlelike bearing. The fifty-foot diameter seemed exceedingly narrow for their dignified height: like purling needles taunting the cavern ceiling. The towers gleamed silently, sheer walls splendid and unbroken, offering no discernable imperfections. If their sole purpose was to intimidate, to inspire, to instill grandeur, they succeeded admirably.

A change took place as I passed between those waiting sentinels. The air formed a cushion, like the slight resistance of a spider's web. I advanced unafraid. My skin was embraced with a cool, tingling sensation. Then I broke through and the pressure and coolness were gone, the barrier behind me. I had been admitted past the fortress gates, beyond the charged, ephemeral portcullis.

A secret power source was activated and the city brightened perceptibly, as if eager to greet, after all these years, a creature of flesh. Somehow, I knew that I had been tested, that if I had failed the test, the power of the portals would have blocked my entrance. My mere presence was proof that the city had opened its heart, unfurled its soul, given up its body — to me. Now the city wanted to show off its wonders.

Everything seemed new and clean and antiseptic, the city suffused with a dull, whitewashed light. The sun overhead was not a light source itself, but a reflector of the city's aura.

The first building I encountered was short and squat, with a domed roof — but it was fifty feet in the air. Like a giant lemon gumdrop, it stood on intricately designed pillars that glistened like gold, but appeared to the touch to be made of plastic — pure, unblemished, untarnished, unravaged by the effects of time. The wispy stiltlike supports, four in all, hardly seemed staunch enough to support the immense weight of the building. Dark openings like empty eye sockets leered down at me from the golden floor, but there was no plausible means of attaining the somber trapdoors.

Crossing the boulevard, I found myself in a wide, decorated plaza. Dominating the center of the extensive square was what appeared to be a beautifully crafted fountain — dry these five million years. It was surrounded by finely wrought statuary that was odd, compelling, almost surrealistic in its shapelessness. Whatever it represented could only be fathomed by the alien mind of the mighty civilization that had created it.

I walked on polished stone that was smooth as marble, but with the texture of velvet. Its looks belied its feel, for it gripped the bottoms of my boots with clutching tenacity. I wended my way along the perimeter of the plaza, openly admiring the fanciful if unimaginable artwork.

I came upon a group of structures that resembled a mosque. The outer walls were rectangular and even, fashioned of smooth, purplish plastic but inlaid with bright, highly reflective amethystine triangles. The pointed, bulbous domes and the lofty portals were a deep, sapphire blue, the round minarets adorning each corner of the faintest turquoise. The soft, cerulean domicile oozed serenity, security, reverence. I rejected the religious significance as part of my Earthly background. Surely such an advanced race had no need for God or religion.

I went completely around the blue mosque, eventually returning to my point of origin without encountering any visible means of entry. Windowlike openings ringed the outer walls but were much too high to be reached or looked into. The sleek surface was unscalable.

A hundred yards away stood another, small mosque, this one predominantly red. Sharp, vermilion cornerstones rose tall and fiery above the hundred-foot-high roof, while the walls between embraced all the shades from blood red to pale pink. Triumph, I thought, must be the theme. And when I had encircled this building and found no possible ingress, I wandered away.

After a while, I found myself back on the broad avenue. I encountered the first intersection, but resisted the urge to explore the side streets. It would be too easy to get lost in the maze of mansions and crisscrossing lanes. I lingered momentarily, then proceeded along the main thoroughfare toward another building that resembled a modern skyscraper, except that each succeeding tier was wider than the one below. It looked alarmingly awkward, as if it might topple over any minute. Protruding casements were tiny pearls set against the milky, opalescent walls.

And so it went, from building to building, from street to street: each structure an entity unto itself, each idiosyncratic in its own artistic way. Paralleling the course of the main boulevard, I delved deeper and deeper into the Utopian city.

There were buildings of dark, defiant ebony that thrilled the soul; of scintillating silver, solemn and austere; gleaming bronze with a tint of verdigris; bright orange, breathing fire like the faraway sun; bold Vienna green. Each one told a story, yet each held its secret. The endless variety of sizes and shapes vaulted the imagination, and I could but guess what sumptuous treasures were housed within those enchanting kaleidoscopic asylums.

Yet, although many had what I took to be windows, none would allow my trespass. I had to be content to merely gape at their spectral beauty, and marvel at their unknown function. That these coruscating towers may have become effete since their construction meant nothing. The simple fact that they had endured all this time was miraculous enough to earn my praise.

In all my Odyssean wandering, I never ceased to be amazed by what manner of scenery happened to lie around the next corner. Now, surfeited with wonder, I must alter my levels of perception in order to comprehend the spectacle that rose before me.

It must have been the flashing, moving rainbow that first attracted my attention to the central spire. From a distance, the magnitude of the grand monolith had been obscured by my own preoccupation. Now, I paled in the enormity of it. It stood almost as tall as the twin spires that guarded the approach to the magical city. And as I drew close, I saw that the main boulevard whose course I was following went *through* it. Like the Colossus of Rhodes, it rested on two broad pedestals, each hundreds of feet square, and tall-masted sailing ships of the past would have had no trouble cruising under the massive arch. Irresistibly, I was drawn to it, like a loose iron filing to an electromagnet, lost in a moment of enduring ecstasy.

Half a mile to the left, I saw the origin of the varicolored arch: a golden sphere that gleamed brilliantly, vacillating as with an electrostatic charge. Like a royal diadem, it launched into the sky, touched the peak of the cathedral-like tower, and arced across to another golden globe half a mile to my right.

This, I knew, was the commemoration of the Martian's crowning achievement, the culmination of all their struggles, the pantheon of their once great race.

And this temple, of all I had seen, was open to me.

Sanctimoniously, I promenaded down the broad

avenue under the penumbra of the colossal structure. Once underneath it, I approached the inner wall. A ramp, wide and ornately balustraded, rose to a yawning doorway the size of a hangar. Two intricately carved pilasters braced the entranceway, their flowery but alien design distinguished with heraldic bearing. Scylla and Charybdis, I thought, as I passed between those lonely pickets as close to the middle ground as possible.

Again,I felt that thrilling, electric force that had greeted me at the city's main gate. But those silent watchers were tamed, and I was allowed to penetrate the sacred portals.

I looked up at the alabaster lintel, saw waves of pure force hanging like a curtain from a slit in its middle. Gossamer threads streamed down upon my face, entered the material of the exposure suit, caressed my brain. I knew that the neural pattern of my mind was the key that had opened the gates of the city to me, and that it now led the way into this palatial residence.

Somehow, it was as bright inside as it had been outside. I paused in an auditorium-sized atrium. A great circular ramp started at one end of the room and, like a grand staircase, wound round and round the perimeter seemingly forever upward. I almost fell over backwards as I leaned to see the ramp terminate hundreds of feet above my head. Studding the opposite wall was a bank of openings, ten feet square, that must have been doorways. I went to investigate.

I jumped back from the first door, appalled at what it held: it was a shaft that plummeted straight down into the bowels of the planet. Its walls were smooth, silken, silent. When I regained my composure, I again peered into that awful abyss.

It did not seem as deep as I had at first thought, but the idea of depth was still frightening. On impulse, I glanced overhead and saw that the shaft soared hundreds of feet upward, with similar openings spread evenly all the way to the top of the building.

I knew then that these awesome pits represented

some kind of vertical conveyance between levels, operated not by cages as in Earthly elevators, but by the
pure energy of thought. Had the power source of this
ancient city still been fully operational I knew that I
could have stepped into that aperture without fear, and
risen or fallen to the desired floor.

But even more astounding, I knew that this entire,
enormous city was only the pinnacle, the merest tip, of
a much larger complex that lay hidden below. Like the
top of an iceberg that protrudes above the blue-green
waters of the ocean, the magnificent structures within
this titanic cavern were only a fraction, the mere osten-
tation, of what was underneath the smooth, marble
floor.

With untoward difficulty, for the second time in as
many hours, I vaulted my plane of thinking into a new
dimension.

How did I know these things? What evidence was
there to support such vagrant allegations? What
caused these thoughts to take shape in my mind? Log-
ical questions all, but the answers were fleeting, vague,
evanescent, as if some familiar sight had inspired a forgotten past, sparked a dormant memory. I confess that
I did not understand — but somehow I *knew*.

The sound of my breathing accompanied me up the
pearly white ramp. The railing was uncomfortably high,
almost to my chin, as if designed for a giant. The balus-
ters were thin ribbons of iridescent metal. The ramp
went three-quarters of the way around the room, coun-
terclockwise, to the first landing. It was here that I
entered the gallery of wonders.

The arched vestibule was edged with two carved
columns, each representing an animal caricature that
reared upon two legs, impossibly long, the forearms
forming the top of the arch. Perhaps, I thought, they are
not caricatures at all, but statues of real animals that
once lived upon the surface of Mars millennia ago. They
looked not unlike polar bears with sharp, outstretched
claws and growling, angry teeth. Or, they could just as
easily have passed for prehistoric ground sloths. Yet

the creatures were timid, harmless.

I ducked under the twenty-foot-high paws, stepped into the spacious room beyond. I knew at once that I was in a museum. Transparent cases of various sizes and shapes were situated randomly throughout the great hall. The outer walls were exquisitely decorated with frescoes, depicting scenes such as no Earthly being had ever beheld. As I studied them they became more familiar, more recognizable. They really were not so foreign, just different.

The scenes, done in sharp, bright colors, were all of mechanical contrivances. They might have been ground vehicles or airplanes or space ships; I had no way of telling. The only common denominator was the attachment of wheels, so I knew that some time during their maneuvers, these things were meant to move on the ground.

The glasslike cases contained models, to what scale I do not know, of strange inventions whose purpose I could not venture to guess. When I looked closer, I saw that the cases were not glass — nor were they cases. Rather, like the coffins that I had seen in the Caves, they were solid blocks of some transparent material that completely encased the models in a permanent and perfect state of preservation.

After circulating through the room, gawking at the incomprehensible designs, I returned to the ramp and continued on around and up to the next level. It, too, was guarded by two monstrous beasts, alien yet tantalizingly familiar. I recalled some of Dr. Keppert's dissertations on parallel evolution, and some of the many fossils that had been unearthed in the past two decades. Such was the similarity of evolution that I could easily have been misled to believe that these were creatures from Earth's own past.

This room was occupied by what I would call scientific achievements. Not that they were any more comprehensible than the marvels that I had seen on the lower level, but there was a spell of grandeur that bordered on the occult. A Neanderthal man visiting the

Smithsonian Institution could not have felt any more out of place than I, and certainly would have been no more enlightened.

If I were asked to describe any of those unearthly inventions, I could not. As if in a fog, my powers of perception were dulled, overloaded by the immensity of it all. Nowhere was there written explanation to be found, not even in some aboriginal tongue. Perhaps they had superseded the need for written language; or perhaps there was some other, more advanced method of communication, long since defunct. Whatever the answer, there was not one printed symbol anywhere to be found. It was as if writing had never been invented.

Understanding nothing of this, I climbed the ramp to a room that was even more unintelligible. Here the walls were embellished with gaily colored panels, overlaid with a rich blend of bronze and burnished gold, and lighted by a mysterious, all-encompassing whiteness that came from everywhere, yet from no one particular spot. It was indirect lighting to the nth degree.

The expansive floor space was filled with three-dimensional objects of art: hanging mobiles, surrealistic sculpture, odd, amorphous carvings. Apparently, the artistic inclination of the ancient Martians leaned away from the mundane. The more oblique and shapeless it was, the more aesthetically satisfying it became.

On the next level, the numerous cases scattered promiscuously across the floor were filled with teeming specimens of plant life from Mars' luxuriant past — an almost animated vivarium. I could hardly believe that Mars had ever been so profusely populated. Yet, I recognized some varieties of shrub and leafy foliage from previous paleontological studies.

How I wished that Phyllis Trimble could be there to guide me through that exotic jungle of trees, bushes, vines, creepers, and grasses. Impressive dioramas contained complete scenes of lush vegetation, mostly desert species, but some definitely of tropical origin. Each diorama was encased in a block of transparent plastic.

So lifelike were they that I could almost hear the rustling of wind through the large, green, thickly veined leaves; almost see tall stalks swaying in a gentle summer's breeze; almost envision flowers, bright and grasping, reaching out thirstily for the dim, distant sun; almost smell the fragrance of the Martian spring. And I knew, in the concerted sixth sense with which I had been endowed since my intrusion into this alien domain, that all the native flora in this room had been gathered alive, and frozen forever in these immutable crystalline cases.

The next level, and the next, and the next, were similarly filled with further examples of endemic plant life, all laid out in labyrinthine passageways, like a psychologist's maze. Half of one entire floor was one huge plastic block, as if a piece of forest had been neatly sliced out and sealed in place. I even found a small cube containing the weird and enduring areolichen.

Up the ramp and through another arched portal I went, this time into a chamber that surpassed in volume Noah's Ark. Crowded together were all manner of animals, indigenous creatures that had not lived upon the face of Mars for millions of years. I saw horned, reptilian beasts with snakelike necks; fat, ruminating herbivores on legs that were long and lean, but under Martian gravity provided more than ample speed and endurance for long migrations; wizened, plantigrade, big-jowled mammals with tremendously furrowed brows and rounded heads, reminding me of swamp dwellers; mouselike marmots with tails three times as long as their emaciated bodies. Whole blocks of crystal friezes contained conglomerations of animals of all kinds, living in their natural habitat. Some were caught as in a snapshot, masticating fronds in blubbery lips, with saliva dripping.

Representatives of all the major classifications were there: mammals, fish, reptiles; large, small, and mediocre; fierce-looking, complacent, and indifferent. One whole floor was devoted to insects, an order that proved both multitudinous and multifarious. The total spectrum of life on the Red Planet, a compendium such as had never been collected in all the museums and zoos of Earth, was exhibited in startlingly lifelike reality, sealed for eternity in pellucid blocks of crystal.

I wandered through many chambers and many levels for time unlimited. I saw animals that were commonplace, and some that were stranger than fiction could have made them. I saw creatures that walked on four legs, ran on two, hopped, skipped, crawled, slithered, and rolled. But nowhere were there birds or flying insects. It was a sad truth that those brave and beautiful and delicate animals that defied Earth's gravity could never have evolved in the thin and tenuous atmosphere of the sun's fourth planet. Flying on Mars, by the pressure of muscle against air, was blatantly impossible.

Level upon level upon level, and an endless parade of fauna, passed me by. My sense of time was so distorted that I knew not whether an hour or a year had passed since my entry into this magnificent palace. The miracles of the moment had so filled my senses that I lost all meaning of reality.

I became aware of a growling stomach, but dismissed it along with my still aching muscles as unimportant. My mind was gorged with wonder, more than enough to allow me to put aside such materialistic feelings as simple pain and hunger pangs. The sweet nectar of knowledge was more fulfilling than ambrosia to a connoisseur.

The domed ceiling, visible only as a white speck from the entry far below, now loomed close. The pinnacle of the great building was at hand and slowly, almost reluctantly, I climbed the last ramp to the culmination of my journey. I knew when I saw the decorated column that adorned the final portal that this was the long awaited denouement. The carved arches that bestrode the vestibule were made into the likenesses of men — the men of Mars.

Chills ran along my body; I trembled slightly. I was shocked to see a real, almost live, Martian. He stood upright in silent retribution, immobilized in a block of hard, transparent crystal. He stood tall and stately for a full eight feet, but he was thin and cadaverous by human standards. He was simply caparisoned in a long, billowy robe of light ultramarine, contrasting gently with his milky skin and round, faint blue eyes. The holy vestment extended from the square, bony shoulders almost to the floor, but was swept to one side as if caught in a perpetual breeze.

The feet were overlarge, ducklike in their width but exceptionally long, and terminated in digits that were nearly finger length and seemingly dexterous. The elongated arms reached forward and bent at the elbow, the forearms parallel with the floor. The palms faced up as if begging for alms, and they could easily have wrapped around a basketball with the tapering fingers touching on the opposite side. The nails were clipped short, the hands snowy white with clean, fine lines, but no veins. Despite the lean appearance of the body, the skin itself was thick and pudgy: a natural insulating layer against a frigid existence.

How shall I describe the face? To say that it was inhuman would be the height of vanity. To say that it was angelic would be anthropomorphic. It was large and wan and oddly distorted — as a penny placed on a railroad track and flattened by a train. The chin was wide and round, the mouth firm, the lips thin and colorless, the eyes deep, pale, passionate, set far apart, the ears ludicrously elephantine. The large jaw was encumbered with loose, flaccid cheeks that sagged leeringly.

Wrinkles, either of age or sun or sagacity, shrouded the face in mystery. The bald pate was domed, almost as if to make room for extra creases of gray matter. The head, the face, the hands and feet, intimated megalocephaly. But the countenance was imbued with intelligence, compassion, gentility. He could have been a prophet, or a Grecian scholar, or the Son of God beseeching his disciples.

Tears welled in my eyes as I gazed up at this saintly patrician, surely a king among his kind to be held in so revered a station. In that wise, waxen face, I divined more than the humility of a single Martian — I saw the reflection of a race, the pride of a people, the nemesis of a civilization. I felt humbled in his presence.

How long I venerated that immobile, imploring paragon, I do not know. I know only that when my muscles cramped and I was forced to shift unsteadily from one leg to the other, I had been lost in thought for many minutes. I walked around the sepulchral case to examine the other great members of the long vanished culture. The room was filled with their bodies, much as an Earthly hall of fame would be studded with bronze likenesses. In each and every one, I witnessed the dignity and esteem of a superior civilization. And I cried because that race was no more.

If only I had the power to bring them back.

I roamed up one aisle and down the other, past crystal caskets of great men and women. Men, I thought, not Martians. I call them men as if they were my brothers. I felt a curious consanguinity with these beings of the past, for were not all species of intelligence my brothers? Was not sapience in itself kinship? Was the mere shape of body, or the origin of race, any different than the inherent goodness of a people? No, they were my brothers, my comrades in arms, and more than my equal in civilization. I could do no better in my own mind than to call them men, and knew as I did that it uplifted my own cultural standards.

There must have been hundreds of them: men, women, and children, exalted all. The poses struck were so real, so vital, so natural, that they might have been caught in the instant of a photographer's flash. The room was an allegory of strength and pride and hope, captured in the penetrating, lifelike eyes. I dared not to touch anything in the room for fear that, like Galatea, one would come to life and step out of his crystal block to admonish me for my foolishness.

I felt the weight of millennia upon me. It seemed like an eternity had passed since I had entered this great building, and that I had learned so much in that time. Yet, I knew that only hours had gone by, and that I might spend a lifetime seeing and learning all that the city had to offer.

I passed out of that hall of the living dead, and stood upon a wide, encircling balcony. The floor was polished marble, the railing ornately gilded.

Above me rose the apex of the building: a twice life-size caryatid, the vestal virgin of the Martian race whose crown supported the central arch of the polychromatic rainbow. I felt, as Moses must have on Mount Sinai, that here I could confer with the gods of this ancient race.

Below, the city sprawled at my feet, visibility illimitable. From my vantage point, I could see miles in all directions; could see the broad avenue leading back to the abandoned crawler, could see the colorful panoply of fantastic buildings, seemingly stretching to some phantom horizon.

It was then that I understood what this city was, what its purpose had been, what its future would be. This building, as well as all the appurtenant structures, had never been lived in, had never been *meant* to be lived in. As each room I had just passed through represented some aspect of Martian culture, so did each building that I could see from my lofty perch. And the huge complex that lay deeper underground, the other ninety percent that was invisible to my searching eyes, encapsulated the heritage of the past, the uplifting of a civilization, the life and history of not just a single race, but of an entire planet.

The city was one gigantic museum.

But who had built it, and why? Surely a race that could have been moved to such magnificent heights of construction could have saved themselves from catastrophe, could have found a way of enduring, could have fled a planet that had become inimical to their way of life.

This was the penultimate truth, but a piece of the puzzle was missing.

Extragalactics, Dr. Keppert had said. Did he say it in truth, or in jest, or in placation? Had the Martians died out, or had they moved on, to vanish in the vast reaches of interstellar space? Was this the secret that Major Tarkington had been leading up to?

As if in answer to my mental questioning, I heard a soft, sibilant voice wafting through my head. It was an intrusion, since I had grown used to the empty, airless silence, and the sound of my own labored breathing.

I discounted the noises in my head as the fancy of a weary brain. How long of a night had it been? How many miles had I driven? How far had I walked? How much had I seen and learned? I was lost in the immensity of it all: lost and disoriented and lying with my face in the sand — listening to the voice of the Sirens. And it was the same voice.

Instantly I was alert. Instinctively I cringed away from the seeming unreality. Disjointed snatches of conversation melded into a wild, discordant shrieking. Miles away, against the lichen green of the cavern wall, and at the opposite side from which I had entered the chamber of the city, I saw flashing lights.

I realized that my suit radio was switched on, that the voices I heard were those of people, that the light I saw in the distance was from a group who had just come into visual and radio range.

I tried to forget my aching body. I tried to control my rasping breath. I turned and ran back through that hall of giants: past the revered of that ancient race. When I reached the ramp, I stopped and leaned over the rail, and looked down at the floor hundreds of feet below. Dizzy, I pulled back to the wall, away from that spiraling pit.

I stepped into one of the square portals, stepped into nothingness. For a moment, I stood there, looking down past my feet. I understood what motivated these magic lifts — it was the power of my brain. I willed myself down, and started descending.

Down and down I fell, past arch after arch, alive with their carved reliefs. Past the halls of animals, past the halls of plants, past the halls of art, of invention, of machinery. I slowed when I reached the ground floor, stepped out of the shaft, and stood in the shadow of the great building. Then, although I had miles to go, I ran along the wide boulevard, running exertionlessly in the light gravity.

I ran past more strange buildings, with brocaded fronts and glazed walls and jeweled buttresses. I ran past rising turrets and glassy cupolas and tall pinnacles. I ran past cobalt, spiral structures and green, oasislike parks, and lilac gargoyled castles.

I passed through twin portals, a thousand feet high, the force field no stronger than a puff of wind. I walked for a mile along a broad avenue, toward a tunnel opening that shimmered in its own invisible barrier. I slowed to a walk as I neared the light and the noise and the commotion. I stepped onto the lichen-covered rock, laid out like a green carpet for a homecoming king.

The voices stopped. The figures came to attention. I could not see their faces inside the exposure hoods, but I already knew who they were. I had heard their voices, and matched them to the sizes and shapes and bearings of those who waited. I felt the sheer power of the magic city behind me, of the energy barricades in front.

"My god, it *is* Doug," Doc Reynolds said, in astonishment.

"I told you," Keppert replied.

Major Tarkington surged forward, came to an abrupt halt at the secondary barrier. "Son, what's happened to you? Are you all right?"

I stopped ten feet in front of them. They stood on one side of the force field, I stood on the other. They were unable to pass through it, I was unwilling. Linda shook her head slowly, as if in disbelief. Deep in my loins I felt the tingle of longing for her companionship, her warm body, her understanding caresses, her — love.

The time for open-mindedness was now. The place for understanding was here. The moment of great truths had at last arrived. The final clue, tugging at my memory, was about to unfold.

Chapter 21

My body itched all over, as if in anticipation; or as if my skin were stretching, or shedding. I could not scratch through the material of the exposure suit.

Linda flung herself forward, arms outstretched. The invisible barrier held her back. "Doug, how did you — I mean — are you all right? I — we thought — you might be in trouble . . . "

I stared at her blankly, disguising my churning emotions.

"Son, how can we help you?" The concern in the Major's voice sounded real. He swallowed so loudly that I heard it over the radio.

Doc fidgeted with his hands. "You should be back in the infirmary, under my care. We don't know what's going to happen to you."

I did not like the sound of his voice. "What could happen to me?"

His face was tormented. "You might — die. The transformation — "

"I doubt it. I feel too alive, too — powerful."

"But we don't know what effect — that is — You were close, but a relapse is possible." He glanced at his companions. "Explosive decompression can have lasting effects on the body: strained organs and blood vessels, weakened lungs, an overstressed heart. Recompression, no matter how immediate, cannot reverse all the adverse physical debilities."

"I seem to have recovered quite well."

"But for how long? You might pass out unexpectedly, or go into convulsions. Doug, believe me, you need to be in my care."

"I've had enough of your care. What I need is more of Dr. Keppert's explanations. He seems to be the only one here without subterfuge."

The geologist took a step forward. "Major, may I?"

Major Tarkington chewed his lower lip, eyes flirting.

He said nothing for a full minute. Then, with a deep sigh, he said, "You may as well. I only hope he's ready for it."

"If he came out of there," the geologist pointed past me, "he's ready to understand."

"I understand that this city wasn't built by the Martians. Nor was the Machine. But I don't quite understand the role of the extragalactics."

"You probably know more about all of this than we do, you just haven't assimilated it yet. But until you do, I'd be more than willing to fill in the gaps."

"Go ahead. I've been waiting to hear this for days."

With a whimsical smile, Dr. Keppert stepped forward, deeper into the force field than any of the others. "Man is not alone in the universe, nor is he unique. But by the nature of his intellect, he *is* very rare.

"Once, five million years ago, another intelligence visited the solar system. They were unimaginably advanced by our standards, and far beyond our ken of corporeal existence. They were long-lived and could travel through space for eons without tiring. They ranged far, exploring the mysteries of the universe, absorbing knowledge for its own sake. But they also had a strictly defined goal: they were searching, always searching, for other intelligences.

"Their entire race had spread itself throughout the universe in this never-ending quest. They wished to find others like themselves with whom to share their knowledge, their science, their technology, their culture, but most of all their companionship. They had no need to conquer, for, by definition of intelligence, they were a nonhostile people. And they understood, as we will some day soon, that all intelligences follow the same rules of logic: a law that is as universal as the law of gravity. The bodies that house them may differ, but the qualities of their being are the same. There is no discrimination in pure thought.

"Yet, in all the wanderings of this noble race, nowhere did they find others like them — until the day they appeared in our solar system. Of the three planets that contained life, Venus' was barely microbial, Earth's was primitive and deadly, but on Mars they found that the rare spark of true intelligence had been ignited. And by some cosmic irony, it was the very coming of those from space that sealed the doom of the Martians."

Dr. Keppert paused. He stood stoically, his hands at his sides, no thought of twitching or stuttering. He was in his element, repeating what he must have repeated many times in his mind.

"They found Mars not a dying world, but a stable one. The Martians clung to their planet tenaciously. There was little doubt that they were on the threshold of emergence, like a flower about to bloom. All they needed was time. But their future was taken away from them.

"When the extragalactic starship dropped below the speed of light into observable space, they were far within the heliosphere where they had no right to be. The resultant dimensional warp destabilized the twin planetary system that orbited between Mars and Jupiter. The planets came together, were torn apart by mutual gravitational stress, their parts scattered throughout the solar system like meteoric shrapnel. The extragalactics calculated that within a century, Mars would no longer be habitable by anything other than the lowly lichen.

"But planets endure, and disasters which may seem a tragedy at the time they occur, are but a blink on the geologic scale, and last but a second of planetary lifetime. In a mere million years, Mars would again be livable, so the extragalactics set about building this grand city for the time when the Martians would return to claim their heritage."

For a moment, I thought that I had fallen asleep and missed something. "Return? Return from where? Are the extragalactics going to bring them back? Are we trespassing on their property?"

"Hardly." Dr. Keppert laughed raucously. "Hardly that, Mr. Martin. Dr. Reynolds, you can explain the biological aspects more concisely than I. Would you like to tell him?"

The doctor's jaw worked soundlessly. He stared at the faces of his friends. "Uh, yes, of course. Well — "

My whale body felt as if it was about to explode. The tingling of my skin was penetrating right to the core of my abdomen. Tears welled in my eyes, but I could not wipe them because of the exposure hood. I spread my stance, fought back waves of nausea. But I did not want help. I was not yet ready to give in.

Doc Reynolds cleared his throat. "Well, most of our lack of understanding comes from not being in touch with ourselves, with our past — because of an artificially constructed mental barrier that has blocked our instinctive awareness."

"You're not making much sense."

"Yes, well — I — first I have to explain something about us, and about instinct." When I made no comment, the doctor cleared his throat again, continued haltingly. "Instinct is a hereditary factor. Every plant and every animal ever grown or born or hatched inherits whatever's necessary to become the creature it's destined to be. Dogs don't have kittens, tomato plants don't grow acorns. But genetics isn't just a system describing how each cell should divide and what it should grow into and how it should function. A dog has to walk like a dog, eat like a dog, bark like a dog, and think like a dog. It's born with a practical dictionary that tells it when to attack and when to run. This is instinct: the memory of what one is.

"Intelligence takes instinct one step further. We generally disassociate intelligence from instinct, but they're really interrelated. Intelligence is also a matter of memory — conscious memory as opposed to subconscious memory. When we put the two together we realize that the true potential of the human brain, the ultimate in awareness, is the conscious knowledge of instinct, what we can call, for lack of a better term, racial memory.

"This is what the Martians possessed. This is what

made them superior to the Neanderthals — a biologic dead end, another dumb ape. When the extragalactics realized that they couldn't save Mars from destruction, that a million years might pass before the world would become livable again, it was a nostalgic awareness of racial memories that nearly denied Martian survival. Because the only place they could live in the mean time was a place of ponderous gravity, crushing pressure, tremendous heat, oppressive humidity, blinding light — the Earth."

I shook my head. "This makes less sense as it goes on."

"Let him finish, son," the Major drawled.

I scowled. Linda pushed forward, closed her eyes, struggled, and fell back. An itinerant blonde curl fell across one eye. "Please, Doug. Listen to him for just one more minute."

"I want facts, not theories. Where's your evidence?"

"Right under our very noses, only we've never been able to recognize the truth." Doc Reynolds placed a gloved hand against his chest. "They were — are — in disguise. The extragalactics were masters in many things, among them genetic engineering. They understood profoundly the functions of evolution. After all, they had forged their own race into what it had become. It was a simple matter for them to collect Martian zygotes, alter the genetic pattern, and transport them to Earth. The physical attributes were easy to manipulate. Where they ran into trouble was with psychological adjustment.

"To the peaceful Martians, being dropped on a hostile planet was like being tossed into the seething cauldron of an irrational hell. Death and suffering hid behind every tree and beneath every rock, Earth was a snake pit, a death world to Martian psychology. The only recourse was a genetic severing of instinct from intelligence, a built-in inhibition which separated the individual from all memory of his true ancestry. But, so that their heritage could be reclaimed when the time was ripe, and so that they could begin again at the departure point of their past glory, this city and the Machine were constructed — not just in their honor, but for their salvation."

I shook my head. I was hearing things like an echo, as if my mind were revealing these facts at the same time, peeling back the blinders. "Are you saying that the Martians have been living among us secretly all this time?"

Doc Reynolds fell silent. Keppert smiled whimsically. The Major grunted, trying to say something. But it was Linda who spoke.

"The Martians are here — under the influence of the Machine. It's that influence that breaks through the psychological barrier that tells us who we are. Doug, *we are the Martians!*"

Chapter 22

Man, the indefinable animal: not a miming link, but an entirely different chain; the eternal antagonist of ancient primates, when brain proved stronger than brawn; a naked body in contrast to the hairy great apes. Man stands alone, an irreconcilable creature of divine intelligence, deposited on a world where, because of its bestial environment, true intelligence could never evolve.

"You're crazy, all of you. You've let this go too far. Just because you've lowered the thermostat and air pressure, and carried out some mad experiments in Martian atmosphere, doesn't make it all true. You aren't Martians, and never will be. You're just sick."

"Son, I know it's hard to grasp, but don't fail us now. We need you. Think how hard it will be for us to convince those on Earth who haven't had your conditioning or first hand knowledge."

"You're deluding yourselves. You want to believe all this so much that you're letting that Machine hypnotize you. Your powers of logic have been deranged. Doc, for god's sake, you of all people should be able to see the difference between delusion and reality."

"*You* must recognize when there's enough evidence to form a conclusion."

"And *you* are too close to the problem to see it in perspective. You have no *tangible* proof."

"Your life is the best proof there is. Without the chemical injections that altered your physiology, and the exposure to the Machine that released your inhibited mind, you would have died yesterday."

Yesterday?

"You've accomplished more of a change in five days than we did in months. You were able to absorb from the Machine everything it could pour into your brain. Doug, you're way ahead us. Your mind is only now beginning to realize its full potential."

Had the shuttle already departed?

"With your mental barriers finally flung wide, you'll be the first to remember a world where there was no war, no pestilence, no disease, no crime, no inhumanity, no agonizing mental pressure of any kind."

Was there still time to radio the shuttle to delay departure?

"Even now the prefrontal lobes of your brain are joining with the cerebrum, bringing out the perception of racial memory which we all share."

I saw a vivid picture of my own brain. I felt new synapses forming where none had been before. Tenuous threads reached out gropingly from every neuron, uniting that which for millions of years had been separate. I perceived a past that had long lain dormant, and a bright future that was bound to be.

"You're on the verge of marrying the group consciousness of your ancestors, while retaining the individual structure of your personality."

Lies. Nothing but lies. They were all insane, unbalanced by the monumental nature of their discovery.

I plunged through the shimmering force field, crashing between Doc Reynolds and Dr. Keppert, pushing them into Linda and the Major. I kept running while they were still recovering their balance. My radio cackled in a chaos of confused voices.

"You fools, you let him get away."

"I wasn't expecting him to hit me . . . "

"Doug . . . Doug . . . "

"Stop him before he contacts the space shuttle."

"Let him go. The boy is scared half out of his wits."

" . . . Doug . . . "

"Suppose he radios for help?"

"Then let him. Maybe that's best."

" . . . Come back . . . "

"He's pretty mixed up right now, I think we should . . . "

"We never should have told him until we had him safely in our hands."

" . . . Please wait, Doug. I want to help you . . . "

I ran for all I was worth. My head felt as if it was going to explode, my skin crawled in agony. But I ran — through the narrow tunnel, past those clouded, crystal caskets, over green pads of lichen, poisonous lichen. I stamped, crushing it, grounding it into dust with every step.

" . . . Doug . . . Doug . . . Please wait for . . . "

With the strength of fear, my legs worked like pistons. I fought off nausea, shook cobwebs out of my head. The ground waved sinuously before my eyes. I gasped for air, cranked open the oxygen valve.

"Let him go. Let him go. That's an order. Don't anybody get in his way."

I leaped off the marble slabs, into the larger cave, among the ruins. In the shadows I detected movement, headlamps. Several exposure-suited people were closing in on me, barring my way.

"Please . . . wait for me, Doug."

I never slowed down. I lowered my shoulder, charged like an express train into the small group of people. But they made no attempt to stop me. They parted down the middle, faded back, stepped aside. I sped through the gauntlet.

I passed a crawler, red and blue figures emerging from the airlock. They watched, but made no aggressive moves. I ran past a milling crowd, hand tools lying idle. They looked on, heads turning at my passing.

I ran through the ruins, along deserted alleys, over rubble. No one raised an arm in offense, no one got in my way. The people simply stood and stared, faces lost in the glare of exposure hoods, identities emblazoned on gleaming plastic foreheads. Oh, they were all here, all six hundred of the missing. Of that I had made sure. But they had been unhinged by that alien — Machine.

I veered triumphantly toward the opening of the Caves, running hard, gasping uncontrollably for air, reaching out for that point of light. I opened the oxygen valve wider. My muscles racked with pain, my head felt as if it was going to split apart. My chest heaved. But still I ran.

Daylight touched the bottom of the rill. I raced past a group of crawlers. All those who should have been sleeping in them were outside watching me go by. I ignored them. I hit the incline, started climbing. The pitch was steep, wearing on my legs, but I scaled the loose talus toward the greater brightness above.

My skin burned with an acid fire, my organs baked. Every step was a nightmare throb. I felt as if I were bursting apart, like a lobster molting. I hurt all over.

But still I ran.

"Doug. Please come back, Doug."

Up and up and up I ran, the sky lightening, the stars fading. I moved like a charging cheetah in the lesser gravity. I burst out of the rill, onto the plateau, in the predawn light, ran from that evil pit, out across the field of sand, flat and unyielding. I gasped, could not catch my breath. My body seethed in heat. I opened the oxygen valve until it would open no more — or was I closing it instead?

I cranked up the radio power, stumbled to my knees, panting like a beaten dog. I groped along the sand blindly, my eyes squeezed tight because of the pain behind them. My body was such a source of agony that I wanted to get out of it.

I pawed at my face, gloved hands raking across my vision plate. I was literally boiling within the suit, suffocating claustrophobically. I writhed in agony, wrenching hoses and tearing fabric in my delirium. I could not stand much more — I must either die or pass out from pain.

I could not have lost consciousness for more than a few seconds. When I came to, it was into a world of pleasure. I opened my eyes and stared at my hands in the sand, felt the grit under my nails. Slowly, I lifted my hand to my face, inserted a finger into my mouth, tasted the bittersweet particles. I breathed easily.

A body lay next to me, propped up on a small dune, shrunken and lifeless. Red and blue material jerked in the mild, cooling breeze. Through tear-filled eyes, I read the inscription above the faceplate: Doug the Martian.

I rubbed my eyes with sandy palms, reveling in the feel of skin on skin. When my vision cleared, I saw that the suit was in tatters, flung aside like a useless chrysalis.

I pulled my lean body together, stood up boldly, renascent with newfound strength. I took in great gulps of pure, fresh air, bathing my unprotected body in the cool dryness of the desert. The wind trickled through my loosened hair, rippled under my arms and between my legs, dragged away the clinging sand.

Looking down, I glared at my reflection in the plex-iglass faceplate, saw a cruel anamorphosis, but one which needed no mechanical encumbrance.

"Doug."

The word came dimly, shrilly, not through the electronics of the suit radio, but through the thin medium of the Martian atmosphere. I saw a vision out of a dream. Across the flowing sands, as if wafted on a puff of wind, drifted a specter of loveliness.

Naked to the world but nude for me, Linda stood atop a low dune. Her soft features were unhampered by hood or bulky hoses, her body was unadorned except by skin which shone and glistened in the fawning light. She stood simply, arms at her sides, expectant smile on her face.

I stuttered, testing my new voice. "How — how long . . . "

"Minutes at first. An hour, as the body transforms." She shrugged. "But you're beyond us. Who knows . . . ?"

"But we can't — change — permanently. We'll always need — we'll always be men."

Behind her, the faraway sun peeked over distant mountains, framing her head like a golden halo. "But our children — "

A rumbling blast shook the ground as a fine filament of light left the desert in front of the mountains, and soared into the sky. On a white, lambent flame, and exactly on time, the space shuttle separated itself from the gravitational attraction of the Red Planet and started its long, lonely voyage back to Earth.

But now I did not care. I staggered forward, threw my arms around my betrothed, hugged her tight, nestled in her flowing curls, kissed her radiant lips.

My mind was growing, expanding. Forgotten knowledge was coming back to me like a dream after waking, crystallizing, clarifying. After a five million year odyssey, I was the first to return to Mars. It felt good to be home.

To make available for life every place where life is
possible.

To make inhabitable all worlds as yet uninhabit-
able, and all life purposeful.

Herman Oberth (1894-1989)